BANISHED SOUL

J.L. WENNING

GYPSY PUBLICATIONS

Published in 2013, by Gypsy Publications
Troy, OH 45373, U.S.A.
GypsyPublications.com

Wenning, J.L.
Banished Soul / by J.L. Wenning

ISBN 978-1-938768-14-9 (paperback)

Library of Congress Control Number
2013935636

Edited by Jon Williams
Cover and Book Design by Tim Rowe

PRINTED IN THE UNITED STATES OF AMERICA

I would like to thank my wife, Vickie and our two daughters, Brianna and Lauren for their patience and understanding through the process of writing this novel.

CHAPTER 1

Charlie was born in the late 1930s to poor parents. His father died a tragic and brutal death, leaving his mother to raise him. He was raised to be a good God-loving Catholic, but that soon changed when he saw his mother brutally raped and murdered, leaving Charlie an orphan at 10. He was placed in the state's custody at an orphanage, but he was never adopted. At the age of 16, losing all hope in the church and God, he ran away. Struggling to make it on his own, Charlie ran into a fellow named Sam, an older gentleman in his forties. He took Charlie under his wing and treated him as a son. Charlie was almost ready to turn 18 when Sam told him he had a special surprise for his 18th birthday. Charlie was told simply that they were going on a trip and that he needed to pack because they were leaving that night.

Sam and Charlie drove through the night, then stopped in a very secluded area. Sam told Charlie that the surprise would be in this place tonight. Throughout the day, people kept arriving, none of whom Charlie had ever seen before. Charlie was getting suspicious, so he approached Sam.

"Who are all these people?" Charlie asked.

Sam replied, "These are my guests for the festivities of the evening."

Charlie asked, "You mean they are all part of my surprise?"

"Yes, especially that one," Sam replied, pointing out a beautiful woman to Charlie. Sam told Charlie that he should go and get to know her, and that her name was Charlotte. Charlie went over to Charlotte and introduced himself.

"Hi, Charlotte, my name is Charlie. How are you doing today?"

Charlotte replied that she was a bit nervous. She said that today was her 18th birthday, and that her parents brought her out here for some sort of surprise. Charlie told Charlotte that today was also his 18th birthday and that Sam had brought him out here for a surprise too. Both Charlie and Charlotte were confused. The two of them sat through the day wondering what sort of surprise awaited them.

As the day passed with the two of them alone together, they began to care for one another, as if they were destined to fall in love. Then it was almost 8 p.m. Sam called for Charlie and told him that he needed to get ready for the surprise. At the same time, Charlotte's parents called for her to get ready also. Throughout the day almost one hundred people had arrived, and Charlie thought to himself that this was going to be one big party.

At 9 p.m. Sam told Charlie that it was time.

"I'll be right there," Charlie replied.

Charlie and Sam walked together toward the bonfire at the same time Charlotte and her parents were doing the same. Charlie noticed Charlotte and waved and Charlotte waved back. As Charlie waved he felt something for Charlotte that no one should feel after knowing someone for only a few hours. As he thought these things, the two parties came together at the fire. The two young people were then told that at the stroke of midnight they would be married and that they both should go get prepared for the wedding. Charlie thought it was very odd to be brought together in this way, but both had the feeling that they couldn't be apart anymore, so they agreed to be married. Charlie knew he loved her and would do anything for her.

Charlotte went with her mother back to their campsite and began preparations to be married. Charlotte's mother told Charlotte that she had been waiting for this day for a long time and was very proud of her.

"I have your dress," Charlotte's mother told her. "Let me go and get it."

At Charlie and Sam's camp, Sam was letting Charlie know how proud he was of Charlie and that Charlie had grown into such a great man under the circumstances of his childhood.

Charlotte's mother returned with Charlotte's dress, but it wasn't the traditional white dress that Charlotte had expected. This dress was black and looked very old. Charlotte asked, "Why is my dress black?"

Her mother replied, "This is a tradition in our religion."

It was now 11:50 p.m. Charlie and Sam were heading back toward the bonfire where Charlie was to be married to Charlotte. At 11:55 the ceremony began. Charlie was shocked when Charlotte came down the aisle in a black dress, but he was so blinded with love that he didn't let it bother him. The ceremony consisted of a lot of chanting of words and phrases that neither Charlie nor Charlotte understood. At the stroke of midnight Charlie and Charlotte said their vows and were married. The reception was short and they were informed that they must consummate their marriage immediately in front of the gathering, as dictated by their religion. The young couple was shocked! But any protests they made were met with reassurances that this was all part of the religious process, so Charlie and Charlotte reluctantly and clumsily consummated their union in front of the gathering. All during the process, the gathering sang and chanted and made weird gestures. After the process ended, they were told to go to a camp especially set up for them and wait and someone would be there at 2:30 a.m.

At the given time, Charlie and Charlotte were awakened by one of the men of the gathering. Charlie and Charlotte followed him back to the bonfire. Once there, the couple saw that all the men were dressed in costumes of Satan with masks on their faces. Only their penises showed. Charlotte was told to get undressed and lie down on a huge stump. Charlie was tied to a tree facing Charlotte. One of the men danced around Charlotte chanting some sort of chant. At the conclusion of the chant he raped Charlie's new bride right in front of him. The same act was repeated over and over. Altogether Charlie was forced to watch thirty-five men rape his new wife. Charlie was then told that in nine months he and Charlotte would be having a baby, but it wouldn't be Charlie's. It would be a special baby that would change his life. He was also told that if he tried anything to end the pregnancy that Charlotte would be killed right in front of him. He was also told that Charlotte wouldn't remember any of the events that took place after they fell asleep and that Charlie was not permitted to speak of them.

As morning came, Charlie and Charlotte awoke in their tent. Charlotte looked so beautiful and innocent, making it more difficult for Charlie not to discuss the previous night's proceedings. The couple left the campground and went into town for breakfast. Charlotte was everything that Charlie could ask for, but the secret was eating him up inside. Meanwhile, the couple was enjoying a meager breakfast and discussing their living predicament, Charlie worried that his money would soon run out.

When the waitress brought the bill, Charlie opened his wallet to pay and found a note. It read, "To the newlyweds from the flock: Go to the bus station and look for locker

66. You will find the key in the glove compartment of your car. Everything that you need will be in the locker."

Charlie and Charlotte went to the car and found a key in the glove compartment. Then they proceeded to the bus station and located locker 66. Opening it, they found another note and a key. The note said that the flock had bought them a house for their wedding gift, and included the address: 607 Hoying Street. Enclosed with the note was a map to their new home. The note also told the couple the details of their domestic life. Charlie was to work at the local meat market and Charlotte would be a stay-at-home wife; the flock would make sure that they were taken care of, and they would want for nothing .

The couple left the bus station and headed to their new house. When they arrived they saw a small, white, two-story dwelling, a suitable starter home.

A couple of weeks had passed when Charlotte noticed that she was late for her monthly cycle. She told Charlie that she was going to go to the doctor. Charlie already knew that she was pregnant, but he feigned excitement when she came home with the news. Charlie liked his job as a butcher at the meat market, but the stress of knowing the truth about the conception of Charlotte's child continued to gnaw at him. As a result, he kept to himself at work and made no friends.

The months went by and Charlie and Charlotte prepared for the new arrival. One day Charlotte told Charlie that the car needed new brakes. Charlie, being a Mr. Fixit, changed the brakes himself.

Later that week Charlotte decided to go to her parents' house. Charlie was unable to get off work, so Charlotte headed out on her own. Her parents' house was over two hours away. Charlotte kissed Charlie goodbye and told him that she would see him later. Charlie came home from work that night, made supper, and anticipated Charlotte's arrival home, but she never came. Charlie called Charlotte's parents. They informed him that she had left over three hours ago, and that she should have been home by now. Panicked, Charlie called the Highway Patrol to see if she had been in an accident. The dispatcher told Charlie that Charlotte had indeed been in an accident. Charlie asked the dispatcher what happened; the dispatcher told him that an officer was on his way to Charlie's house to explain.

About fifteen minutes later came a knock on the door. The officer told Charlie that Charlotte's brakes had failed and that she ran a stop sign and went under a semi trailer. She was decapitated and died instantly.

Charlie dropped to his knees in pain. He spent the whole night crying. He must have finally fallen asleep, because the telephone rang the next morning and awakened him. It was Sam. He did not offer condolences but told Charlie that he was wanted at 4949 Cut Deep Road in Hickstown. Charlie got dressed and headed for his destination, wondering what was to become of him. When he arrived he noticed several cars parked around the house as if some sort of meeting was taking place. Charlie went up to the door and was greeted by Sam.

"Come in," said Sam. "We need to talk to you."

As Charlie went into the house he noticed the leader of the flock sitting at a desk and the other members of the flock sitting in a circle around the desk. The flock leader ordered Charlie to come to the desk. Charlie approached cautiously.

Charlie asked, "Why was I summoned here?"

The flock leader replied, "It is about the death of Charlotte."

"I had nothing to do with Charlotte's death. It was a freak accident," Charlie insisted.

"We think differently," replied the flock leader. "You

were the one to change the brakes on the car. Your conscience was getting to you and you thought you could end it this way and that we wouldn't think you were involved. You are here for sentencing, Charlie, and we have all agreed to your punishment. Do you have any last words?"

Charlie could barely get the word out as he cried, "No!"

"The other leaders and I have decided that you are going to be responsible for the passage," detailed the leader.

"What is the passage?" Charlie asked.

The leader explained, "The passage is where evil can come to this world without detection. When you arrive home tonight, go upstairs to the bedroom closet, open the door, and the passage will be at the attic entrance. You will quit your job and you'll never be able to leave the house. Also, to make sure you're too embarrassed to leave, we have a second part to your punishment."

Just then a beautiful woman came out of the kitchen chanting something unfamiliar to Charlie and waving her arms. A cloud of black smoke appeared and Charlie fainted.

A couple hours later Charlie awoke in a bed. Sam handed him a mirror.

"Look, Charlie. Look at what we had to do to you since you were so irresponsible," declared Sam.

Charlie looked in the mirror and it was an awful sight. They had deformed his face by crushing one side, making it look like he had only half a face.

Sam handed Charlie a note as he said, "Read this, Charlie."

Charlie began reading the note. "This punishment is to remind you that your life is half over. If you fail on this assignment you'll find your life is fully over."

Charlie was confused. If he was so irresponsible, why would he be guarding the passage? He went back upstairs to the attic passage looking for answers. Upon his arrival

J.L. Wenning

he noticed an evil spirit exiting the passage. Charlie tried to communicate with the spirit but the spirit never heard him.

Charlie was determined to figure out what the passage was and how he could communicate with the spirits. Charlie spent the day with thoughts of how he would crack the mystery of the passage and what the spirits wanted that passed through the gate. It was getting late so Charlie decided to sleep on it. "Maybe something will come to me while I sleep," he hoped.

CHAPTER 2

Charlie awoke the next morning no further along than he had been the night before. So he went back upstairs to the passage and again, time after time, he had no luck communicating with the spirits. He spent that afternoon thinking and then it hit him. 'The library!' he thought. But he wasn't able to leave the house so that couldn't be possible.

Charlie sat in his chair, pondering over the idea. Hours later he decided he would go at night and break in. He'd experienced his share of stealing while living on the streets before he found Sam. Charlie wondered if he still had it in him.

Rising suddenly from his chair, he felt determined. He decided he would sneak to the library the following night. That settled, he headed for bed. Charlotte came to him in his dreams and helped him determine a plan to get to the library without getting caught.

Charlie awoke, his mind reeling with the details. First he was to call Sam and say he was having horrible pain in his side. So first thing in the morning he called Sam. Sam told Charlie he would be right over to take him to the hospital. Charlie then lay on the floor in front of the door holding his side as if he were in pain.

Soon Sam arrived and came through the door yelling, "Are you okay Charlie?"

Charlie moaned, "No, I'm in so much pain I can't stand it. Take me to the hospital, quick."

Sam explained, "I can't take you to the hospital, but I can call the flock leader and have him send a witch over to help."

Charlie then put phase two into play. He cried, "You never cared for me, did you, Sam? You just took care of me because I was to help raise a Satan spawn!"

"That's not true!" Sam argued. "I do care for you, Charlie."

Charlie groaned in reply, "Then take me to the damn hospital before I die."

Reluctantly, Sam agreed and took Charlie to the hospital. When they arrived they were greeted at the front desk by a receptionist asking, "What seems to be the problem today, sir?"

Sam answered for Charlie, "He is having severe pain in his side."

She escorted Sam and Charlie to a small room, and told them, "The doctor will be right with you."

The doctor, an older man with very little hair, arrived shortly after and asked Charlie, "What is the problem, son?"

Pointing to his right side Charlie replied, "I have been having pains in my right side."

The doctor palpated the side, saying, "Hmm, you could be having appendicitis. We will have to run some tests and see for sure. We'll have to keep you overnight."

Charlie was relieved the plan so far had fallen into place. After filling out the paperwork Charlie was hooked to an IV and given some medication for the pain.

The nurse approached Sam and told him, "You might as well head home. We will have to run some tests to determine what is going on with Charlie. It could take a while."

With that Sam walked into Charlie's room and said, "I

am going to head to your house and watch the passage. I will be back later. You get better. Fast," he ordered.

The hours went by as doctors performed a barrage of tests on Charlie. Soon it was evening and Sam had returned. He told Charlie, "Things are fine at home, and no one knows you are out of the house."

Just then the doctor came into the room and informed them that it wasn't appendicitis like they thought. The tests had determined that Charlie had a bacterial infection and the doctor still wanted Charlie to stay the night and get a good start on antibiotics. Sam and Charlie chatted for a few minutes, then Sam left. Charlie lay in bed plotting the final phase of his plan: how to get out of the hospital without being caught and break into the library.

Soon it was midnight and Charlie was ready for action. He first took out his IV, being careful to shut off the alarm before the nurses could be alerted to his antics. Then he went and put on his clothes. Slowly he opened the door, looked both ways to make sure that no one would see him, and started down the hallway. Suddenly, Charlie realized that he would have to pass the nurses' desk to get out.

He thought for a moment, then went into the closest room and hit the nurse's call button. He waited behind the door for the nurse to come into the room, then sneaked out the door as the nurse was checking the patient. He went down the elevator, out the door, and on his way to the library.

The town was deadly quiet as he tried to use the alleyways, so as not to draw any attention to himself. Charlie finally reached the back door of the library. He then reached into his pocket for his trusty skeleton key—but it was gone! Thinking quickly, he remembered that he had seen a tire dealer on his way to the library. He thought he might find a tire iron in the dumpster. It was a long shot, but worth the risk.

Walking down the alley toward the tire dealer, Charlie noticed a screwdriver lying in a mud puddle. "This will get the job done," he thought to himself.

Returning to the library, he spared no further time, quickly manipulating the lock and letting himself in the door. He went straight to the card catalog to find what he needed. Charlie found four books on Satanic cults and demon worship. He tucked them into his jacket and headed quickly for home.

He made it home with no problem, and decided to go to sleep and read the books in the morning. He was awoken by Sam.

"What are you doing home from the hospital?" Sam asked.

Charlie replied, "I was released early this morning. The doctor said that he misdiagnosed me and that there was nothing wrong with me. Maybe supper just upset my stomach."

"Well, whatever," Sam replied, but he looked skeptical. Charlie knew that Sam didn't buy his story and would head to the hospital to find out what really happened.

Sam did indeed go to the hospital to find out what happened. When he arrived he noticed a police car out front, so he went to the front deck and asked to visit with Charlie. The receptionist told Sam that Charlie had escaped the night before and they had officers looking for him. Sam thanked the receptionist before she could mutter another word. He wanted out of there before she could summon the cops to talk to him.

Sam was on his way home when he noticed police cars in front of the library as well. Sam asked an onlooker what was going on. The man told Sam that someone had broken into the library the night before. Sam thought he knew who was behind this, so he headed back to Charlie's house.

Sam arrived at Charlie's and barged right in. "What the hell are you thinking, boy?" demanded Sam. "I know you escaped from the hospital and broke into the library! What do you have to say for yourself?"

Sam then noticed the books on the coffee table.

"So you think you can outsmart the flock, boy?" yelled Sam, as he picked Charlie up by the scruff of his shirt.

Before Charlie could reply Sam started beating him relentlessly, punching him in the ribs, then the face. After roughing Charlie up, Sam headed out the door yelling that he was on his way to the flock leader and that Charlie would pay dearly for this.

Charlie lay dazed on the floor for a moment, then shook the cobwebs out of his head and quickly grabbed the phone. He called the flock leader and told him that Sam had let him out of the house and that Sam was on his way to the leader's house. He explained to the flock leader that he had called Sam to his house because he was having side pains, and when Charlie suggested that Sam call to get a witch doctor that Sam disapproved and took him to a hospital. He also went on to explain that when Sam left the hospital that Charlie had escaped to get back to the passage. The flock leader told Charlie that he would be waiting for Sam and thanked him for informing him of the events.

Charlie slumped in his chair, wondering if he had done the right thing by lying to the flock leader. What sort of punishment would Sam receive?

"No time to dwell on what's done," he thought. He quickly decided to read up on the spirits.

Meanwhile, Sam had arrived at the flock leader's house.

"Ah, Sam, what brings you here?" asked the leader.

Sam replied, "It's Charlie. He tricked me into taking him to the hospital. Then he escaped from the hospital and broke into the library."

"Interesting," said the flock leader. "I've recently had a conversation with Charlie. Won't you come in? We'll discuss this."

Sam followed the flock leader into his office. Both men took seats by his desk and began to discuss the situation.

"So why did he break into the library?" asked the flock leader.

Sam replied, "I don't know, but I did see a few books on spirits and Satanism on his end table."

"Interesting," considered the flock leader. "He is trying to research his situation."

"If I may ask, what was your conversation with Charlie?" Sam asked of his leader.

"Oh, nothing much, Sam. He just tried to convince me that you were responsible for this whole hospital situation. I told him I would take care of it, so we have to think of something to make him think that we haven't figured him out. Let's go have a drink on this."

Back at Charlie's house, he was so intent on his reading that he forgot to check on the passage. He muttered an expletive as he headed upstairs. There he again tried to communicate with a spirit with no success.

"Well, back to my reading," thought Charlie, heading back to his recliner.

Sam and the flock leader pulled up to the local strip bar. "This should help us relax," said the flock leader.

Sam replied, "Oh yeah, nothing better," as they headed in.

Once in the bar the two of them picked a secluded table away from the stage area so no one else could hear them and ordered some beers from a very stressed-looking waitress.

"So what do you think we should do with Charlie?" asked Sam.

"Well, let's see," said the flock leader. "Does he still have father-son feelings for you, Sam?" Sam just shrugged as the waitress arrived with their drinks.

"Well, let's enjoy the scenery while we think, Sam. You pick out the girl and I'll buy the lap dance," offered the flock leader.

Sam gestured to a lovely brunette. "She looks good," he said. The flock leader made the request, then Sam and the woman disappeared into the back room for his private dance. When Sam was out of sight the flock leader went and talked to the owner of the establishment.

"How much for the girl for a couple days?" he asked.

"A thousand for three days," the owner replied. The two men shook on the deal, then money was exchanged.

"She'll be a nice addition to our little get-together for the next three days," the flock leader mentioned. "We needed a little entertainment."

After about twenty minutes Sam and the lady came out of the back room.

The flock leader told Sam, "I've figured out the plan. I just reserved this young lady for the next three days. We're going to give her to Charlie."

'What? Why?" exclaimed Sam.

"I'll explain on the way home," the leader told Sam. He turned to the bar owner and said, "I'll be here tomorrow for her at noon." Sam and the flock leader went out to the car. Sam was anxious to hear the flock leader's plan.

"Okay," began the flock leader, "we send the girl to Charlie's house for three days and she pretends to like him. With the condition that Charlie is in, he'll fall for her quickly. If he doesn't, we can always rely on our black magic. She can find out what Charlie is up to and then tell us. She'll be the perfect spy. Then we can determine Charlie's punishment." Sam thought it was a great idea and was hopeful that it would work.

Charlie was asleep in his recliner when a loud noise woke him. It was storming, and he looked at the time and noticed it was 11:30 p.m. He decided to go up and check the passage before he turned in for the night. While checking the passage he saw a spirit that he hadn't seen before.

It was a child. Charlie tried to communicate with the specter, but had no luck. The small, wispy figure didn't seem to see or hear him. There was nothing threatening or evil about the spirit, just a deep feeling of sadness.

"I need to figure this out as soon as possible," Charlie said to himself. "I'll set aside all day tomorrow to research."

Charlie went to bed wondering what that child had done to end up at the very gate of Hell. Through the night Charlie dreamed about this child. He dreamed there was a huge fire, with a lot of people screaming. The child was holding matches. Could that child, who looked so innocent, be responsible for the fire and the deaths of all those people?

Chapter 3

The next morning Sam received a phone call from the flock leader instructing Sam to meet him at the strip bar to pick up the woman. When Sam arrived at the bar the flock leader was already there waiting. The two of them went in together. The flock leader went to the bar owner and asked if she was there yet and the owner said she had just arrived and would be out shortly. After a few minutes she appeared from the back room. The flock leader told her they wanted to surprise someone with her as a gift, and that they could discuss the agenda on the way. The three of them headed out to the flock leader's car, where they introduced themselves.

"My name is Nemrak," said the flock leader, "and this is Sam. What is your name?" The pretty brunette replied softly that her name was Francisca, but everyone called her Fran for short.

"Well Francisca, here is our plan. Our friend Charlie is very lonely. He recently lost his wife in a car accident, along with an unborn child. He was very traumatized by the accident, so he is very cautious of going outside. We want you to give him some companionship. Get to know him and what interests him, to get his spirits up. You don't have to have sex with him or anything of that nature. We would just like you to be friendly to him."

Francisca nodded, listening to her instructions intently.

Nemrak continued, "We would like you to go to his house and introduce yourself as a friend of his deceased wife, Charlotte. Tell him that you wanted to visit her. When he tells you of the tragedy, fall to your knees in emotional pain, then do some acting from there. Also," added Nemrak as an afterthought, "tell him you are stuck in town and need a place to stay." Nemrak went on to explain to Fran that they were concerned that their friend Charlie was ready to go off the deep end, and that he was exhibiting some odd behavior. He asked Fran to take note of any odd behavior of Charlie's that might be a sign of depression.

Francisca was so grateful for work, was willing to do anything. She went over the instructions in her mind, making sure she understood what she was to do. When she was sure she understood her assignment, she told Nemrak and Sam she was ready.

Outside Nemrak's house she hailed a cab to take her to Charlie's house. She gave the cabbie instructions to go to 607 Hoying Street. The cab driver tried hitting on her, but she was focused on her task. When they arrived Francisca paid her fare quickly and hopped out. She went quickly up to Charlie's door and knocked, before she lost her courage. She silently prayed she wouldn't forget any of the details Sam and Nemrak had given her.

Charlie answered the door and Francisca had to swallow hard. How was she going to spend the next three days with him?

Charlie asked, "Can I help you?"

"Is Charlotte around?" she asked, pasting on a fake smile.

Charlie looked stricken for a moment, then asked, "You haven't heard?"

"Heard what?" asked Francisca innocently.

"Charlotte died in an accident a couple months ago," Charlie whispered sadly.

"God, no!" cried Francisca as she fell to her knees on the front porch. She hoped her sobbing seemed realistic. Charlie stepped outside, got down on his knees, and tried to comfort her. Fran felt terrible inside, knowing that really she should be the one comforting him. She let her tears slowly disappear.

After it appeared that she had settled down, Charlie asked her, "Who are you, and how did you know Charlotte?"

Francisca explained simply that she was a high school friend of Charlotte's and had been traveling for business nearby. She thought she'd come to visit her only friend left in the area.

After considering for a moment, Charlie asked her to come inside. Francisca followed Charlie into the house, where she started to cry again. This time the tears were real. She was so nervous about making a mistake in her acting. Then she remembered the rest of her assignment with Charlie.

"Oh no!" she whimpered. "I'll have no place to stay tonight!"

Charlie apologized, but told her there was no way that she could stay with him.

"Well… maybe I could rebook my flight in the morning, if I could just stay with you for the night?" she asked hopefully.

Charlie reluctantly agreed to let Fran stay with him. "But just for one night," he warned her.

Charlie helped Fran bring her luggage into the house. He took it to the guest bedroom but warned her that under no condition could she go upstairs.

"Why not?" she asked.

Charlie told her it was none of her business. Fran considered pushing the issue, but Charlie turned on his heel and was gone. So she unpacked her things, then returned to the kitchen. She noticed Charlie reading and asked him about his book. Charlie didn't even look at her, but shrugged and said, "Just some books on my religion."

She sat across from him at the table and began asking questions about Charlotte. Charlie looked up from his book and stared at Fran for a moment. Then he said, "Charlotte was a good wife. Everything was fine until the accident."

"The accident?" Fran asked.

"The one that killed her," Charlie whispered sadly.

Fran asked a few more questions, trying to get Charlie to go into more detail, but he didn't seem comfortable enough with her. His quick, one-word answers weren't getting her anywhere. Fran decided that she would get up from the table and look around the house. She looked around for an hour or so and then decided to turn in for the night. Charlie was still sitting at the table reading when Fran went to bed.

When Fran awoke in the morning Charlie was still asleep so she snooped around the house a little more. By the time Charlie interrupted her, asking what she was doing, she had made her way to the kitchen. Fran smiled and said she was just trying to find the bowls.

"I'm a little hungry," she explained innocently. Charlie showed Fran to the bowls in the cupboard and then asked if she had made new arrangements to get home. She frowned and then lied, saying that the one and only plane at the tiny airport was having mechanical problems and she wouldn't be able to fly out for a couple more days.

Despite the trouble he knew could come, Charlie told her that she could stay, but no one could know he had a guest. Fran agreed happily, thinking her assignment would surely be a success. Then she asked Charlie, "Why are you so serious?"

Charlie said, "Ever since Charlotte died in the car accident I have been lonely." Fran immediately realized that her question was silly. Obviously grief was driving Charlie to be such a serious man.

"Let's do a project that would have made Charlotte happy," exclaimed Fran.

At first Charlie looked as if he would say no. Then he slowly said, "Since we're going to be roommates for the next few days, that's not such a bad idea."

"I noticed that the front of the house was kind of drab. I thought that maybe the two of us could plant some flowers there."

Charlie hesitated for a few moments, then said, "All right, that would be fine, but you will have to go and get the flowers because I am unable to leave the house." A look of surprise crossed Fran's face, but she masked it with concern.

"Why can't you leave the house?" she asked.

Charlie said simply, "It's a long story."

So Fran agreed to go and get the flowers after breakfast. They finished eating and Fran took Charlie's car and headed to the flower store in town. A feeling deep inside her told her never to return. The night before she kept hearing strange noises coming from upstairs, but she knew she would go back and complete the job. She needed the money.

Fran went to the flower store and picked out some nice white petunias. Charlie reluctantly came outside and helped her plant the flowers. After digging in the dirt for a while, Charlie discovered he was enjoying the task and simply having someone around to talk to. Fran finished patting a plant into the ground, then told Charlie she was going in to use the bathroom. Charlie had grown so relaxed, he forgot that he had left something in there.

As Fran was using the bathroom, she looked to her left side for toilet paper and saw the two books that Charlie was reading. One was on Satanic cults and the other was a

Satanic spellbook. This was very freaky to Fran, but also very interesting. Now she had some evidence to take back to Nemrak and Sam. She leafed through the books, then carefully put them back.

She went back outside to help Charlie finish planting the flowers. When they were done both Fran and Charlie stood on the edge of the road and admired them. Charlie thanked Fran for bringing some happiness to his life after the accident.

"You're welcome, Charlie," Fran said warmly. "But I have one more surprise for you!" Suddenly Charlie looked at his watch and jumped up. He was back in the house and upstairs before Fran knew what was happening. Fran went back into the house too, and was tempted to go upstairs… but she was now gaining Charlie's trust and she knew that the best way to a man's heart was through his stomach. The supper she had planned for the two of them would, she hoped, gain more trust from Charlie.

Soon Charlie came back downstairs and asked Fran what the big surprise for tonight was. Fran said that since Charlie had been so nice to her that she wanted to make him a special supper. Charlie told her that would be great, especially after eating his own cooking for so long. Fran laughed at Charlie's comment and Charlie chuckled with her. The two of them talked a little but Charlie kept going upstairs. Fran thought to herself that she needed to get upstairs and see what was going on up there. But she looked at her watch and decided it was time to start supper. She began preparing her specialty, cheesy spaghetti bake, when she realized that she forgot the mushrooms. She called for Charlie to come down to the living room, then asked if he could go to the store for her.

"I told you before that I can't leave the house," said Charlie.

"Oh, you only have to pick up some mushrooms! Just

go in, grab them, pay for them, and leave. You'll be gone for no more than ten minutes!" she laughed.

Charlie began to whine, but Fran explained that she needed to watch the supper and didn't want to ruin the surprise. Finally, Charlie agreed to go to the store. All the way to the store Charlie wondered what would happen if someone from the flock saw him. He just swallowed deep and plowed ahead.

Back at the house Fran was busy looking for Charlie's books when she stumbled into the closet where the passage was located.

At just that time, a spirit was passing into this world. Startled, Fran screamed, then hurried out of the closet and back downstairs. She watched the doorway to make sure whatever it was hadn't followed her. After she calmed down she began to realize why Charlie had been so secretive with her. She now understood the importance of the two books she saw earlier that day. She began to put the pieces together. She thought Sam and Nemrak's flock must have something to do with the spirit she saw. Maybe Charlie was the guardian of the passage and was trying to learn more about what he was guarding. Fran decided she might be getting in over her head.

Charlie located the mushrooms and was on his way to the checkout when he heard a familiar voice. He nervously turned around and to his surprise it was Jake from the meat market.

"How are you, Charlie? It's been a while," said Jake. Charlie smiled cautiously and replied that he was doing all right. As he was paying for his mushrooms, Jake told Charlie that it was nice seeing him and Charlie replied in kind, then hurried out of the store. Back in his car Charlie wondered if Jake was part of the flock and if he would tell Sam or the flock leader. All the way home Charlie pondered the thought in his head that maybe Jake was part of the flock.

Arriving home, Charlie was met by a frantic Fran at the door. "We need to talk," she said.

"What's wrong?" asked Charlie.

"I saw it," exclaimed Fran.

"Saw what?"

"In your closet, a spirit crossing over to our world," explained Fran breathlessly.

"What were you doing in my room?" demanded Charlie.

"Let me explain," insisted Fran. She pulled him by the arm and guided him to the sofa. They sat down and Fran told Charlie her story: being hired by Sam and Nemrak to get to know him and report back. She went on to say that she never knew Charlotte and that she accepted their assignment because she needed the money.

"They told me that Charlotte was killed in an accident in which you were deformed, but when you told me about Charlotte's death and that you weren't in the vehicle I knew something wasn't right," Fran explained. She went on to tell how she saw the books in his bathroom, and that she had lied to him about her plane having mechanical problems. Charlie's expression became tighter and more withdrawn, and Fran could see that his anger and hurt were pushing him away from her.

"I want to help you, Charlie!" said Fran.

Charlie snorted, looking skeptical.

"I'm also beginning to have feelings for you," admitted Fran, shyly.

Charlie was speechless at first, then he said carefully to Fran, "You know if you stay here and Sam or Nemrak find out we will both be punished. Maybe you should sleep on your decision tonight."

Fran and Charlie said nothing to one another as they ate supper. Charlie headed upstairs soon afterwards to check on the passage. As usual some spirits were passing through but nothing out of the ordinary (at least for the passage). Charlie thought to himself how nice it would be to have Fran around but wondered if it would be worth it if Sam found out. He still wondered if Jake was part of the flock or not.

Charlie dozed off in his chair by the doorway, but was awakened in the middle of the night by another disturbance in the passage. It was the same spirit as before. This time it spoke to him.

"Charlie, you will not defeat me. You are my slave and you will obey my every command. Let Fran stay with you. No one will know. She will not be of any use to you in your quest to defeat me, but you can have a good time with her. I know you care for her, and that will be your downfall."

Charlie was puzzled by what the spirit said and knew that something was not right. He realized that the spirit didn't seem evil and he wondered why. Charlie pondered the words of the spirit. He thought that maybe the spirit wasn't the same one that came to him the other night.

Chapter 4

He must have dozed off as he was thinking. When he opened his eyes again, it was morning. He heard Fran scurrying around downstairs. Charlie rolled out of bed, checked the passage, then headed downstairs to get some coffee. He met Fran in the kitchen and asked her how she slept last night.

Fran replied, "I hardly slept at all. What happened in the middle of the night? I heard you moving around upstairs."

"Do you really want to know?" he asked.

When she replied that she did, Charlie told her he needed to know her decision. She told him she had decided to stay and help him.

"I was afraid of that," Charlie said. He went on to explain that he was visited by a spirit the night before. "He first came to me the other night and told me he was my master and that I needed to serve him. Last night he appeared and told me that you and I wouldn't be able to defeat him but that I should let you stay and we should have a good time. But last night he seemed different. It could just be my imagination, though. I'm not sure."

Fran told Charlie she believed together they could end this terror so he could live a semi-normal life. She then told Charlie that she would read the book on Satanic cults and he could read the other book and then together they could win. Charlie hesitantly agreed.

Sam was at home eating breakfast when he received a phone call. It was Nemrak.

"Sam, how are you doing today?" said Nemrak.

Sam replied that he was doing fine. Nemrak then asked Sam if he had heard anything yet from Fran. Sam replied that he had not heard anything yet. Nemrak told Sam to meet him the next morning at the bar where they had found Fran. They would see if she was there or had been there for work. Sam replied that he would be there, and hung up the phone.

After hanging up with Sam, Nemrak placed another phone call to the high priest in his flock.

"Hi James. I may need a favor from you. We hired a woman to go to Charlie's house and find out what he has been up to. We haven't heard from her yet, so I may need you to summon a spirit to see if she is still at Charlie's and see what they are up to. I would send Sam but I don't want to make Charlie suspicious that we are onto him."

"Just let me know when you need me," James said. "I'll be available."

Charlie and Fran decided to take a break from reading so they could eat. They put together some cold meat sandwiches and decided to go over their notes with each other.

Fran told Charlie that Satanic cults not only worship Satan but also have the ability to talk to spirits; the only member that can talk to spirits is the high priest.

"That's what I got from my reading also," Charlie said. "We need more information. Let's scan through the books tonight and see if we can find any information on how to communicate without being a high priest."

Through the rest of the afternoon and into the early evening the two of them scanned through the two books. They finished at about the same time.

Fran spoke first. "Nothing more in here."

Charlie said he didn't find anything either. Fran told Charlie that she was going to run to the store and pick up something for supper. She also wanted to know if Charlie had a Bible around the house. Charlie replied that he did not, and that the house had been fully furnished when they moved in. Fran said that she would stop by a church while she was out and ask the priest if she could have one. Charlie said that would be fine and that while she was gone he would check on the passage.

Fran arrived at the church just as mass was letting out and noticed a priest greeting people out front as they left. She patiently waited for everyone to leave before she approached the priest.

"Hi, Father. My name is Fran and I was wondering if I could have a Bible." She told him that a friend of hers was having some problems and she thought reading some Bible scriptures might help him.

The priest said he would be happy to give her one. As they walked into the church he introduced himself as Father James Wilson and said if she needed anything else to call the church and ask for him. Fran got the Bible and thanked the priest, then headed to the grocery store. While Fran was in the store she noticed that she was running low on money and that she might have to go pick up her check later. Fran picked up supper and a bottle of wine and headed back to Charlie's.

Charlie greeted her at the front door. "Did you get the Bible?" he asked.

"Yes I did," replied Fran. "I also picked up something special for supper. Here is the Bible, go ahead and read it while I make supper."

Charlie hurried to his desk, wondering where he should start. He decided just to browse around in the Bible to see if he could locate anything useful.

As Fran was preparing their meal, she heard a commotion from upstairs. She checked the study, but Charlie was gone. She went up to Charlie's room to see what all the noise was about. When she arrived upstairs she saw the spirit that Charlie had been talking about: it was speaking to Charlie. Fran ran back down the stairs and into the kitchen, frightened.

Later Charlie came back downstairs. He had just sat down to scan through the Bible again when Fran summoned him to the kitchen, saying that supper was ready. The two of them sat down to a nice supper, neither of them bringing up the spirit. After they had eaten Fran told Charlie it was time for his surprise. She took the chilled bottle of wine from the refrigerator and asked Charlie to join her in a toast.

"To the two of us, and how together we will defeat the passage and free you, Charlie." Charlie toasted with Fran, and as the night went on the closer the two of them became. That night before bed Charlie and Fran exchanged a goodnight kiss.

In the morning Charlie awoke to the sound of Fran leaving. He hurried down the stairs to try to find out where she was going but he was too late. Charlie then decided to make some toast and coffee and scan through the Bible.

An hour had passed when Fran returned to Charlie's house. He got up from his desk and met Fran at the door, asking where she had been and telling her he was worried sick about her.

Fran laughed as she said, "It's good to see that you care. I was running short on money and had to run to my employer to get my checks."

Charlie said he just wanted to know where she was going. They then sat down together to look over the scriptures in the Bible.

Joe the bar owner was working on getting things ready for that night's events when the phone rang.

"Hello, Joe's Strip Bar, Joe speaking. How may I help you?"

"This is Nemrak," the voice on the phone said to Joe.

Joe replied, "How may I help you, Nemrak?"

Nemrak told Joe that he was the one who had bought Francisca's services and was wondering if she had reported back to work yet or if he had seen her recently. Joe said she had been in this morning to pick up her paychecks and had asked to take a two-week leave of absence and gave no reason why. Nemrak told Joe thank you and goodbye. Joe wondered if Francisca was in trouble. Why would Nemrak be checking on her? Joe called Fran's house but no one answered, so he left a message.

"Fran, I think you may be in trouble. A man named Nemrak called looking for you and sounded very disappointed when I told him that you were on a leave of absence for two weeks. Please call me back when you get this message."

Nemrak wasn't done making phone calls. He dialed the number of the flock's high priest, James, and left a message. "James, this is Nemrak. We need to set up a mass to summon a spirit to spy on Charlie, because the girl we hired just blew up in our face."

Then Nemrak called Sam to let him know what was going on. Sam asked Nemrak if he should go check on Charlie. Nemrak said it wouldn't be necessary, that he was in the process of summoning up a spirit to spy on Charlie.

Sam said, "If you need me for anything, call me."

Later, James the high priest called Nemrak back. They discussed the meeting, and set it up for Thursday night at midnight, when the moon would be full. James and Nemrak called the rest of the flock to set up the meeting, and all were told not to mention anything to Charlie if they had contact with him.

Charlie and Fran spent the whole day, Tuesday, looking through the Bible and they were still no further along than they were before. Fran suggested that she go back to the church on Wednesday and talk to the priest, to see if he could help her. Charlie agreed that maybe their only option. They ate a late supper and then headed off to bed.

Charlie went and checked the passage. No unusual activity this night, but it was only last night when an evil spirit that claimed to be his master had visited him.

Charlie pondered what the spirit had said to him: "Be careful whom you trust, Charlie. Trust no one, only me. I will lead you to your freedom."

Charlie was puzzled by the message the spirit had given him. Was it trying to help him or trick him?

Fran lay in bed trying to figure out why she was having feelings for Charlie. She had always been one for whom looks and material items meant everything, but somehow she was able to see through Charlie's deformities to the caring person he was inside.

CHAPTER 5

The next morning Fran joined Charlie in bed, awakening him.

She said, "Charlie, I don't understand my feelings for you, but I want to make love to you."

When they finished, Fran said she was going to get a shower and then go to the church to talk to the priest.

She arrived at the priests' house and asked to talk to Father Wilson. The receptionist said Father Wilson was out for the day with funerals, but that Father Sandler could help her out. Fran waited as Father Sandler came down from upstairs. He introduced himself and asked how he could help her. Fran explained that her friend had a spirit problem, and wanted to know how he could communicate with it to see what it wanted. Father Sandler told her that the Catholic Church didn't believe in exorcists or spirits and that he would be no help to her, but if she left her name and phone number he could set her up with someone that could. She was to mention to no one how she found out about this person.

Fran wrote her name and number on a piece of paper and handed it to the priest. She told him it was her friend's number where she was staying.

Fran headed back to Charlie's to see if he had found anything out. Charlie told her he had discovered nothing. Fran told him that the church wasn't able to help but the priest knew someone that might so she gave him her name and Charlie's phone number.

Charlie asked, "Why did you give him my phone number? What happens if they find out?"

Fran said, "I'm sure Sam and Nemrak won't find out."

Charlie kept thinking to himself about what the spirit said to him about trusting no one. Would Fran be one not to trust? The priest? Charlie was so confused because he was falling in love with Fran and couldn't stand not to be with her.

Charlie said to Fran, "Would you like to know what the spirit said to me the other night?"

Fran said, "I already know. I went upstairs after you and heard the whole conversation. You can trust me, Charlie." Fran then went on to say she may be crazy but she was falling in love with him. That made Charlie a little more at ease.

Later in the day, at the rectory, Father Wilson was going over the paperwork for the day when he saw that Fran had been in, inquiring about spirits and communicating with them. He asked Father Sandler what she had been inquiring about. Father Sandler told him she had a friend with spirit problems and was interested in trying to communicate with them.

"I told her the Catholic Church doesn't believe in spirits or exorcisms and let it go at that," said Father Sandler.

Father Wilson said that he did. He thanked Father Sandler and went on with his business.

Charlie and Fran spent the evening on the couch, snuggling and watching television. A few hours went by before the phone rang.

"Charlie, who's calling?"

"This is William Hurst. Father Sandler told me that I

needed to call at this number."

Charlie told Fran that the phone was for her.

Fran answered, "This is Fran."

William told Fran that he was the person that Father Sandler had recommended and he wanted to meet with her and her friend Friday afternoon. Fran said they would be there all day.

William said, "How's 3 p.m.?"

Fran said that would be fine and she would see him then. She then gave him directions.

Charlie and Fran retired to bed together that night after they both went and checked the passage.

Early Thursday morning, Sam's phone rang. It was Nemrak.

"Sam, we have gotten a break. One of my old friends called me about a woman coming to him about a friend with spirit problems, wondering how to communicate with them."

Sam said, "Did he give a name?"

Nemrak replied that he wasn't able to locate the name, but he thought it might have something to do with Charlie.

"We need to hope for the best tonight when we summon the spirit to spy on Charlie," he said. Sam agreed and told Nemrak that he would see him at the cemetery.

Charlie and Fran were sitting at the table eating breakfast when Charlie said to Fran, "I'm falling in love with you yet I barely know you. Could you tell me about yourself?"

Fran said she was born into a strong Catholic family, her mother and father were very religious, and she had two brothers. She went on to say she lived a very normal life, her mother was a stay-at-home mom and her father worked to support the family, and her two brothers were altar boys with the local Catholic church. "It was very tight around our house. People from the church tried to help us out, and my brothers mowed the lawn for the church. One day, though, my oldest brother came home and told my mom that Phillip, my youngest brother, was in trouble at the church and she needed to go to the church and pick him up. She told Matt and I to stay home, that she would be home with Phillip shortly, but she never came home. We were told that she had a heart attack."

She continued, "The three of us were put into an orphanage and all split up to different families. My foster father sexually abused me and my foster mother let it happen until I turned sixteen. I ran away from home and became a stripper at Joe's Strip Bar and that's where I've been since."

They sat in silence for a moment.

"What about you, Charlie?" she asked.

Charlie stuttered for a moment and then began. "I, like you, was born to a very religious Catholic family and, like yourself, my parents died while I was very young. My father was mixed up in some sort of mafia or something and had a hit put out on him. He was shot in the head and dumped in a river with cement blocks tied to his legs. Then they raped and murdered my mother right in front of me.

"I was placed in an orphanage under a different name to protect my identity but was never adopted. When I turned sixteen I broke out and that's when I met Sam and you know the rest."

Fran said it was weird that their childhood memories were so alike. Charlie agreed.

"When I found out Charlotte was pregnant, I was very happy even though I knew the baby wasn't mine," said Charlie.

"What do you mean, the baby wasn't yours?" Fran asked Charlie.

"That's the part I left out when I told you about Charlotte. She was raped by the members of the flock and one of them was the father. Sam told me that the baby Charlotte was carrying was a special baby."

Fran thought for a moment and realized, "She was carrying the new flock leader when she died. Charlie, that's why you were punished so severely. It's all coming to me now." Fran told Charlie they would discuss more in the morning, that she needed to research the books a little more after finding out what he had told her.

At the cemetery, the flock was all showing up. It was 11:45 p.m., and the high priest was setting up for the ceremony to call the spirit into action. Sam and all the other members chanted as the witches danced around chanting spells to encourage the spirit to come. At 11:55 p.m., Nemrak started the ceremony by telling the flock that he thought Charlie was trying to betray them and that he needed all their help for the high priest to summon the spirit.

"Let's pray," said Nemrak.

The whole flock joined Nemrak in prayer. When they were done, the high priest started chanting. "Join us, cruel spirit. Join us in making Heaven and Earth in Hell. We ask this through our lord Satan, father of the spirit."

Just as the high priest was done chanting, a child spirit appeared.

"Spirit, I ask you to help us find the one who betrays our flock," chanted the high priest.

The spirit snarled and motioned that he would do the work in the name of Satan. He was gone just as fast as he appeared.

The high priest said, "I will summon the spirit again on the last night of the full moon, so we can see what Charlie is up to."

Charlie was awakened by the sound of Fran leafing through the books. "I think I may have found something!" she yelled.

Charlie hurried down the stairs. "What is it?" he asked.

"It says here that a spirit can only be summoned and spoken to on a full moon," she replied.

"Really? The full moon just started yesterday, so we have a few days to try to communicate," replied Charlie.

The couple was excited, thinking they were closer to freeing Charlie. They decided to go upstairs and try to read some prayers in front of the passage. They hoped the prayers would get the attention of a spirit that was willing to help them. They spent the next few hours reading prayers in front of the passage, to no avail.

At exactly 3 p.m. the doorbell rang. "Go to your room," Charlie told Fran.

The gentleman at the door introduced himself as William Hurst. Charlie invited him in and called for Fran. She entered the living room.

"Can you explain your situation to me?" William asked Charlie.

After Charlie and Fran finished their story, William pondered for a moment. "I believe the only solution to the problem," he said finally, "is for Fran to go to Rome and become a nun." "What for?" Fran asked. "How is that going to help?"

"You will learn how to deeply interpret the scriptures as you go through your training. You will understand their meanings better, and this should help you find out exactly what you need."

Fran thought for a moment, she looked at Charlie. He nodded to tell her he would be fine.

"So when do I leave?" she asked.

William replied, "Tomorrow at noon."

"Tomorrow!" exclaimed Fran. "I have a lot to get done

before then."

"Then it's settled. I'll pick you up tomorrow at noon. I'll take care of all the affairs on my end. You two get any loose ends taken care of on yours," said William.

Fran immediately started flying around the house, getting her things together. Charlie tried to help but got in the way more than he did any helping.

"I need to grab a few things from the store. Is there anything you need me to grab for you before I leave?" Fran asked Charlie.

"Nope, I have everything that I need here. I get deliveries every week," Charlie replied.

"Okay, I'll be back shortly."

Charlie stopped her before she headed out the door. "Promise to marry me when we get things straightened out," he said.

Fran said she promised and went on uptown to the store.

Charlie went off to check the passage: no unusual activity. So he went to bed, waiting for Fran to come home from running errands.

Fran stopped in at the bar where she worked and told Joe that she was quitting, that she was leaving the country with personal issues. Joe asked if she had gotten his message; she told him she hadn't. Joe said he was worried about her safety, that Nemrak was calling to check on her and ask when she was coming back to work. Fran assured Joe that she would be fine and headed back to Charlie's. When she arrived at Charlie's, she noticed the house was dark, so she headed upstairs to the bedroom. Charlie was already asleep so she didn't wake him up, she just lay beside him, holding him and crying. She couldn't help wondering if Charlie would be all right while she was gone.

Charlie awoke the next morning with Fran lying right next to him. He glanced at the clock and saw it was 9 a.m.

He knew that Fran was leaving at noon so he thought he should wake her up. Fran awoke frightened by Charlie nudging her.

"What time is it?" asked Fran.

Charlie replied, "It is 9 a.m. What do you have to do before you leave, Fran?"

Fran replied that she was done packing and taking care of all the other errands she had to do. "The rest of the morning I want to spend with you Charlie," said Fran. "I want to lie in bed with you and have you hold me. I feel so safe when I'm in your arms."

Neither uttered a word until 11 a.m., when Charlie told Fran it was time for her to get ready. Fran got out of bed and headed to the shower. Charlie got out of bed and checked the passage, then headed downstairs to make lunch for Fran and himself.

After her shower, Fran looked up into the mirror. A woman she had never seen before appeared in the mirror and warned her that the flock had found out about her and Charlie's intentions, that she needed to leave as soon as possible. Fran was frightened by the words of the spirit, but the only people that knew were Charlie, William, and herself, so she should be safe until everything blew over. When Fran came out of the bathroom she noticed that Charlie had made lunch.

"What a surprise," Fran said to Charlie.

Charlie said, "What, me cooking? You think I ordered out all the time? I can cook."

Fran said, "No, it's just a surprise that you are making lunch for me before I leave. It's very romantic."

Fran and Charlie sat down and had lunch. Just as they finished eating the doorbell rang. At the door was William. He asked if Fran was ready to go. Charlie said that she was and she would be right out. Fran came out with her luggage. She gave Charlie a kiss and told him that she loved him, then she headed out the door. Charlie told Fran that he loved her too and that he would miss her. He waved as they pulled away in the car.

Fran had just left and already Charlie was missing her company. He was worried about her, but it was for the best. She would be safer in Rome, away from him and the flock. When she came back she would know all they needed to know to free him from the flock's grip.

Fran and William were on their way to the airport when Fran asked William if she was doing the right thing. William asked Fran if she loved Charlie; Fran said she did and William told her that love was all the assurance she needed.

Fran smiled at William and said, "You're right."

William smiled back and went on to tell her that all the arrangements in Rome had been made for her. A taxi would pick her up at the airport and take her to the seminary. William again assured Fran that she had nothing to worry about, and that she would be home with Charlie before she knew it and they would be free to live a normal life.

It was about 3 p.m. when Fran arrived at the airport. William dropped her off out front and gave her the tickets. "These are your flight tickets. You'll need to go to Concourse C to catch your flight. It leaves at 5 p.m., so you should have plenty of time.

"Oh yeah," he continued. "One more thing. Here is a calling card so you can keep in touch with Charlie. You should probably let him know you're here."

Fran thanked William and headed into the airport. Inside, Fran checked her luggage and headed to her concourse. She found it with no problem and decided to sit down and have a drink. While she sat at the bar she debated whether she should call Charlie or if she should wait until she got to Rome. She decided to wait.

Charlie, meanwhile, was home pacing, waiting for the phone to ring, wondering if Fran had made it to the airport all right.

"I wish she would call," Charlie thought. All sorts of thoughts were going through Charlie's head: maybe Fran and William had been in an accident; or maybe they left together in a secret rendezvous. But the most awful thought going through Charlie's head was that maybe William was a fraud, and he had kidnapped Fran and raped her and left her in the gutter for dead.

He couldn't stand it anymore. He decided to call information to get the airport's number. Just as he was ready to call information, the phone rang. It was William.

"Charlie, I just wanted to let you know that Fran made it to the airport all right. She will be departing from Concourse C, and the phone number for the airport is 123-555-2345."

Charlie hung up with William and called the airport right away. When the attendant picked up, Charlie asked if he could speak to a Francisca Martin. The attendant said she could page to see if someone by that name was there, if Charlie would hold for a minute. Charlie held.

"Francisca Martin, telephone," echoed through the concourse. Fran approached the desk.

"I'm Francisca Martin," Fran said to the attendant. The attendant handed Fran the phone.

Fran said, "This is Francisca. May I help you?"

Charlie answered on the other side, "How are you holding up, Fran?"

Fran replied she was fine. Then Charlie asked why she didn't call him. Fran replied that she wanted to wait until she got to Rome because she was nervous about flying. Charlie told Fran she would be fine and that he loved her and wanted to hear her voice. Fran said she loved him too but her flight was boarding and she had to go.

Fran boarded the plane with no problem. As she waited for takeoff she began to feel less nervous about her decision to go. She felt like she wasn't alone in this ordeal. It was like someone was right there with her, helping her to relax.

After getting off the phone, Charlie went upstairs to check the passage, where he noticed Charlotte. She told Charlie she was happy he had found happiness with Fran but he needed to be aware that the flock was stronger than estimated. Charlotte then disappeared and another spirit showed up. This spirit showed Charlie a fireball falling from the sky before disappearing. Charlie, frightened, called out for Charlotte to see if she could help him figure out what was going on. But Charlotte never replied. Charlie went back to the kitchen and paced, wondering if the fireball was Fran's plane or what else it could be.

As he had supper, Charlie kept wondering about what the spirit had showed him, what it meant. He decided to go back through the Bible to see if anything in there could help him understand. He leafed through the Bible for a couple of hours and found nothing. He decided that it was time to turn in for the night, knowing that Fran would be calling early the next morning.

As he slept that night a familiar voice came to him in his sleep. It was Charlotte. She appeared in a dream to inform him that Fran had made it to Baltimore and that her flight was on its way to Rome, but she had more important news.

"Charlie," Charlotte said, 'Fran loves you a lot and I am happy for you two, and want to wish you the best." She smiled. "You are going to be a daddy. Fran is pregnant." Charlotte also wanted Charlie to know she missed him and that she would try to look out for both Fran and him.

Charlie awoke the next morning anxious to hear from Fran. He sat down to eat breakfast when the phone rang, but it wasn't Fran, just some salesperson. He sat back down, thinking about what Charlotte had told him in his dream.

CHAPTER 6

Sam was also having breakfast when his phone rang. It was Nemrak. He told Sam to gather the flock for a ceremony at 11 p.m. for the recalling of the sprit. Sam told Nemrak he would inform the flock members of the change in time and would see him that night. Sam hung up the phone with Nemrak and began calling the flock members.

Fran arrived in Rome and decided to call Charlie. The phone rang twice before he answered. Fran asked Charlie how he was holding up. Charlie relied that he was doing fine, but he missed her deeply. Fran told Charlie that she also missed him, and she just wanted to let him know that she had made it safely to Rome, and she was on her way to the seminary. Charlie then told Fran that Charlotte visited him in his dreams, and that she was happy for the two of them. Then Charlie grew silent. Fran asked what else she had said.

He replied, "She also told me that you were pregnant."

Fran's jaw dropped. "Not that I know of," she replied. "I've had no problem to make me believe that I might be."

Charlie asked Fran if she would be able to take a pregnancy test. She reminded him that she was studying to be a nun, and that none of this could surface or she would be expelled from the classes, and all that they had worked for would be ruined. Fran then told Charlie that she was supposed to start her period on Monday, and if she didn't she would inform him when she got into town the following weekend.

Charlie said that sounded fair. Fran told Charlie it was time for her to leave for the seminary, and that she would call him next Saturday when she got back into town.

"I love you, Charlie," Fran said.

Charlie replied, "I love you too, Fran."

Charlie was leafing through the Bible when he finally realized that what he was looking for wasn't in there. He went upstairs to the passage and tried to communicate with Charlotte. He kept calling Charlotte's name into the passage. He was finally answered, but not by Charlotte. The spirit that appeared told Charlie that Charlotte was an angel, and that only demon spirits were in the passage.

The spirit hissed at Charlie and said, "I control you, Charlie. She can't save you." Then it disappeared.

Charlie stumbled away from the passage. He hurried downstairs to catch his breath and try to figure out why she couldn't save him. He then decided to read over the demon worship book to look for any clues to what the demon had said. As he read through the books he couldn't help thinking about Fran and if she was pregnant, and how she would conceal it for the three months she would be in Rome.

He read page after page until all the words jumbled together and made no sense to him. He decided to turn in early that night, hoping that Charlotte would come to him again in his dreams and help him make sense of everything.

Sam arrived at the cemetery at 10:45 p.m. and began preparing for the ceremony. Nemrak and the high priest came over to Sam and asked, "Sam, did you hear anything about any flock members not showing up? We need everyone here for tonight's ceremony."

Sam replied, "All members are to be here tonight."

Nemrak remarked, "Good. The high priest said he invited a voodoo princess to the ceremony tonight."

Sam asked, "What for?"

"For Charlie," Nemrak replied.

It was now 11 p.m. and time for the mass to start. The high priest stood behind the altar and said he was grateful for the gathering.

"Let's bow our heads and look straight to Hell and pray," said the priest. "Oh Satan in the highest we praise you, we put you on the pedestal where you belong. We offer you this sacrifice tonight in the name of all that is evil."

After the prayer was over Nemrak headed up to the altar for the night's reading: "'In the early times before there was good and evil God and the Devil ruled Heaven equally. God became jealous of the Devil and banished him to Earth where the devil became disgruntled knowing that God had betrayed him and banished him from the throne in heaven. He plotted his revenge on God every day of his life on Earth. God created the Earth around the Devil to be beautiful without conferring the Devil first. This enraged the Devil more. Then God sent his son Jesus to rule the Earth and this fueled the hatred of God more. As we know the Devil had his disciples just as Jesus did. As the story goes Jesus died for the people to save all mankind but really the Devil destroyed him. God was then outraged and sent Satan to hell.' The struggle against good and evil, passage 10 Satanic Pentagram. Let us pray."

After the flock prayed a member brought a lamb to the altar.

The high priest looked at the ground and said, "Satan take this Lamb of God as we your people aim to please and help you regain what God has taken from you."

A masked man chopped the lamb's head off and the priest filled a cup with the blood. He took the cup and again looking at the ground he praised the devil. "This is the blood of the Lamb of God that gives your spirits the ability to go between heaven and hell to help you Satan regain your rightful position." The high priest then added water to the blood and passed it around the flock members. "Take this all of you and drink from it. This is the blood of the Lamb of Satan. Help us regain control over God."

The high priest and the flock were dancing and chanting around, then the high priest put his hands in the air, and the whole place grew silent.

"We have a special guest tonight. This is Mildred. She is a voodoo princess. She is new to the flock so let's give her a warm welcome."

The whole flocked hissed and spat at Mildred. "She will be assisting our witches in black magic," he continued.

Now they were ready to start the ceremony to recall the spirit to spy on Charlie. "The minds in fear, the minds in fear, the minds in fear," the whole flock was chanting.

Suddenly the spirit appeared above the altar. The high priest offered the spirit some lamb's blood. The eldest witch approached the altar, where she put a spell on the spirit. The spirit then flew into the crowd and entered the body of a young boy. The boy was then told by the high priest to approach the altar. The flock was in awe as none of them had ever witnessed a possession before.

The boy's mother cried out, "Why my son?" The high priest assured the mother that her son would be fine. The high priest then told the crowd that he had put the spirit in the body of the boy so that all could understand the spirit.

At the altar the boy began to speak, and then the spirit took over. The high priest asked the spirit what Charlie was up to. The spirit replied that he wouldn't tell him anything. The high priest then asked the question again, and the spirit replied with the same answer again.

The high priest said, "I'll ask you one more time."

The spirit said that he didn't need to tell the priest anything, that he knew what was going on inside.

"You just need to look inside yourself for the answer," said the spirit. After the spirit was done talking he left the body and the boy fell to the ground.

Nemrak asked the high priest what the spirit was talking about, but the high priest couldn't respond to him. Nemrak then called Sam over to the high priest.

"What do you need?" asked Sam.

"I think something might be wrong with James," said Nemrak. Sam looked down at the high priest and noticed that he was convulsing. Sam told Nemrak that they needed to get James to the hospital.

Nemrak and Sam took the high priest out of his ceremonial clothes and loaded him into Sam's car to take him to the hospital. On their way, the high priest went in and out of consciousness, rambling on about God and the Devil. Neither Nemrak nor Sam was able to make sense out of anything he was mumbling. They were almost to the hospital when James started praying the rosary. Sam and Nemrak were very confused. Why would James be praying the rosary?

When they arrived at the hospital they informed the ER staff that James had started having convulsions. The nurse in the ER asked if James was taking any medication. Nemrak said he didn't know but would go check in the car. Outside in the car Nemrak feverishly rummaged through James's ceremonial dress to see if he could find any medication. He looked in the left pocket and found what he was looking for and headed back into the hospital.

"Let's see what this is," said the nurse. It was lithium. The nurse took the medication and asked Sam and Nemrak to go have a seat in the waiting room while the doctor attended to James.

"We'll just go find a place to eat. Here's my phone number. Contact us if there are any changes in James's condition."

Just as Sam and Nemrak left, the doctor came in to see James.

"Hi, Father Wilson. How are you tonight?"

James hissed at the doctor, "Father Wilson is dead. I'm James Wilson, the High Priest of Satanism."

The doctor asked the nurse about the medication.

"It's lithium, just as I figured. Multiple personality syndrome."

"Where are the two men that brought him here? I have a few questions for them," said the doctor.

Just then, James jumped up out of his bed and headed out the E.R. door. The doctor and nurses tried to stop him but were unable to. One nurse came back in to tell the secretary to call the police and report a psych patient escaped. The secretary called the police department and told the dispatcher what was going on; the dispatcher then asked for a description of the patient. As the secretary described the patient, the dispatcher said it sounded a lot like Father Wilson. The secretary said they thought the same.

"We will get all available units looking for him," the dispatcher told the secretary.

James found a phone booth not too far from the hospital and called a close friend of his.

"William, this is Father Wilson. Could you come and pick me up? I'm at the phone booth on the corner of Main and Market."

William said he would be right there. James waited there until William came and picked him up.

Sam and Nemrak finished eating and headed back to the hospital to check on James. When they arrived they were notified that James had escaped and that the police were looking for him. Nemrak told the secretary to call the police back and tell them they weren't needed. The secretary said she couldn't do that. Nemrak just held his hand up in the air and the secretary made the call. On their way out of the hospital Sam asked Nemrak how he had done that.

"Just something I learned from a witch. Comes in handy every now and then."

James got into William's car and noticed that he had no medication in his pockets.

"William, can you take me to my brother's guest house tonight? It's late and I don't want to wake Father Sandler. He has the early mass in the morning so I'd rather not disturb him."

William agreed and headed toward James's brother's house. When they arrived, James told William he knew where the spare key was and would let himself in.

"Thank you, William," said James. William then headed home.

Sam and Nemrak left the hospital looking for James. They drove around for almost an hour before they decided to go check his house. Sam pulled into James's driveway and Nemrak went up to the door. Nemrak rang the doorbell. Noticing lights and movement, he rang the doorbell again. Suddenly there was an answer through the intercom.

"Who is it?"

"It's me," Nemrak replied. "Open the door, James."

James replied, "I don't know you. Go away before I call the cops."

Nemrak was angered and yelled to James, "What do you mean you don't know me? You open this door right now."

James refused to open the door. "I'm on the phone with the cops right now. Leave now or they will be on their way."

Nemrak said, "Fine, I'm leaving." Sam and Nemrak headed back to Nemrak's house.

CHAPTER 7

The next morning James awoke in his brother's guest house wondering what had happened the previous night, how he had ended up at the phone booth. He called William to see if he could bring him to church to get ready for mass. William said that he would be right over to pick him up. After James hung up the phone he took the last pill he had.

Charlie had awoken and gone to check the passage when he heard a loud noise downstairs. He went down the stairs to see what caused the noise. He checked the kitchen and noticed a spirit.

The spirit told Charlie, "The one you trust the most will be the one who ends up costing you in the end."

Charlie asked if it was Fran. The spirit replied that it wasn't Fran but that both of them knew and trusted the person. Charlie was about to ask the spirit another question when it disappeared. Charlie then went back up to check the passage. There was no unusual activity, but he did notice a lot more spirits than usual. He went back downstairs and sat in his recliner, wondering who the one that they trusted was.

William arrived to pick James up to take him to get ready for church. He asked how James was feeling. James replied that he was confused on how he ended up at the phone booth last night.

William said he didn't know how he ended up there, "but I did notice you were acting funny last night."

"The only thing I remember is going to sleep at 10 p.m. and I barely remember a hospital room, then I ended up at the phone booth calling you."

William said, "Maybe you need to rest after mass today."

James said that he would, and wondered if William could refill his prescription. "I've misplaced the bottle I just got and took my last one this morning." William said he would bring it by after mass today.

Fran was at the seminary preparing for her first day of class after church. During church Fran kept wondering if she was pregnant or not and how Charlie was holding up. After church she was heading toward the cafeteria when she ran into another woman there to be a nun. Fran introduced herself to the woman.

"Hi, my name is Marcy."

Fran asked Marcy if she wanted to eat lunch and get to know one another better. Marcy said that would be splendid. The two of them headed to the cafeteria. At the table, the two of them started telling each other about themselves; of course, Fran made up her story. The two of them bonded really well over lunch and became instant friends. Fran thought to herself that having a friend at the seminary would make the time go quicker.

James made it through both masses and was waiting for William to show up with his medication when he started having flashbacks of the night before. James was sweating bullets when William showed up.

"Are you all right?" asked William.

James replied that it was time for his medication and

asked William if he could get him a glass of water while he sat down. When William returned, James took his medication and in a matter of minutes was back to his normal self. James then asked William what he had been up to. William replied that he had taken a woman to the airport the other day, to fly to Rome to become a nun.

James replied, "Really? Well, who was she?"

William said, "You should know her. She was in here asking you and Father Sandler about an exorcism."

"I remember her," replied James.

"Well, her friend happened to be her boyfriend. What an ugly guy. His face was severely deformed. They are trying to save him from some spirits or something."

"Kids these days are weird," James said. William and James spent the next couple of hours talking about Fran becoming a nun to save her boyfriend.

Sam was at home recalling the past night, wondering why James told Nemrak that he didn't know who he was and threatened to call the cops on them. Then the phone rang. It was Nemrak telling Sam he wanted him to come over and take him to James's house. Sam said that he would be right over. Nemrak replied that he would be waiting.

Sam went outside and jumped into his car and was heading to Nemrak's house when he passed the rectory. Sam drove by the rectory and had to do a double take. He swore that James was on the porch talking to someone. Nemrak's house was only a mile away and they would have to pass the rectory again on their way to James's house, so Sam continued to Nemrak's house.

Nemrak was outside waiting for him and got into the car. Sam couldn't wait to tell Nemrak about what he saw. On the way to James's house, Sam told Nemrak about how he thought he saw James on the porch of the rectory. As they passed the rectory no one was on the porch. Nemrak then told Sam that James had a twin brother that was a priest and that maybe he was in the area visiting the parish. Sam said he never knew that James had a twin brother.

Nemrak replied, "That's because James doesn't like to talk much about him."

They arrived at James's house and realized that no one was home. Nemrak decided to go ring the doorbell anyway and there was no answer. He got back into the car and asked Sam to take him to get his car.

Fran and Marcy had just finished lunch, and the two of them headed off to class. Fran was thinking to herself what a nice woman Marcy was. Too bad I have to lie to her about myself, but I have to protect Charlie and me. Fran and Marcy entered the classroom and noticed that the class only consisted of four women. The instructor entered the room and introduced herself as Sister Stephanie.

"Today we will go over the rules and regulations of being a sister. We prefer to be called sisters rather than nuns because we are a sisterhood of God. The following rules are: no smoking, no sex, and no drinking will be tolerated. If you are caught in any of these actions you will be automatically expelled. We will teach you everything you need to know on how to help your local church, help your local communities with prayer and understanding in the ways of our Lord."

Sister Stephanie then handed out Bibles to everyone in class.

"This is your study guide. I'll teach you all how to interpret the words the way they were intended."

Sister Stephanie then asked the class to introduce themselves. She started in the back of the room and Rachael introduced herself, then there was Marcy, then Francisca, and finally Lisa. Lisa asked Stephanie why there were only four students in the class.

Sister Stephanie replied, "It is hard for us as humans to let go of some of life's pleasures. Only the ones who truly believe in God and his ways come here."

Sister Stephanie then gave an assignment: "Read the first 50 pages of the Bible and interpret what you think they mean. We will go over it in class tomorrow."

William decided it was time to go. James said he would walk him out. Sam and Nemrak were on their way home at this time, and were just getting ready to pass the rectory. Suddenly James fell to his knees, holding his head.

"Are you okay?" William shouted to James.

James didn't reply. William called for Father Sandler to come out and help. James was going into convulsions, speaking of the devil and how he was going to take over the world, that God underestimates the power of Satan. William had a confused look on his face when Father Sandler came out to help him.

"Don't worry about him, William," said Father Sandler. "This happens every once in a while. His medication causes it."

Father Sandler and William got James into the rectory and laid him on the couch. Father Sandler told William that he would take care of James and that he should go home.

Sam dropped Nemrak off and decided to pay Charlie a surprise visit. He arrived at Charlie's house and let himself in. Charlie was in the recliner reading a book on Satanic cults when Sam walked in.

"What have you been up to, Charlie?" asked Sam.

"Reading," replied Charlie. "Just trying to understand our religion better and why we do the things we do."

Sam told Charlie he could explain everything he needed to know, if Charlie would tell him the real purpose of his readings. Sensing a trap Charlie politely declined Sam's offer. Sam stayed for about 45 minutes and just talked to Charlie. Sam then headed out for the day.

Charlie was worried. Was Sam onto him and Fran? Would Fran be all right? Charlie was pondering these thoughts in his head as he headed upstairs to check the passage. The spirits were unusually quiet, so Charlie went to bed for the night.

Fran was up reading verses in the Bible, trying to make sense of the words and what they meant.

"How does Stephanie want me to interpret the readings?" she wondered.

Over and over Fran was reading the verses, jotting down her thoughts. The whole time she was worrying about Charlie and how he was doing. Suddenly there was a knock at the door. It was Marcy, and she was having problems with the reading. Together the two of them analyzed the readings the best they could. Marcy and Fran then sat down and began to talk.

Marcy started telling Fran how she didn't belong at the seminary. Fran asked Marcy why she didn't think she belonged. Marcy told Fran that she couldn't tell anyone about this, and then she decided to drop the whole thing and head back to her own room. After Marcy left, Fran headed to bed wondering why Marcy didn't think she belonged. Fran tossed and turned all night, finding it more difficult to sleep in the strange place.

Fran awoke in the morning and reread the interpretations of the scriptures she had done. Something seemed funny about the interpretation but she wasn't sure what it was. She looked at the clock and noticed she had just enough time to catch a quick bite to eat before class, so she headed to the cafeteria. She noticed Marcy, and approached her about the previous evening, Marcy asked Fran to come over to her room after supper and they would talk. The two of them headed off to the classroom.

Sister Stephanie walked into the classroom shortly after Fran and Marcy.

"Class, let's get out our interpretations and get ready to turn them in."

Fran was hesitant to turn in her assignment; she looked at Sister Stephanie and took a deep breath. Stephanie looked up at Fran and asked her if she was all right. Fran said she just had a long night and handed in her assignment.

"Class, the assignment for tonight is to read the next fifty pages and interpret it. Class dismissed."

Fran left the classroom and headed back to her room to get an early start on her assignment, since she was to meet with Marcy later that night. She flipped through the pages of the Bible, jotting notes as she scanned through each and every word. Time seemed to fly by. When she looked up at her clock she noticed that she had worked right through lunchtime. She knew that she should get up and walk to get a snack and a break. She went to the cafeteria, grabbed an apple and a juice, and headed back to her room. After a couple of hours she was finally done with the homework and ready to go to Marcy's room.

On the way to Marcy's room Fran met Marcy heading to the cafeteria for supper. Marcy asked her to join her. Fran accepted. During supper Marcy told Fran that she wanted her to meet somebody.

Marcy said, "She is a friend here checking out the seminary and maybe joining our class."

Fran was eager to meet a new person at school. After supper the two of them headed back to Marcy's room. Marcy opened the door and let Fran in. As Fran walked in she noticed a woman sitting in a chair. Marcy introduced the woman to Fran, saying, "This is Daphne."

"Hi Daphne. My name is Fran. How are you tonight?"

Daphne didn't say anything. Fran looked at Marcy with a dumbfounded look.

Marcy told Fran, "She has to trust you before she talks to you."

"Okay," said Fran. "So, about last night. Why don't you think you belong here?"

Marcy opened her mouth but no words came out. She just looked at Daphne. Fran was puzzled for a moment. Then she asked Marcy if they were lesbians. Marcy said that wasn't it.

Marcy then said to Fran, "You're very hesitant to be here too. You act as if you have something to hide. You can trust me."

Fran looked at Marcy and said, "When you tell me what you are hiding then I'll tell you."

Suddenly Daphne stood up and said that Fran should leave. Fran asked why and Marcy told her to just leave.

This left more questions in Fran's head. She desperately wanted to speak to Charlie but it was only Tuesday and she wasn't allowed into town until the weekend. She was flustered and decided to go back to Marcy's room. She was bound and determined to see what Marcy and Daphne were hiding.

Fran noticed a sweet smell coming from Marcy's room. She had never smelled anything like it before. Fran knocked on the door and then everything went blank. Fran awoke the next morning in her bed, with Sister Stephanie at her side.

"What happened?" asked Fran.

"We don't know," said Stephanie. "I was doing my rounds when I found you in the hallway in front of Marcy's room. You were unconscious and Father Pelfrey helped me bring you to your room. I've been here all night with you to make sure you would be all right."

Fran said, "I don't remember how I got there last night.

I don't remember anything after supper."

"Fran, I made you an appointment with Doctor Collins for after class."

Fran replied that she felt fine and didn't need to see the doctor. Stephanie said it was up to her if she wanted to see the doctor or not. Fran, knowing that she could be pregnant, told Stephanie she would see how she felt after class and decide then.

Stephanie said, "Well, then, I'll see you in class."

Fran said, "See you then."

Fran was very suspicious of Marcy; she had only told Stephanie that she didn't remember anything from the night before so she wouldn't trigger any alarms. Fran took a shower and got ready for class. On her way she ran into Marcy in the hallway. Marcy asked Fran how she was feeling.

Fran replied, "Fine, but why would you care?"

Marcy looked at Fran and apologized for the night before. She told Fran to come back to her room Friday night and all of her questions would be answered.

"Trust me," said Marcy. The two of them went into class and took their seats. Stephanie then came into the room and discussed their assignment.

CHAPTER 8

Charlie had some uneventful days after Sam visited. He was leafing through the book on Satanic cults, and learned that the High Priest had a sworn enemy. It wasn't any priest, bishop, pastor, or any other clergy. It was a High Priestess. She was used as an avenue to help people having a spiritual episode to embrace God. Charlie also learned that a High Priestess would be able to close the passage. But how would he find one? Did people still practice it today? How would he find out?

Charlie pondered those thoughts while he went to check the passage. The activity level was below normal, which caused him some concern, but he just blew it off.

He began searching through the Bible, hoping to find some information in it. He leafed through it for about an hour, and then he heard a ruckus upstairs. He went upstairs to investigate and noticed the child spirit. The spirit looked weaker, and for some reason that bothered Charlie. Maybe it was because Fran might be pregnant. Charlie tried to communicate with the spirit, asking if there was anything that he could do for him, but the spirit just looked at him dumbfounded.

Charlie went back downstairs to research the Bible more. He couldn't get the child spirit's face out of his mind. Something looked familiar about the spirit but Charlie couldn't put a finger on it.

That night, Charlie was awakened by a voice in his dream saying "Pagan."

He racked his brain. "High Priestess and Pagan…what do they share in common, if anything?" Pondering this in his mind, Charlie fell back asleep.

Fran was just leaving class when Stephanie flagged her down and asked her if she was going to see Doctor Collins. Fran told her she felt fine and didn't need to see him, but wanted to thank her for her concerns.

"I'll stop by later to see how you're doing," Stephanie told Fran.

Fran headed back to her room. What did Marcy mean about finding out everything on Friday night?

Fran was leafing through her assignment when she heard a knock on the door. It was Stephanie.

"I told you I would be by to check on you," said Stephanie. "So how are you feeling?"

Fran replied that she was fine and that she was in the middle of her assignment. Stephanie said she would see her tomorrow in class, and to let her know if she needed anything. Fran said she would and let Stephanie out of her room. Fran wished the weekend would come soon, so she could speak to Charlie and let him know how she was and how things were going.

James had a miserable night due to his medication not working. In the middle of the night he ended up seeing Satan and his followers taking over the world. James ended up in his car by morning. A cop, wondering if he was all right, woke him. James replied that he was fine and told the cop to leave him the hell alone. James decided to head back to his house to try to contact Nemrak to set up another sacrifice.

Back at the church Father Sandler was frantic. "Where's

James taken off to? He was supposed to do confession this morning!" He was supposed to work with pre-Cana couples. How would he do both? He prayed to God for the answer as he frantically searched for James. He decided he would cancel the pre-Cana couples until later that afternoon so he could do confessions. During mass he tried to cover his worries about James, but it was very hard to do. James had been acting strangely lately. Father Sandler decided after confessions that he would call the police and the archbishop if James didn't show up.

It was now Wednesday morning and Fran had just awoken. She showered, finished up her assignment, and headed to the cafeteria, where she ran into Marcy. Fran asked her how she was doing.

Marcy muttered, "I don't know why I'm here," and left the cafeteria. Fran shrugged off Marcy's comment and went to get her breakfast. Sitting down to eat, Fran again leafed through her assignment. She finished breakfast and headed to class. When she arrived at class, again she saw Marcy, and again something didn't seem right with her. Just as Fran was going to approach her, Stephanie came into the room. Stephanie noticed right away that something wasn't right with Marcy.

"Marcy, are you okay?"

Marcy replied, "No."

Stephanie then told Marcy to go back to her room and rest, and that she would send someone to her room later with the assignment. Marcy left the room. Stephanie then called the class to order. Everybody handed in their assignments and received that night's assignment. Stephanie then told the class it was time for mass, and that they all needed to attend.

After mass Stephanie asked Fran if she would go check on Marcy and let her know the assignment. Fran said she would and headed to Marcy's room. She was shocked to see Daphne answer the door.

"Is Marcy feeling better?" Fran asked.

"She is sleeping right now," replied Daphne. Fran then told Daphne the assignment for that night and left.

Charlie spent most of the day pondering the words high priestess and pagan. He looked at his watch and to his surprise it was almost 11 p.m.

"I haven't eaten yet," thought Charlie to himself as he headed into the kitchen. He sat down and ate a bowl of cereal. Charlie then went to check the passage; again the child spirit was present. Charlie just hung his head, wondering what happened to that kid, because every time the spirit showed up Charlie was overcome by sadness. Charlie then headed off to bed. Just after falling asleep, a voice came to him. "Hermes!"

Charlie awoke with the three phrases looming in his mind. "What do they mean?" pondered Charlie, "and how would he find out." He thought about sneaking into the library again, but he would have to make a new plan. Charlie lay in bed plotting ideas on how to sneak into the library without being caught.

In the morning, as Father Sandler was preparing for the funeral service, the phone rang. It was the archbishop, letting him know that he would have a replacement for James that night. Father Sandler asked the archbishop what had taken him so long; the archbishop replied that this had happened before and James always showed back up. Father Sandler, being new to the parish, had his suspicions about James leaving at night but never mentioned anything about it.

Fran was already awake; she was still worried about

Marcy. She went to her room to check on her and was greeted at the door again by Daphne. Fran asked if Marcy was feeling better. Daphne replied that Marcy was already at the cafeteria getting breakfast. Fran noticed the necklace that Daphne was wearing. It was a circle with a star in it. Daphne noticed Fran looking at her necklace, and hurriedly tucked it into her shirt. Fran then snapped out of her temporary state of mind and said she would go meet Marcy for breakfast. On her way to the cafeteria she thought about Daphne's necklace.

"I know I have seen that symbol before, but where?" she thought. Fran was racking her mind thinking about it until she reached the cafeteria. Fran found Marcy and sat with her.

"How are you feeling today, Marcy?" Fran asked.

"Much better, thank you," replied Marcy.

"Did you get your assignment done last night?"

"Yes I did. Daphne helped me," said Marcy.

Nemrak was sitting at his desk reading when the phone rang. It was James asking if he had arranged for the sacrifice that night. Nemrak said it was all taken care of. Then James asked Nemrak if he was able to find the sacrificial lamb for the All Hallows Eve Sacrifice. Nemrak said he had gone through the flock's families and found what they were looking for.

Nemrak then called Sam. "Why don't you bring Charlie to the ceremony tonight?"

"Why would you want me to do that?" asked Sam.

"He needs to stay in touch with his religion," Nemrak answered.

Sam called Charlie. Surprisingly, Charlie agreed to accompany Sam to the ceremony.

"I'll pick you up at 11 p.m.," Sam told Charlie.

After hanging up with Sam, Charlie was still wondering how to get the information that he needed. Maybe I'll see or hear something tonight at the ceremony.

It was a quarter after ten when Charlie went upstairs to check the passage. Again the child spirit was there but this time he seemed happier. Charlie couldn't figure it out.

Charlie was getting changed for the ceremony when Sam came and knocked on the door. Charlie hurried and pulled up his pants to go answer the door.

"You're early," Charlie told Sam.

Sam replied, "I know."

Charlie invited Sam in as he went upstairs to finish dressing. Luckily Charlie had put all his books upstairs so Sam couldn't see them. Charlie finished dressing and went downstairs.

"What's the hurry?" Sam asked him.

Charlie replied, "I thought you were ready to go."

Sam said he thought the two of them could sit and talk. He asked how Charlie was doing.

"Not bad, considering the circumstances," Charlie replied.

Sam then asked Charlie what he had been up to.

"Looking after the passage. What else could I be up to when I can't leave the house?"

"That's right," Sam sighed, and became quiet. Ten minutes of silence passed before Sam said they should be leaving.

The car was silent on the way to the ceremony. As they got closer, Charlie grew nervous. The scenery grew more and more familiar and Charlie began having flashbacks of Charlotte. Sam looked over at Charlie and asked him if he was all right.

Charlie took a deep breath and replied, "Considering what took place here, I'm fine."

They parked the car and headed to the congregation of people. Charlie listened to the conversations going on as they passed through. Suddenly he heard the word "pagan." He grabbed Sam and told him he wanted to sit here. Sam replied that he wanted to sit up front. Charlie told Sam that he was too uncomfortable being here and would prefer to sit here. Sam agreed that they could stay here. They took their seats and Charlie concentrated on the conversation of the two flock members.

"Those Wiccan witches can save the world from the coming of the Antichrist. They think they can hide behind their pagan religion and their high priestess for protection."

Charlie then realized what he needed to look for as he heard three of the five words said to him in his sleep. He was hoping to hear more but then Nemrak began to speak.

"Faithful followers, let us give thanks to our lord." All the flock members looked down at the ground and began to pray to Satan.

"Satan our lord help guide us to be loyal followers in your name, help us lead our lives to help you rise from Hell and reclaim your rightful ruling of Earth."

After they were done with their prayer James came up to the podium and told the flock to be seated. He went on to say how tonight they had a special sacrificial ceremony planned. James told Nemrak to bring the sacrificial lamb to the altar. Nemrak brought the lamb to the altar as James had one of his witches lay a black cloth on the ground in front of the altar as she chanted a spell. James then began chanting and raised his hands in the air for the flock to rise again.

"Satan take this sacrifice as our gift to you as you strengthen yourself to take your rightful rulership."

The witch came out with a black dagger and handed it to James. He took the dagger, looked at the ground, and began chanting some more. Then with one swipe of the dagger he sliced the throat of the lamb. As the witch collected the blood in black urns the whole flock began chanting and dancing, just as on the night that Charlie and Charlotte were married.

This angered Charlie and made him more determined to put a stop to the nonsense. He had to bite his lip not to say something.

James held one of the urns in the air. He took the urn of blood to the altar and began chanting in a language that Charlie didn't understand. He motioned the urn counterclockwise around the cloth three times and the urn disappeared; he took a second urn and said, "Enjoy your feast of our sacrifice Satan, let us join you in your feast of returning to power." James drank from the urn, and then the flock members took turns drinking the blood of the lamb.

Charlie tried to avoid having to drink, but, not wanting to make a scene, he went up and drank the blood. As he approached the altar, he noticed that he was being watched by one of the witches. Charlie avoided eye contact with her, but he felt like her stare was penetrating him. He tried to clear his mind as he returned to his seat with Sam.

Charlie wasn't able to sleep that night. Going to the ceremony brought up so many memories of Charlotte that he was crying. He needed Fran now more than ever before and she had only been gone for about a week.

Charlie was looking through old photos of him and Charlotte. The more he saw the angrier he got.

"Look what they did to me!" Charlie was so upset that he began ripping the pictures of himself, only keeping those of Charlotte. That person no longer lives until I seek my revenge on those who took her life.

Charlie thought for a while. I know there is a connection between pagan, Wicca, and high priestess. It must be a religion, but why isn't it mentioned in the Bible? Where do I need to go to get the information? Hopefully Fran would have answers on Saturday when she calls.

CHAPTER 9

Fran was awakened by a commotion in the hallway. She heard Sister Stephanie telling someone to get Dr. Collins. Fran opened her door and went to investigate. She found Daphne lying on the floor unconscious. Fran went over to see if she could help Sister Stephanie.

"Go check on Marcy," Stephanie told Fran. Fran nodded and noticed the medallion on Daphne's neck; she was finally able to get a good look at it. Then she went into Marcy's room and found her crying on the bed.

"What happened?" asked Fran.

Marcy replied, "We got into an argument and I slammed the door on her. I didn't mean to hurt her." Fran comforted Marcy for a little while. She stayed until Marcy fell asleep, then headed to Sister Stephanie's room.

"How is Daphne doing?"

"Okay," replied Sister Stephanie, "but how did you know her name?" Fran answered by saying she was introduced as Marcy's friend and that she was here checking out the seminary, thinking about becoming a nun.

"We don't allow visitors here, you know that. As soon as she recovers she will have to leave. Does anybody else know of her being here?" asked Stephanie.

"Not that I know of," said Fran.

"After class tomorrow, I want to talk to you and Marcy," said Stephanie.

Fran left Stephanie's room thinking of the medallion that Daphne was wearing. It looked so familiar but she couldn't place it. Maybe she could ask Marcy about it in the morning.

The next morning, Fran showered and headed to the cafeteria for breakfast, hoping to catch Marcy before class, but Marcy was nowhere in sight. Fran ate breakfast and then headed to class. Marcy was coming down the hallway hollering for Fran. Fran turned around to acknowledge Marcy.

"We can't meet tonight," said Marcy.

"Why?"

"It has something to do with Daphne. I'll explain after she recovers," replied Marcy.

Fran told Marcy that Sister Stephanie was going to make Daphne leave after she recovered, because no one was supposed to have visitors. Marcy sighed with a lost look in her eyes.

"They can't make her leave. I'll no longer be able to be here without Daphne," she said.

Fran went to ask Marcy why she couldn't be here without Daphne, but Marcy darted off before she could get the words out of her mouth. She took her seat just as class began. They went over their previous assignment, and were given an assignment for the weekend. Stephanie reminded the class that they were able to go into town on Saturday, and that Sunday they were expected to be at mass and make communion. Stephanie then dismissed the class except for Marcy and told them to have a great weekend.

Marcy tried to sneak out but Stephanie caught her and told her that they needed to talk. Fran also stayed in class and asked Stephanie if they could talk. Stephanie told her she would talk to her after she talked to Marcy, and that Fran should go back to her room and she would meet her there.

Marcy and Stephanie went into Stephanie's office. "Who

is this woman that we found unconscious in the hallway in front of your room?"

Marcy denied knowing who she was, or what she was doing at the seminary at all.

Sister Stephanie knew what Fran had told her and was confused. "You're saying that you don't know who she is or what she is doing here?"

Marcy replied, "Yes. May I be dismissed now?"

Sister Stephanie reluctantly agreed and Marcy went back to her room.

Sister Stephanie decided to head right to Fran's room to see if she told the same story she did the night before. Fran answered the door and invited Sister Stephanie in.

"So who was that woman we found in front of Marcy's room last night again?" she asked Fran.

Fran replied that her name was Daphne, and that she was a friend of Marcy's. She was here checking out the seminary, she was thinking of becoming a nun.

Sister Stephanie said, "Okay, but how did you know about her?"

"Marcy introduced her to me, that night I fainted and you found me in front of Marcy's door," Fran replied.

"Do you remember any more of what happened that night?"

"Just a sweet smell coming from Marcy's room. It was nothing I've ever smelled before."

Fran then asked Sister Stephanie about Daphne's pendant. "It looks familiar to me but I'm unable to place it, and it bothers me."

Sister Stephanie told Fran she would check it out when she went back to check on Daphne. "One more question, though: do you think anyone else knows about Daphne?"

Fran replied, "I don't think so because I have never seen Daphne outside of Marcy's room, and Marcy didn't talk to anyone else in class."

Sister Stephanie left Fran's room and headed to check on Daphne. She ran into Dr. Collins along the way.

"How is Daphne, Dr. Collins?" asked Sister Stephanie.

"She had a concussion and will need a few days to rest. She is sleeping now."

Stephanie went to Daphne's room and saw she was sleeping, just as Dr. Collins had said. She decided this would be a perfect time to look at Daphne's pendant. It was a pentagram but the point was up, not down. This confused Stephanie. She had never seen one with the point up. She decided to seek Father Pelfrey's advice, but he was out until Sunday morning. It would have to wait.

Charlie had slept in; he awoke to a commotion in the passage. He went to check it out and noticed the child spirit. The spirit looked stronger than ever. Something still bothered Charlie. It was how the spirit looked so familiar to him, but he couldn't place the reason why.

Charlie was still angry from what took place at the ceremony the night before, and all the memories that were brought back to him. He couldn't wait until Saturday to hear from Fran. He was frustrated from not hearing from Fran in the two months that she had been gone and still wondering if she was pregnant or not.

Fran was very curious about what Marcy had told her, so she decided to make her way to the medical rooms to try to talk to Daphne to get an explanation. She met Dr. Collins and Sister Stephanie, who told her Daphne was sleeping and that no one could see her. Fran decided to write Daphne a note and asked the nurse to give it to her when she awoke; the nurse said she would do that.

Fran then headed back to her room and began working on her assignment. She was very frustrated with the whole situation going on. She had no idea if she was pregnant or not. She hadn't had a period since she had been there but she hadn't had any morning sickness. I hope I can get the privacy tomorrow to call Charlie and just hear his voice, she thought.

Father Sandler was worn out from doing all the masses and funerals by himself; he was relaxing when the doorbell rang at the rectory. He answered the door and to his surprise it was the replacement for Father Wilson. Finally!

"You must be Father Sandler. I'm Father Carey." Father Sandler sighed with relief and invited Father Carey inside. The two of them sat down, planned a schedule, and got to know one another. Father Carey told Father Sandler to take the rest of the day off and also Saturday.

"Just show me around and I'll handle it from there," said Father Carey.

"Are you sure?" asked Father Sandler.

"Yes, I am sure. You've had a rough two months. It's the least I can do for you."

Father Sandler thanked Father Carey and told him that he would inform him about the Father Wilson situation Saturday night. The two priests went over to the church and Father Sandler showed Father Carey around. Father Carey decided to look more around the church to get familiar with it and do some praying.

"Go rest, Father Sandler," said Father Carey. "I'll be fine here."

Father Sandler agreed and headed back to the rectory. Instead of resting, though, he had filing and paperwork to catch up on. He stumbled upon Fran's paperwork, and noticed her address, and also how it was conveniently misplaced. It was unlike Father Wilson to be disorganized, Father Sandler put the file where it needed to go and filed the instance in the back of his head.

Fran was studying when she heard a knock at her window. She looked out and saw Marcy.

"What's going on?" Fran asked.

"I'm leaving. I don't belong here. I just wanted to let you know something, Fran."

"What's that?"

Marcy replied, "Demands are fear."

Fran was puzzled as Marcy took off into the night. It was past curfew but Fran knew she needed to let Sister Stephanie know what was going on. She frantically pounded on Stephanie's door.

"What's wrong, Fran?" asked Stephanie.

"Marcy has run off!"

"What?"

Fran told Stephanie about her encounter with Marcy at the window.

"What did she want to let you know?" asked Sister Stephanie.

"All she told me is that 'demands are fear,' and as she ran off she kept chanting 'demands are fear.' I don't understand what she was talking about."

Sister Stephanie said that Fran should go back to her room, but Fran didn't want to. Sister Stephanie then said that Fran could stay with her, since she was shaken up. Stephanie decided she would have to contact Father Pelfrey and let him know what was going on. She put some pillows and blankets on the couch and told Fran she would be right back.

Since Father Pelfrey was out of town, Sister Stephanie went to her office to call him. Sister Stephanie then went to get Dr. Collins. She told him what was going on and said they should go check Marcy's room to see if she may have been playing a prank on Fran.

Marcy's door was unlocked. They let themselves in and called for Marcy but there was no sign of her. Dr. Collins noticed some clothing wrapped up on the table. As he unrolled it he found some kind of herbs wrapped in the cloth.

"Stephanie, what is this?" Stephanie looked and shrugged her shoulders.

"I'll keep these until Father Pelfrey returns," he said. "I can run some tests and look through some medical journals to find out what they are. Why don't you head back to your room and get some rest. I'll look outside to see if I can find Marcy."

Dr. Collins took the herbs and cloth back to his office and called the police to report that one of the students had run off. He was informed that unless he felt the student was in immediate danger that they wouldn't fill out a report until 24 hours had passed. Dr. Collins said he would let them know if she returned and hung up. He then decided to do a quick check of the seminary grounds, but there was no sign of her, so he decided to go back to his lab and run some tests on the herbs he found.

Sister Stephanie was awakened by a knock at the door. It was Father Pelfrey. He had returned from his mission.

"Has there been any change since we talked last night?" he asked. Stephanie informed Father Pelfrey about what she and Dr. Collins found in Marcy's room.

"Where is the stuff?" asked the priest.

"Dr. Collins has it in his office," Stephanie replied.

Father Pelfrey headed to Dr. Collins office.

"Hi, Father Pelfrey," said Dr. Collins. "I have some news for you. The herb we found was opium, but this cloth we found still puzzles me."

"Let me see the cloth," said Father Pelfrey. He examined the cloth and to his surprise it was a Wiccan ceremonial altar cloth.

"What was Marcy doing with this, let alone the opium?" he wondered. "Have you called the police yet,

Dr. Collins?"

"They told me they were unable to do anything until she was gone for at least 24 hours, unless she was in immediate danger."

Father Pelfrey replied, "I'll call them and get them moving on the investigation."

Father Pelfrey called the police department and told the dispatcher what was going on. She informed Father Pelfrey that they were aware of the situation and they were going to send an officer the next evening if Marcy didn't return.

"I think you need to send someone here now," Father Pelfrey said. "We found something here that makes me believe she may be in trouble." The dispatcher said she would send an officer right away.

Dr. Collins and Father Pelfrey were discussing the possibilities of the opium when they were informed that a police officer was there for them. The officer made out a report and asked if they had any pictures of Marcy.

"Just the class picture," Father Pelfrey replied. "It's almost two months old but that's all we have." The officer took the picture and assured them that they would find Marcy.

Sister Stephanie tossed and turned all night. She had just fallen into a deep sleep when she was awakened by Fran.

"So did you find Marcy last night?" asked Fran.

Stephanie replied, "No, they didn't find her."

Fran left to get breakfast. Sister Stephanie tried to go back to sleep when there was a knock at the door. It was Father Pelfrey.

"No word yet on Marcy, but you may be interested to learn what you and Dr. Collins found in her room." Father Pelfrey went on to tell Stephanie about the opium and the Wiccan ceremonial altar cloth.

"What are they for?" she asked.

"The ceremonial cloth is used by a Pagan High Priestess, and the opium would be used to help ease the mind so they could control the person they were dealing with. They used opium in the old days to make people believe they had a spiritual experience."

"What would Marcy be doing with that?" asked Stephanie.

"I haven't figured that out yet," Father Pelfrey said, "but I am taking the stuff into town with me today and asking an old friend about them just to make sure all my cards are in a line."

Just as Father Pelfrey was about to leave, Sister Stephanie remembered Daphne's pendant. "Father Pelfrey, come with me. I need to show you something."

Father Pelfrey followed Stephanie to the medical area. Dr. Collins was checking on Daphne when they arrived.

"How is she doing?" asked Father Pelfrey.

"I have her sedated. She became conscious during the night but she was in a lot of pain," explained the doctor.

"When do you think we will be able to talk to her?" asked Sister Stephanie.

"Probably Monday," said Dr. Collins. Father Pelfrey asked Stephanie what she wanted to show him. Stephanie pointed at Daphne's pendant.

Father Pelfrey looked and raised his eyebrows with interest. He put his hand on his chin and said, "Just what I thought."

"What?" demanded Stephanie.

Father Pelfrey said, "Let's go to town with the students. Let me talk to my friend and I'll explain later."

Fran was excited. She had been in Rome for almost two months with no chance to call Charlie, or get a pregnancy test. The potential of finally getting the privacy to talk to Charlie overshadowed her thoughts. When they arrived,

Fran hurried to get her shopping done, and headed to the phone booth, but again no privacy. *When will I be able to talk to Charlie again?*

Charlie was waiting by the phone for it to ring, just as he had for the last two months. When Fran didn't call, he began to wonder if she was still okay, and if she was still in classes.

Charlie was going through some papers when he stumbled upon William's number. He decided to call William to see if he knew anything. William answered his phone and informed Charlie that he had the seminary's phone number. Charlie copied it down and thanked William for his help.

Charlie called the number and asked if there was a Francisca Martin taking classes there. The secretary told him there was but she wasn't able to accept calls.

"Just let her know Charlie called."

The secretary told Charlie she would deliver the message but she needed some information from him. Charlie gave her his name, phone number, and address.

He was relieved to know that Fran was still in class. Maybe she was just too busy to call.

The van returned to the seminary in time for supper. Sister Stephanie made it a point to sit with Father Pelfrey instead of with the girls. Father Pelfrey told Sister Stephanie to meet him at 9 p.m., that he had found out all he needed to know about what they had found.

Stephanie went to the secretary's office to screen any phone calls that came in for the day. The secretary told Stephanie that the only phone call that came in was for Fran.

"Who was it?"

"It was a man named Charlie, and he just wondered if

she was still in class."

Sister Stephanie told the secretary to file the information in case she needed it later.

At 8:45, Stephanie headed to the chapel to meet Father Pelfrey, who was already there. The two of them sat in a pew together.

"The altar cloth that you and Dr. Collins found was from a Wiccan High Priestess. Daphne's pendant is one worn by a Wiccan High Priestess."

"Marcy did know Daphne then," Stephanie said. "She told me she had never seen her before."

Father Pelfrey said he had a theory. "Daphne was treating Marcy for something, but I haven't figured that out yet. She used the opium to sedate Marcy into meditation."

"What kind of smell does opium produce?"

"A sweet smell."

"That's the odor that Fran described when she fainted in front of Marcy's door."

"Opium wouldn't make someone pass out by itself. It's more of a sedative or hallucinogen, used to help a person relax. I will be very interested in talking to Daphne on Monday."

CHAPTER 10

Charlie was lying on the couch when he heard a commotion upstairs. Again it was the child spirit, and he appeared even stronger. Charlie peered into the eyes of the spirit. His chest tightened up, and he fell to his knees, feeling an overwhelming urge to cry. He tried to get up, but he was unable.

As soon as the spirit left, Charlie's chest loosened up, and he quit crying. He began having weird feelings; it was as if he knew the spirit but didn't know the spirit.

It was early Sunday morning when Fran awoke very nauseated. She went to the bathroom to throw up, and after she threw up she felt better. She put her hand on her belly and said a little prayer. "Someday with the help of God we will all enjoy our time as a family: you, your father, and I. Thank you Lord for blessing Charlie and me with this child. Please give me the strength to carry on in my mission. I pray to you Lord. Amen."

Fran ran into Sister Stephanie in the cafeteria and asked about Daphne. Sister Stephanie told Fran that Daphne should be able to talk on Monday.

"Can I talk to her?" asked Fran.

"You can, but not until after Father Pelfrey and I do," replied Sister Stephanie.

During mass the other students were informed of Marcy's disappearance; they held a prayer session for her. Before Father Pelfrey ended mass he informed all the students that they were to meet in the cafeteria after supper.

Charlie was moping around when he decided to do something that would help take his mind off of Fran for a little while. He went to the local flower shop to get some mums to plant around the house. He remembered how happy he was when Fran and he planted flowers that spring. He picked out six of the prettiest mums he could find.

"Will that be all for you today, sir?" said the cashier.

Charlie asked if he could have some planting directions with the flowers. The cashier gave Charlie the instructions and told him the total for the flowers. Charlie paid and left.

The day was a perfect one for Charlie to plant the mums. As he planted them it brought back memories of Fran. Charlie began to daydream about Fran and their baby. He was happy again; he couldn't wait to show Fran his handiwork.

As Charlie ate supper that evening the phone rang. It was Sam.

"Charlie, I'm calling to let you know about the All Hallows Eve ceremony. You will be attending."

Charlie wasn't happy that he was being forced to go, because Fran was due to be home November first and he wanted time to straighten up the house. He knew if he had to go to another ceremony that he would be in no mood to greet Fran when she arrived. Sam told Charlie that the ceremony was on October 30th and that he would pick him up at 10:30 p.m.

Father Pelfrey and Sister Stephanie were already in the cafeteria when Fran arrived for the meeting. Father Pelfrey asked the students if anybody knew Daphne, but Fran was the only one who raised her hand. Father Pelfrey expected that because Fran and Marcy were close. He went on to explain the situation in detail. "So if anybody sees Marcy they need to report to Sister Stephanie or me right away."

Rachael spoke up and said she thought she saw Marcy Saturday morning off in the distance as they loaded into the van to head to town. Father Pelfrey said that he would look into it. Sister Stephanie then dismissed the meeting.

Father Pelfrey went back to his office and called the police. He told the dispatcher that one of his students thought she had seen Marcy. The dispatcher told Father Pelfrey that because it was dark, they would have to wait until morning, and that would give them time to set up a search party. Father Pelfrey said he would be awaiting their arrival.

Father Sandler and Father Carey were discussing the day's events when they heard a commotion outside the rectory. When they went up to the front of the rectory they noticed the curtains blowing in with the wind. They knew they didn't leave the windows open, so they began looking around to see if anything was missing. After searching for a few minutes they noticed the day's offering was gone.

"Who would steal money from a church?" asked Father Carey.

"I don't know," replied Father Sandler, "but we need to call the police."

The police showed up and did an investigation, but all they got were some fingerprints. They asked Father Sandler and Father Carey to submit their fingerprints for comparison, and then they asked if anybody else worked there.

"Just Gladys," Father Sandler replied, "but she's sleeping. We'll send her up first thing in the morning to get printed."

Fran awoke in the morning and again she vomited, but afterwards she felt better. She was excited; today she would be talking to Daphne. She ate breakfast and headed to class but when she got there she saw a sign on the door. The sign said that class was cancelled and gave their assignment. Fran headed back to her room.

As soon as Daphne finished her breakfast, Father Pelfrey and Sister Stephanie were in her room, asking for an explanation.

"Where to start? My name is Daphne Blanchor, and I am a Pagan High Priestess, I was assigned to Marcy as a special case. Marcy is a Satanic Princess trying to change her ways. I tried controlling her by myself but her powers overmatched mine. I went to my elders to seek advice; they recommended that we try converting her to Catholicism using my powers and the powers of your God. I kept her in a medicated meditation to help her relax, and it helped her to be able to be here and learn. We were doing fine until she and Fran became friends. It was like she sensed something through Fran, and then she became out of control. I tried doubling her dose of herbs; that's what I was doing that night Fran passed out in front of Marcy's door, but it shouldn't have affected her like it did. Until recently the double dose worked, but then Marcy went berserk and hit me in the head with something, and I blacked out. I knew there should be no visitors here, so I stayed in the room until Fran came over one night and caught Marcy and me in the middle of meditation. I had to be here to keep Marcy under control, that's why the story of me being here to check out the seminary came about."

Father Pelfrey said, "We found your ceremonial cloth and herbs in Marcy's room the night she disappeared."

"What, she's gone?" Daphne shouted.

Father Pelfrey told her about Marcy coming to Fran's window and running off.

"Do you know what that means?" Daphne asked. "It means demons are here. I need to speak to Fran alone as soon as possible. After I'm done talking to Fran we need to get everyone together. It's very important."

Fran was working on her assignment when she heard a knock on her door. When she opened it, she was shocked to see Daphne.

Daphne told Fran that she may want to sit down. Fran sat down and Daphne began telling Fran her story.

"That's why she always said she didn't belong here," said Fran.

"But that's not all," Daphne said. "Fran, I feel you are in grave danger. Marcy sensed something about you. I don't know what it is, but she knows something about you that you may have not told her. She could read it in your mind. What's your secret?"

When Fran didn't answer right away, Daphne continued. "I am the only one who can help you."

"I have a secret, but I want to come clean in front of Sister Stephanie."

"Go get her. We can both hear your story."

Fran found Sister Stephanie talking to the other students. Frantically, Fran told Sister Stephanie that they needed to talk in her room with Daphne. Stephanie replied that she already knew what was going on with Daphne, and she was rounding everyone up for a group meeting per Daphne's request.

"I have something I need to tell you also," Fran said.

Sister Stephanie suggested that she get Father Pelfrey and meet in Fran's room.

When Sister Stephanie found Father Pelfrey arrived, Fran was asking Daphne what Marcy meant by "demands are fear." Without hesitation Daphne replied, "Demons are here."

"Here too?" Fran asked.

Daphne said that now would be a good time for Fran to tell her story.

Fran started speaking. When she got to the part about

discovering the passage in Charlie's house, Daphne spoke up. "You're describing the altar bridge," she said. "It's where spirits can pass from Hell onto Earth. Charlie must be a bridge keeper."

"Not by choice," Fran replied. She told them about Charlie and Charlotte's wedding ceremony.

"A demonic wedding ceremony," Daphne said. "Both Charlie and Charlotte were put under spells. This ceremony is performed when the flock's high priest reaches a certain age, and the baby that Charlotte carried was to be the new high priest."

Fran then told them about Charlotte's death, Charlie's punishment, and her own desire to learn how to help him, hence her presence at the seminary.

"So that is what Marcy sensed from you. She knew you didn't belong here and she wanted to know why."

"But I never told her anything," replied Fran.

"Marcy is a Satanic Princess. She has powers that you can only imagine."

Sister Stephanie looked at Fran. "You being here has all been a lie. You were one of the best students."

"I have no intention of becoming a nun," Fran replied, "but being here has made me more in touch with myself then I ever was. If you feel I need to be expelled, I won't have any hard feelings."

Sister Stephanie told Fran she would have to talk it over with Father Pelfrey.

"Wait a minute," said Daphne. "As long as Marcy isn't under my control Fran will be in grave danger. If she is expelled Marcy will hunt her down and no one knows what will happen."

"We'll take that into consideration when we make our decision."

"I'm pregnant," said Fran.

A deep silence took over all the others in the room.

Finally, Sister Stephanie rolled her eyes, as if to say, "what's going to happen next?"

Father Pelfrey finally spoke. "Fran, you and Daphne can stay until we decide what to do, or until we find Marcy. Fran, you may continue classes with the understanding that you may be asked to leave when a decision is made. You and Daphne will share a room so you are protected from Marcy, and so you can figure out how to find her."

After Stephanie and Father Pelfrey left, Daphne told Fran she thought she could help Charlie. "I've never done anything like that before, though. I would have to return to England to learn more from my elders."

"When will you leave?" asked Fran.

"Not until I know you're safe."

"I'm safe here, aren't I?"

"Well…as you remain in the seminary. If you leave, you are fair game."

"If you come back before Saturday I'll have no reason to leave for anything," said Fran.

"Are you sure prepared to risk your life and the life of your unborn child?"

"I'm prepared to die for Charlie if needed."

"We must start a plan, then. I'll leave tomorrow morning. You must remember, under no circumstances are you to go outside of the seminary, or leave any windows open in your room while I am gone," Daphne said. "Marcy could cast a spell on you if your window is left open."

"Oh," said Fran. "Thank you, Daphne. If it wasn't for you I would still be miserable here living a lie. I am so happy we can possibly save Charlie."

Charlie was almost asleep when he heard a commotion. He got up and checked the passage but there was nothing there. Then he heard the noise again. It was coming from outside. He ran down the stairs and out the front door, only to hear the car peel out as it sped away.

Charlie looked around outside and noticed his flowers had been torn up, and there was a note in his mailbox: "Charlie, you are trying our patience. Remember we have people all over. Follow the rules and you won't be hurt, keep disobeying us and we'll make you pay."

Charlie sat on his front porch step and cried, not because of the threat but because of his flowers, they were all he had to help him cope with missing Fran. His anger grew although he knew it was only a few weeks before Fran returned home.

As he started inside, he accidently cut himself on the screen door. Charlie wrapped his bleeding hand in his shirt and ran up the stairs to check the passage. Does it ever end?

The child spirit again had appeared, and this time he appeared stronger than ever before. The spirit reached out, grabbing Charlie's shirt and ripping it right off of him. "Now I will control you," hissed the spirit.

Charlie was shocked. Before he could say or do anything the spirit had vanished. Charlie wondered what the spirit would want with his shirt, until he looked down. "My hand," he mumbled out loud. "I had my hand wrapped in my shirt and now the shirt contains my blood."

Charlie lay in bed, wondering how long he would be able to keep his sanity with everything going on. He had just begun to fall asleep when he began saying, "Charlotte, Charlotte, help me Charlotte." But Charlotte's spirit never answered him.

CHAPTER 11

Fran and Daphne woke up early. Daphne took a shower and called a cab. While Fran showered, Daphne left her a note reminding her to watch out for herself and not to leave windows open.

While Fran was getting ready for class, there was a knock at her door. Fran answered the door and it was Sister Stephanie. "Is Daphne here?"

"No, she left to go back to England and consult with her elders on the situation."

Sister Stephanie told Fran that since Daphne had left that Fran was to stay with her. Fran reluctantly agreed; it was better than being by herself. She also told Fran that Dr. Collins wanted to examine her after class.

Charlie awoke still concerned about the previous night's events, and with Charlotte not coming to him in his dreams. He was also troubled by the spirit taking his shirt. He had read about possessions, and spirits didn't need personal possessions or blood to possess a human. Charlie was puzzled by the whole situation. Did he over-look something in his reading? He decided to re-evaluate the situation and study up on it.

Father Sandler had the afternoon off so he decided to go eat at his favorite restaurant. On his way to the restaurant he thought he saw Father Wilson with two men unfamiliar to Father Sandler. The men were in front of the old five and dime store. He had an urge to stop but since he didn't know the other two men he decided not to.

When he arrived at the restaurant, he asked to use the phone. He told the dispatcher who he was, and that he thought that he saw Father Wilson.

"I'll send a patrolman to the scene," said the dispatcher.

Fran was on her way back to her room when she heard a voice calling her name. The voice wasn't familiar; already stressed, Fran ignored it and continued on her way. In her room, she began packing her stuff and fantasizing that she was packing to go home to Charlie.

Fran was deep in her daydream when she was interrupted by Rachael. "Marsha had a message for you."

"Who's Marsha?" asked Fran.

"She is the operator here. She told me she tried to catch you in the hallway, but you just ignored her and headed into your room."

"Oh, she was the voice I heard. I am so paranoid right now, and I didn't recognize her voice."

"She wanted to let you know that Charlie called for you. He must have called on Saturday. She thought the news might help brighten your spirits."

"It worked," Fran said, blushing.

Rachael started helping Fran pack. As they worked, Rachael asked Fran where she was from.

"I am from a little town in Ohio called Anilec Charlie and I live together there."

"I was fascinated by the story you told the other night," Rachael said. "Generally Catholics don't believe in possessions and evil spirits but I do. I've seen it happen before."

"Really?"

"I'm from California. My brother was a priest in Sacramento. He had a family come to him about their house. They saw ghosts. Being a Catholic priest his beliefs told him there was no way the story was true, but he gave them a phone number of a paranormal expert that he knew from college. The expert went to the house and his equipment went off the wall with paranormal readings. He told the family that one of the members must be a medium, meaning that the spirits channel through them. The paranormal expert then contacted my brother and let him know what he had discovered. He wanted my brother to do a cleansing ceremony on the couple's youngest girl that he believed that was a medium. He talked my brother into it, but the ceremony only angered the spirits. My brother did some research on exorcisms."

"If he didn't believe in exorcisms why did he research?" asked Fran.

"Catholics want you to believe that the only spirit is the holy spirit, and that spirits will only be able to walk on Earth when Jesus rises from the dead. Catholic priests perform exorcisms, but they tend to hide it and pretend it didn't happen."

"Why's that?"

"Back in the early years you were considered to be a witch if you talked to spirits, and as punishment you were hung or burned at the stake. As the Catholic religion grew they began to help people, but they'd cover it up as if nothing happened."

"I'm beginning to understand now. Like doctor-patient confidentiality," said Fran "Do you think he could help us?"

"I'll call him on Saturday and ask him."

Fran headed to Sister Stephanie's room and was surprised to see two beds in the room. Sister Stephanie laughed and said, "Did you expect to sleep on the couch the whole time?"

Fran debated whether she should tell Sister Stephanie about what Daphne had said. She decided not to, and
agreed to let Sister Stephanie have the bed by the window.

Charlie spent the whole day reading up on why the
spirit may have taken his shirt, to no avail. It was getting
late so Charlie decided to turn on the television and relax,
but as soon as he did the telephone rang and it was Sam.

"Charlie, with All Hallows Eve approaching we need
room for some of our witches to stay. You have a three-
bedroom house and you're the only one living there, so
next week you'll be hosting witches from out of town."

Charlie wanted to tell Sam to forget it, because he
needed to get the house ready for Fran coming home, but
he knew he couldn't, so he just agreed and told Sam that he
would talk to him later. I have to get rid of the books and
anything of Fran's. Where to put it?

Charlie knew the witches could come and go as they
pleased, so he would have to hide the items very well. He
decided to use the loft in the garage.

Charlie put the stuff in the garage and was heading
back to the house when he heard a neighborhood dog
howling. Without any control of his own Charlie began
howling back. He scared himself back into reality. What
the hell? He hurried inside the house, where he pondered
the experience for a little bit. Then he checked the passage
and turned in for the night.

When Fran awoke, she noticed that Sister Stephanie
was already gone. She took a minute to wake up, stretch-
ing on her bed and thinking of how close she was to being
back with Charlie and letting him know she was pregnant.
Daphne would be back in a day or two, and Rachael would
talk to her brother on Saturday. Things were starting to
look very good. Then suddenly everything went blank.

It was time for class to begin, but there was no sign of Fran or Sister Stephanie. Rachael was concerned, but Lisa said maybe they just overslept. Rachael said she would wait five minutes. When that passed, they decided to go and check the cafeteria, but Fran or Sister Stephanie weren't there.

They headed to Sister Stephanie's room. They pounded on the door and got no response, so they went to find Father Pelfrey.

"I bet Marcy has something to do with this," Rachael said.

That remark made Lisa a little nervous. "Weren't you with Fran yesterday?"

"Yes, I was," answered Rachael. "Are you saying I had something to do with this?"

The two of them began to argue. Just then, Father Pelfrey was walking down the hallway.

"Ladies, calm down. What's going on?"

Rachael and Lisa wouldn't let one another get a word in. Father Pelfrey was getting frustrated with them, until Dr. Collins showed up. Father Pelfrey asked if he could take Lisa with him and get her story, and he would do the same with Rachael. Dr. Collins agreed and took Lisa with him to his office. After Lisa left Rachael's attitude changed. Father Pelfrey asked what was going on.

Rachael told Father Pelfrey they couldn't find Fran or Sister Stephanie.

"What were you and Lisa arguing about?"

"Honestly, I couldn't tell you," replied Rachael.

"Well, that explains why you're not in class. I'll go to Sister Stephanie's room. If no one's there, I'll get Dr. Collins and we will get the key."

Dr. Collins and Lisa were on their way to Sister Stephanie's room when they ran into Father Pelfrey. He told them there was no response from Stephanie and that Lisa should return to her room. Father Pelfrey and Dr. Collins headed to the secretary's office to get the key to Sister Stephanie's door.

"What do you think is going on here, Father?"

"I don't know," replied Father Pelfrey, "but we need to get to the bottom of it."

When they opened Stephanie's door, there was no sign of Fran or Sister Stephanie. They were confused. Why would Fran and Sister Stephanie run off together?

"Dr. Collins you go to Lisa's room and I'll go to Rachael's and inform them to make travel plans to head home. We will not have another instructor in time for them to finish."

Father Pelfrey went to Rachael's room and told her what they had found.

"I want to stay and help you find them," Rachael told him.

"Okay, but make your travel arrangements. You need to be gone by Saturday."

Dr. Collins told Lisa she should make travel plans, and Lisa agreed to leave as soon as possible. Dr. Collins left Lisa's room and headed to Father Pelfrey's office.

"We should call the police," said Father Pelfrey.

Dr. Collins agreed.

"Twenty years here and nothing like this has ever happened before. What should I do?" said Father Pelfrey.

"All we can do is contact the authorities and pray," responded Dr. Collins.

Father Pelfrey called the police. "We will send an officer to make out a report and get descriptions and pictures."

"What's going on?" asked Dr. Collins.

"They are sending an officer, but until they're gone for 24 hours, not much else."

When the officers arrived, Father Pelfrey showed them to Stephanie's room and then went back to his office. The officers took pictures and duster for fingerprints, gathering up anything that may help give them a theory of what happened. After a few hours uncovered nothing out of the ordinary, they sat down and wrote their reports, and then reported to Father Pelfrey's office.

"Well, what did you find out?" asked Father Pelfrey.

"There is no sign of forced entry or a struggle. They must have left willingly together or with whoever else may be involved."

Father Pelfrey didn't buy the story for a minute, but these were seasoned veterans. They knew what they were doing.

"We will put out an A.P.B. after they are missing for 24 hours. We'll find them."

After they left, Father Pelfrey went to tell Dr. Collins what they had said.

"Why would they leave together?" asked Dr. Collins.

"I don't think that's what happened," Father Pelfrey replied, "but I really can't put my finger on anything right now."

Charlie had one week to prepare to have the witches over to stay. He was becoming stressed, and was getting a tension headache so he took some aspirin and went to bed.

As he slept he saw images of trees moving, as if he were moving through them, but not as if he were walking. He felt some strange cloth on him but couldn't make out what it was. Suddenly it was dark and cold. This startled Charlie, and he awoke in a cold sweat.

What was that all about? I don't understand any of this, and I have no one to talk to about it. I could use a beer. He wasn't old enough to buy any, but he knew one of his neighbors kept some in his garage.

Charlie went over and stole some beer and brought it back to his house. He began chugging the beers until he passed out. As he lay passed out on the couch, the cold, dark, eerie feeling came over him again, this time accompanied by some chanting he couldn't understand, and a smell he had never smelled before. Then suddenly there was a blood-curdling scream.

Charlie jumped up off the couch. What were his dreams telling him? He looked at the clock and saw that it was 1 a.m., so he decided to go and check the passage. There was above-normal activity, but nothing unusual.

Charlie went to bed but couldn't fall asleep. He was too freaked out by his earlier dreams to close his eyes.

Chapter 12

Father Pelfrey was eating lunch when he was told he had a phone call. When he answered the phone it was Chief Ward. He wanted to let Father Pelfrey know he had decided to go ahead and put out an A.P.B. and call in a search party around the seminary grounds. Father Pelfrey asked if he and Dr. Collins could assist in any way; the chief said they could use as many volunteers as they could get. "We'll meet at the seminary at 6 p.m.tonight to setup base, and we'll begin searching tomorrow morning at sunrise."

Father Pelfrey said he would prepare the seminary to handle everyone. He then went to Dr. Collins's office to let him know what Chief Ward had told him. Dr. Collins asked if Father Pelfrey wanted Rachael and Lisa to help. Father Pelfrey said that Lisa had already left, and that Rachael should help Marsha answer the phones.

After talking to Rachel, Dr. Collins went back to his office and called the local churches to see if they could round up volunteers to help with the search. Father Wilcox told Dr. Collins he would do the best he could to round up volunteers, and that he would contact a few other churches for him. After making a few other phone calls Dr. Collins headed to Father Pelfrey's office, but Father Pelfrey wasn't there. He found Father Pelfrey in the church, praying. He decided he would just go to Father Pelfrey's office and wait for him to return.

Charlie heard a commotion upstairs. When he reached the passage there was the child spirit again. Charlie said, "What do you want with me?"

The spirit laughed with an evil hiss and disappeared. Charlie lost it and began throwing things into the passage. "Come back here you son of a bitch, I wasn't through with you yet!"

Charlie had tossed everything he could get his hands on into the passage, when he became short of breath and sat down. He began taking slow deep breaths; before he knew it he was asleep.

He again dreamed that he was in a cold, dark place. There was just enough light to make out an image of a woman that looked like she had her throat slit, but Charlie wasn't sure. Again it all went blank, and then he was moving through the trees again, and again it all went black.

Charlie felt someone poking at him. "Wake up, boy," said Sam.

Charlie was freaked out because he was now on his couch. "Did you put me here, Sam?"

"Do you see anybody else here with me? I didn't carry you down here by myself."

"What are you doing here?"

"I stopped by to let you know that the witches are only going to be for three days instead of four."

"That's great," Charlie said. "Are you looking forward to All Hallows Eve?"

"Always. It's the only night that evil spirits can be on Earth and raise Cain."

"But spirits pass through the passage here all the time. Where do they go?"

"Those are all the spirits called up by cults all over the world to do their dirty deeds. But how are you doing, Charlie?" Sam asked

"I've been feeling funny lately," Charlie replied.

"It's just your soul preparing you for the festivities. You'll be fine."

After Sam left, Charlie went upstairs. For some reason he wasn't paranoid anymore. It was like all the weight had been lifted from his shoulders.

Father Pelfrey sat with Dr. Collins and Chief Ward, going over the plan for the next day. Chief Ward said they would spread the volunteers over the seminary grounds, close enough together that they could hold hands, and they would comb through the whole grounds. Every square inch would be checked. "When they are done with the seminary grounds we will make a five-mile perimeter around the seminary, and break it into smaller sections and check them as thoroughly as possible. This will be a lengthy process with the number of people we have."

"We'll have to round up more volunteers," said Father Pelfrey.

"Yes, that would help. They could be miles away," replied Chief Ward.

Father Pelfrey, Dr. Collins, and Chief Ward mapped out the areas to brief the volunteers. Marsha and Rachael copied pictures to pass out to the volunteers so they would know who they were looking for.

Chief Ward stood in front of the crowd of volunteers and went over his plan. "Anything that may be evidence, stop and notify one of my officers. If you know anyone else who may want to help, we appreciate all the help we can get. It is very important that we all work together. These days will be long and stressful. Prepare for the worst."

Charlie awoke very refreshed. He got out of bed and went downstairs to get breakfast. On the table there was something wrapped up in a note from Sam. "Charlie, I bet you're feeling pretty good this morning. Inside this package is some Prozac. It will help you with any tension you may have. It will also help you sleep. I know you've had late nights; it's getting close to that time of the year. If you like the way you've been feeling, flush the pills. Remember, Charlie, it's in your soul. Sam."

Charlie pondered the note for awhile, then put the pills by the sink. He would think about it, Charlie decided, but it was nice getting a good night's rest.

Dawn was approaching in Rome, but there were even fewer volunteers than they expected.

"This doesn't look good," Father Pelfrey said to Dr. Collins.

"I know," Dr. Collins said, "but we used up our resources for volunteers, and there are so many rumors floating around town, people may think it's a lost cause."

"What kind of rumors?"

"Mainly that the girls left willingly and staged everything."

"I can see why people could think that. The Catholic religion has had its share of criticism." Father Pelfrey was about to say something else, but Chief Ward spoke up instead.

"I'm disappointed in the turnout here, but I want to thank everyone who showed up. We need to plan on adding a few more days to the search. Again, please try to recruit more people if possible." With that, the search began on the seminary grounds.

Charlie spent the day watching TV and pondering the idea of the medication. Was it a trick? Sam knew Charlie wasn't happy about having the witches over, and he also knew Charlie was up to something around the house. He probably wanted to medicate him so the witches would be able to read his mind without Charlie being able to block them out.

He had pretty much decided against taking the medication when he heard commotion upstairs in the passage. Again it was the child spirit. As the spirit passed through, Charlie heard something very familiar. "Help me, Charlie!" It was Fran's voice. He heard a baby crying, and then a blood-curdling scream, and then silence.

"No!" screamed Charlie. "Not Fran too!" Charlie fell to his knees crying and pounding his fist on the floor. The whole time, he kept hearing someone saying "daddy, daddy."

Charlie stopped crying and looked up. There was a child standing in front of him. "Hi daddy."

Charlie's heart sank. "I'm not your daddy. How did you get in here?"

Charlie awoke in his recliner. He clearly remembered going upstairs to check the passage; how did he end up back on his recliner? Was it all a dream?

Charlie got up and went to the kitchen to take one of the pills. He was still shaking from the whole experience. He needed something to keep himself busy. He looked out his back door and noticed some leaves that needed raked.

Daphne was spending her last day in England with her elders. She had gathered all the information and obtained all the herbs and potions that she needed. Rosemary, the elder high priestess, warned Daphne that alone she might not be able to close the passage. Daphne blew off the warning. She knew many high priestesses that had performed the ritual successfully on their own.

The search of the seminary grounds was yielding no clues. The volunteers were tired and their spirits had fallen. Chief Ward told Father Pelfrey that if they didn't find any clues soon he was afraid the morale of the group would alter how many people showed up in the future.

"What should we do?" asked Dr. Collins.

"I'll take care of it," said Father Pelfrey.

When the search was done for the day, Father Pelfrey called everyone together. He started by thanking everyone for their hard work. He said he knew not all the volunteers were Catholic and they may be uncomfortable in the church, but they were all God's children, no matter their religion, race, or sex. "Let's pray. Lord, please help us keep our strength and our faith as we step up to the challenge ahead of us. Lord let us come together as one and make our challenge easier. In this we pray to you, Lord. Amen."

Charlie had raked his leaves and was inside for the evening, pondering the idea of taking the medication left by Sam or going without. He had already taken one pill and felt good. Maybe he could take one every other day, and then stop on Monday when the witches arrived.

Charlie was deep in thought when he heard a commotion outside. He peered out his window and saw two of his neighbors playing loud music and drinking. Charlie went outside and asked the two men if they could keep it down, it was getting late.

"What you are going to do about it, freak boy?" asked Mr. Motz. "If we look at your ugly head for a while do we turn to stone or something?"

The comments angered Charlie but he kept his cool as the neighbors went on making fun of him. He asked them again to turn down their music.

Mr. Grey said, "Yeah, freak boy, your wife was fine. Too bad she's dead."

Charlie lost his temper and was ready to pound his neighbors, but somebody stopped him. Charlie looked behind him and saw Mr. Otis holding him back. "Calm down, Charlie. These punks aren't worth your time or energy. I've already called the police and they are on their way. They will probably want you to fill out a report.

"Thank you, Mr. Otis." Charlie went to his house and sat on his front porch, waiting for the police to arrive. He tried to calm down but it was hard for him. Why were people so hateful? Why was it in human nature to put down or make fun of somebody because they were different?

Charlie was pretty calm when the police arrived. They told Charlie's neighbors to turn down their music, and then they came over to Charlie's. "I'm Officer Livingston and this is my partner, Officer Walls. What happened here tonight?"

Charlie explained his confrontation.

"They say you attacked them," replied Officer Livingston.

"I did no such thing," Charlie said. He told them what the men had said, and how Mr. Otis had intervened.

"We will go to Mr. Otis's house and get a report from him. If his story agrees with them, we will have to arrest you for assault."

Charlie rolled his eyes as the officers headed to Mr. Otis's house. It seemed to take forever, but the officers finally came back and told Charlie the stories matched. "We told Mr. Otis, Mr. Motz, and Mr. Grey that if we are called back here tonight for anything we will arrest someone. Let's try to be civil to one another."

Charlie went back into his house. He checked the passage and found no unusual activity, so he decided to turn in for the night.

Charlie had just begun a deep sleep when he heard loud music again. He tossed and turned, even covered his head with his pillow to try to block out the music, and it did for a while. He was fast asleep when again he heard the loud music, but this time a voice came to him in his sleep. "Bring them here let me deal with them."

Charlie got out of bed and headed downstairs, out the

front door, and across the street.

"Hey, it's freak boy again," laughed Mr. Motz.

"He's going to try to kick our asses," laughed Mr. Grey. "I'm shaking in my boots."

Charlie approached them. To their surprise he said, "I'm sorry about earlier. Why don't you come over to my house and have some beer?"

The two men looked at each other. "Okay, man," said Mr. Grey. Charlie led the two men to his house and into his kitchen. Charlie went to his refrigerator and suddenly everything went black. All he could hear was a man screaming.

CHAPTER 13

Another dawn approached in Rome. To the surprise of Father Pelfrey and Chief Ward, they had twice as many volunteers as the day before.

"This morning we are going to search zone 2," Chief Ward announced.

One of the volunteers spoke up. "Shouldn't we search the woods first?"

Chief Ward replied that they had dogs coming the next day to search the woods. The volunteers all lined up in a row, ready to begin their search. Father Pelfrey and Chief Ward hoped to find something, but both of their gut feelings agreed with the volunteer who wanted to search the woods.

What a dream last night, Charlie thought. I thought those pills were supposed to relax me. Charlie checked the passage and was headed downstairs when he heard what sounded like two-way radios outside. He went to the front door to investigate.

Across the street were two police cruisers. He went out on his front porch. He saw Mr. Otis and called him over. "What's going on?"

"No one knows," Mr. Otis replied. "The cops aren't saying anything."

Just then the county coroner pulled up. The coroner was

in the house for about fifteen minutes before two hearses arrived. About twenty minutes later two gurneys came out carrying bodies covered with sheets.

Charlie's jaw nearly hit the ground. Nervously, he told Mr. Otis that he had some stuff he needed to get done, that he would talk to him later.

Charlie paced, thinking the cops were going to suspect him because of the incident the night before. He didn't eat all day. That night, he was going to take one of the pills that Sam gave him but something stopped him. He put down the pills and headed upstairs to check the passage and go to bed.

As he slept he was back in the woods again, with the feeling of moving through the trees. There was a struggle, and Charlie saw two figures wrestling around. One got up and ran away, then there were screams, and everything went red.

"We found something!" echoed in the air.

Father Pelfrey and Chief Ward headed to where the voice was coming from. They arrived to find a piece of black material. Chief Ward put on gloves, picked up the material, and put it into a paper bag, which he marked "exhibit 1."

"I'll need some material from a nun's dress," he said to Father Pelfrey. "We need to compare the two samples to see if they are a match."

The two of them headed back to the seminary to retrieve the sample. After retrieving it, they headed to Dr. Collins's office to use the microscope to compare the two pieces of material. Chief Ward placed the sample that Father Pelfrey provided under one microscope and exhibit 1 under another. Chief Ward went back and forth between the two microscopes, adjusting the magnification on each. After twenty minutes, he declared that the two were a match.

They went back to the search unit. "Nothing else has been found," Dr. Collins said. "Maybe the material was placed to throw us off the trail.

"Maybe so," said Chief Ward, "but we need to follow up on the lead."

The next morning, Chief Ward and Father Pelfrey met before anyone else showed up. "I want to investigate further in where we found the piece of clothing," said Chief Ward.

"Won't that put us behind schedule?" asked Father Pelfrey.

"Not if we split up the crews and search both areas. Each person will be responsible for a few more square feet, but we have the dogs coming today."

Chief Ward and Father Pelfrey ended their meeting just as everyone else began showing up. Chief Ward explained to the volunteers the change in plans. They split into two groups and began their search.

Charlie awoke wondering what was up with his dream last night. He noticed a bad taste in his mouth as he yawned, so he headed to the bathroom to brush his teeth. When he looked into the mirror he noticed a scratch on his cheek. He wondered where it came from.

He glanced at the clock and noticed that it was 11:45 a.m. It didn't seem like he had slept that long. He went downstairs and turned on the television.

"Breaking news in Anilec , Ohio, where a jogger was attacked and killed by a wild animal. Thirty-seven-year-old Kim Robinson was jogging on West Bank Road with twenty-seven-year-old Joyce Stinson when she fell. As Ms. Stinson tried to help her up, a wild animal jumped out of the woods and attacked and killed Ms. Robinson. Ms. Stinson was able to escape unharmed."

Charlie looked at the TV. That's what happened in my dream. What is wrong with me? What can I do? He burst into the kitchen and took ten of the pills that Sam had given him. He was walking back to the couch to lie down when he began to feel nauseated. He ran to the bathroom and vomited up the pills and a lot of blood

Dusk was setting in Rome as the search began to wind down for the day. Nothing had been found. Father Pelfrey told Chief Ward, "This is very disappointing. You would think we would have found more than just one piece of cloth."

Chief Ward replied, "The evidence is pointing to where I thought it would. They must have left on their own. We'll finish the search, but I can guarantee you that we will not find them. They're long gone."

Father Pelfrey took his notes from the search back to his office and looked through them. Sister Stephanie was a young nun, but why she would run off with Fran and Marcy? What influence could those two have on her?

There was a knock at his door; it was Daphne. "Where is everyone?"

"Fran and Sister Stephanie are missing," Father Pelfrey told her. "Lisa went home and Rachael is still here."

"Fran and Sister Stephanie are missing? When did this happen?"

"Sunday night."

"All Hallows Eve is fast approaching," Daphne told him. "Marcy will begin gaining power. Fran and Sister Stephanie are going to be sacrificed to Satan, and we need to do something about it."

" Why don't you stay with Rachael tonight?" said Father Pelfrey. As they walked to Rachael's room, he told Daphne that she was more than welcome to join in the search.

"Fran told me everything," Rachael said after Father Pelfrey left. She told Daphne about their conversation.

"Call your brother on Saturday," Daphne said. "I told

Fran I would save Charlie. I haven't given up on her. Even if she isn't found I'm still helping Charlie."

"We need to get Fran's address."

Charlie woke up and still felt weak. His body ached and he was drenched in sweat. Maybe he was coming down with the flu. He grabbed the phone and called Sam.

"Sam, it's Charlie. Can you get me something for the flu?"

Sam said he would because Charlie needed to be feeling well for the witches coming in four days. He arrived about twenty minutes later.

"Here you go, Charlie. This should help you feel better."

Between coughs and blowing his nose Charlie asked Sam if he could check the passage. Sam did so, then came back downstairs and told Charlie he would be back in the morning to check on him and the passage if needed. Charlie thanked Sam as he headed out the door.

Friday morning approached in Rome. As Father Pelfrey and Dr. Collins prepared for the day's search, they were surprised by Daphne. "Come with me," she said.

They went back to Rachael's room. Father Pelfrey asked what the pillows were doing on the floor, and why there were rocks on the floor, and what was that smell? Daphne explained that they needed to meditate to clear their minds, so they could block out bad karma and only let the good in, that it may help them remember any little clues that they could have missed.

The three of them kneeled on the pillows and Rachael joined them, Daphne lit four candles, then made a cross in the air, saying, "Mother Earth, wind, fire, and water." Then the four of them joined hands. "Now relax, close your eyes, and find a peaceful place."

Daphne began chanting, and before anyone knew it they

had a feeling of floating off to a peaceful place. It grew quiet, and then Daphne began chanting again. The feeling of floating returned; they could see their bodies kneeling on the pillows in Rachael's room.

Suddenly they were back. Dr. Collins spoke up. "Remember when Lisa said she thought she saw Marcy?"

Father Pelfrey said, "Now I do. We've been looking on the wrong side of the property; we need to direct our attention to the north end." They all headed back to talk to Chief Ward.

Chief Ward was giving final instructions when Father Pelfrey interrupted, telling him to search the north end of the property. "One of our students thought she saw Marcy as they were getting into the van. She would have had to see her on the north end of the grounds."

Charlie awoke feeling better than the night before, but he was still concerned about the incident with his neighbors. Any time now, his phone could ring, or there could be a knock at his door, and it would be the police wanting to question him. Charlie was getting ready to shower when the phone rang. It has to be the police.

"How are you feeling?" It was Sam.

Charlie told Sam he was feeling better and that he didn't have to come over to check the passage.

"Boy, is there something bothering you?"

"No," replied Charlie. "I was getting ready to shower so I'll talk to you later."

After his shower, Charlie began frantically preparing for the arrival of the witches. He wished he could find something to help calm his nerves; it seemed that every time he took one of the pills that Sam gave him, something weird happened.

There was a knock at Charlie's door. It's the cops, Charlie thought, but it was just Mr. Otis.

"Charlie I thought you might want to make a donation to help with the funeral expenses of Mr. Grey and Mr. Mott. Since they committed suicide their life insurance policies won't cover any of the expenses."

"Suicide?" Charlie repeated.

"You haven't heard yet? Mr. Mott and Mr. Grey hung themselves in the garage sometime after the cops left that night."

Charlie felt a weight lift off his shoulders. He told Mr. Otis he didn't have any money to spare.

Mr. Otis told Charlie that he understood, and that the funerals were on Monday morning. Charlie just nodded as Mr. Otis left. He shut his front door and let out a sigh of relief. He had been nervous for no reason.

Charlie was just sitting down to supper that evening when he heard a knock on the door. He got up and was met by Sam, who had let himself into the house. "See you're feeling better," he said to Charlie.

"Yeah," replied Charlie, "just a little down." He told Sam about arguing with his neighbors, and the spirit in the passage that had prompted him to invite them over, and finding out they committed suicide that night.

Sam laughed. "The time is coming, Charlie. You're preparing for the upcoming holiday." Sam had said this before, and Charlie still didn't know what he meant.

"Have you been taking the pills I gave you?" Sam asked.

Charlie told Sam he was, but Sam saw right through Charlie's lie. "We'll just have to see about that." He walked into the kitchen and was about to grab the pills when Charlie confessed.

"All right, I haven't been taking them. I don't like the way they make me feel."

"Don't like the way they make you feel? What is wrong with you? These pills help you get into contact with your soul."

Charlie snapped back, "I will not take them and you can't make me take them."

Sam snatched the pills from the cupboard and headed to the door. "I may not be able to make you take them," he said, "but I know someone who will." He hurried out to his car and sped away.

Charlie fell back into his recliner. *I should've kept my mouth shut.*

He was about to doze off in his recliner when he heard his front door open. He leaped up to see who it was, but there was nobody there. *I must have dreamed it.*

Daphne took a couple of volunteers and headed deeper into the woods to search. Chief Ward gave her a radio and told her to let him know if they found anything or if they needed help.

"We found something!" echoed through the morning air. The search party had found Sister Stephanie's rosary.

"Stephanie would never leave her rosary willingly," Father Pelfrey told Chief Ward.

Chief Ward acknowledged the discovery and said maybe his hunch was wrong. "But we haven't found enough evidence to rule anything out yet."

As dusk approached, Chief Ward tried to contact Daphne on the radio, with no response. "Wait a while and try to contact them again," Father Pelfrey told him. "If we don't hear from them, we'll just have to pray for them tonight. It's too dark to send anyone out to find them."

Daphne, Amy, and Tyler were hot on what they thought was Marcy's trail. They were so involved that they barely noticed the darkness settling in. When they finally did, none of them knew where they were.

"Let's not panic," said Daphne. "We need to find shelter. It looks like it might rain tonight." Daphne looked around. "If my hunch is right, Marcy would have had to find a place to stay. She would have had to drag Sister Stephanie and Fran, so she would needto have a place already picked out so she could keep one of them there while she went and got the other." With that thought in mind, they headed deeper into the woods.

Daphne was scouting farther up the trail than Amy or Tyler when she spotted a cave. She hollered for Amy and Tyler. When they caught up, Amy just rolled her eyes and said nothing. Daphne told Tyler to round up some firewood, that she and Amy would scout the cave.

"Boy it's dark in here," said Amy.

Daphne kept feeling around until she determined there was enough room in the mouth of the cave for them to be comfortable. "Well, it's big enough for us to sleep and have a fire," she told Amy. "Let's go find Tyler."

Tyler was out in the woods, but he wasn't looking for firewood. He was daydreaming about being in the middle of nowhere with two women, all the things they could be doing.

Tyler's daydream was interrupted by Daphne's voice. "Where's the firewood?" She made him round up wood and the three of them headed back to the cave.

"Do we have matches?" Amy asked.

"Who needs matches?" replied Tyler. Daphne rolled her eyes as he began rubbing two sticks together.

Twenty minutes later, Daphne was at her wit's end. Tyler was still trying to start a fire and Amy was whining that they were all going to die. She reached into her cloak and pulled out a powder. "Here," she told Tyler. "Put some of this on those sticks, and some on the logs."

Tyler did as she said, and suddenly they had a fire. "The fire will keep us warm for a while," he said, "but maybe we should snuggle together for body heat."

"In your dreams," Daphne said, pointing in Amy's direction.

"Whatever!" Amy said.

"Actually, I was pointing behind you," Daphne told her. Amy looked back and saw a pile of wood.

"How did that get here?" asked Amy.

"Marcy was here," replied Daphne. "We're on her trail."

Sam went to Nemrak's house after leaving Charlie's. He told Nemrak about Charlie's neighbors.

"The pills are working," replied Nemrak.

"But that's the problem," Sam said. "He doesn't like the way the pills make him feel." He reached into his coat pocket and pulled out the full bottle.

Nemrak snarled. "He needs to take those pills, or his soul will never lose the compassion he still possesses."

"He said I couldn't make him take them. I told him I knew someone who could."

Nemrak picked up the phone. "James, this is Nemrak."

CHAPTER 14

When Charlie awoke, he realized the witches weren't coming until Wednesday. *Maybe I should try to make it to Mr. Mott's and Mr. Gray's funeral.*

Charlie got out of bed and was brushing his teeth when he heard a commotion upstairs. He hurried up to check the passage, but there was nothing there. *That's weird,* he thought. *I definitely heard a noise coming from up here.*

Charlie was looking around when he noticed that something was missing. It was a picture of Charlotte while she was pregnant. *Why would anyone want that picture?*

Light was peeking through the mouth of the cave as Amy began to stir. She noticed Tyler waking up also, so she decided to make a torch and head deeper into the cave to relieve herself.

Daphne woke up and asked Tyler where Amy was. Tyler said she had gone deeper into the cave.

"Marcy could still be here," she replied. "We need to find her."

They had gone about thirty feet into the cave when Tyler said, "What's that smell?"

Just then, Amy came toward them around a bend in the cave. "For your information, Tyler, that wasn't me. I just had to pee."

The three of them began to investigate. "It smells familiar,"

Daphne said, "but the dampness hinders it."

Suddenly Daphne realized Tyler wasn't next to her. She turned to find him on the ground, holding his head. Amy, oblivious to what was going on behind her, continued moving deeper into the cavern. Daphne was getting ready to help Tyler up when they heard Amy screaming. Before they knew it, Amy went running by them, almost knocking Daphne down.

"What's wrong with her?" asked Tyler.

"I don't know," replied Daphne, "but we should find out."

When they tracked Amy down, she had a frightened, glazed look on her face, and she couldn't stop crying. "What did you see in there?" asked Daphne.

Amy made no reply. Tyler asked Daphne if she wanted to go back into the cave. Daphne told him they needed to contact Chief Ward and let him know what was going on. "Chief Ward, this is Daphne. Do you copy?"

No response. She tried again, and still no response. She took a deep breath and began to look over the radio, and then she noticed that it wasn't even turned on. She turned it on and heard Chief Ward's voice.

"I hear you," she said. "This is Daphne. Do you copy?"

"Where are you?"

Daphne told him about the cave, and about whatever had spooked Amy.

"Stay put," Chief Ward replied. "We'll find you."

Daphne signed off and looked at Tyler. "How long has this been turned off?"

"I don't know."

She glared at him.

"Okay, ever since you gave it to me last night. I figured, I was with two women in the woods, so…"

Daphne shook her head and sat down on a stump. After a minute, she called Chief Ward back. "Bring some extra people with you. We need to investigate this cave."

Tyler said he wanted to apologize for turning off the radio. "It was very childish of me. If I would have left it on, we wouldn't be in the predicament we're in, and Amy would be fine."

Daphne sighed. "You're cute. I forgive you. If you weren't such an idiot we wouldn't have discovered the cave. I'm almost positive that Marcy used this cave, so there must be evidence inside that may help us."

Soon the search party arrived. Chief Ward asked Daphne how she was feeling.

"I'm fine," she said, "just concerned about Amy. We need to get her back to Dr. Collins."

Tyler asked Chief Ward what they had brought to eat. "All we bought was some water. Dr. Collins wants to check you out before you're allowed to eat anything."

"What?" Daphne asked.

"You heard me. Dr. Collins wants to keep you under observation all night since you were exposed to the elements for over 24 hours."

"What about the cave?"

"I'll leave two of my best men here to secure it until tomorrow we can get more men and some dogs."

Daphne reluctantly agreed. She and Tyler hopped in the wagon where Amy had already been loaded and they headed back to the seminary.

As they entered the seminary grounds, Amy started going deeper into shock. Her skin became very pale, cool, and clammy, and her lips got a blue tint to them. Chief Ward radioed Father Pelfrey to get Dr. Collins to the main entrance.

They pulled up to the main entrance and Dr. Collins was waiting with a gurney and an oxygen tank. They placed Amy on the gurney and put her on oxygen. Dr. Collins gave her a shot of morphine to relax her, so her body could

long enough to get him to take the pills. He took the medication with no problem since he was still under the mind control spell.

"Amy is recovering from her incident and all of her vital signs have returned to normal," Dr. Collins told Daphne and Tyler, who had come to his office. He then took each of them back to the exam room individually to check them over. Tyler seemed fine, but he wanted to give Daphne some antibiotics to prevent pneumonia. She said she would treat herself with herbs and come back for the antibiotics if the herbs didn't work.

From there, Daphne went to Rachael's room. "Can I stay with you tonight?" she asked.

"Sure," Rachael said. "I needed to talk to you anyway."

"That's right," answered Daphne. "I've been so involved in trying to figure out what that smell was in the cave that I totally forgot about that."

"I've got good news," Rachael said. "I talked to my brother Darren. I told him about Charlie and Fran, and he agreed to help us. If we can find Fran."

"Don't give up on Fran. She is a very strong person. We need to start planning the exorcism of Charlie's house to close the alter bridge."

Father Pelfrey and Chief Ward were debriefing the officers about the previous day's events as they waited on the K-9 unit to show up. Daphne and Rachael walked in just as the debriefing was ending. The officers were about to be dismissed when Daphne spoke up. "I know Marcy was in that cave. The smell I didn't recognize yesterday was opium, so she had Fran and Sister Stephanie in there. There should be some clues. We need to begin at the cave and search deeper in to the woods."

It was Sunday morning and volunteers were few and

far between. Father Pelfrey just shook his head as he leaned over to Dr. Collins. "I was afraid of this. The search has lasted too long. Hopefully we find something today to renew the interest of the people."

When the K-9 unit showed up, the handful of volunteers loaded up on a wagon and they all headed to the cave. When they were gone, Marsha came up to Dr. Collins and told him that Chief Ward had a phone call. Dr. Collins radioed Chief Ward, who said he would send an officer to take the call.

Marsha went back inside to take a message from the caller, who described a woman dazed and confused on Highway 32. She was dirty, and her clothes were torn. Marsha went back and gave Dr. Collins the message just as Officer Cortez showed up. Marsha gave him the message.

Officer Cortez said he would get right on it. As he left, Dr. Collins radioed Chief Ward to let him know what was going on. Chief Ward thanked Dr. Collins and said he would pass the message on to Father Pelfrey.

Officer Cortez arrived at Highway 32 and found the woman. He glanced at pictures of Marcy, Sister Stephanie, and Fran, but there seemed to be no resemblance. He approached the woman, taking notice of the blood on her clothes. "Can I help you?" he asked her.

She looked at him. He was about to ask again when she fell to the ground. Officer Cortez immediately called for an ambulance, then went to examine the woman. She had a pulse and was breathing, but she had lost a lot of blood from several cuts on her arms and legs. Officer Cortez retrieved blankets from his cruiser trunk and wrapped the woman up in them until the ambulance arrived.

The ambulance arrived about ten minutes later and took the woman to the hospital. Officer Cortez radioed Chief Ward to apprise him of the situation. "I don't think she was one of the women we're looking for, but until she's cleaned up I remain optimistic. She was taken to the hospital by ambulance. I'm heading to the hospital right now. I'll keep you informed."

Monica was stirring around Charlie's house when she heard a racket upstairs. She hesitated for a moment, and then went to see if Charlie was still on the couch. He was. When she heard the noise again, she ran upstairs and noticed that the noise was coming from the passage.

She opened the closet door and saw the spirit of a child pacing back and forth. Being a young witch, Monica was inexperienced, and a little freaked out. The boy looked at her and said, "You need not fear me. I'm on your side. I'm here to watch you."

"Watch me?"

"Yes," the spirit replied. "My friends and I are relying on you to keep our plans for Halloween. Just keep giving Charlie his medication and all will be well." The boy disappeared as Monica blinked.

Monica thought for a moment. I don't understand… maybe Nemrak can answer some questions when he comes by later.

Monica was giving Charlie another dose of his medication when Nemrak came to the front door. She explained what had happened at the passage.

Nemrak raised his eyebrows. "You shouldn't be talking to the spirits," he said. "They are preparing for All Hallows Eve. You mustn't interfere with their plans, or there will be a price to pay. You don't want to end up like Charlie, do you?"

"I'm sorry," Monica sobbed.

Nemrak headed upstairs to the passage and began chanting until the spirit again appeared. Nemrak pleaded with the spirit, that he must not talk to Monica. "She is young and curious. Your identity could be uncovered and all control we have over Charlie will be lost."

The spirit calmly told Nemrak that he was unaware of the Charlie's circumstances, and that he would be back until all phases of the plan were ready. The spirit's voice grew angry. "You must make sure that your part is taken care of!" Then he disappeared.

On his way out, Nemrak reminded Monica to stay away from the passage. Monica was ashamed of herself. She still had a lot to learn. She tended to Charlie as instructed. One more dose and she would be able to lift her spell, and he would be allowed to wake.

She was prepared to lift her spell from Charlie the next day and let the pills do their work. She would only have to supervise him to make sure he took the pills for two more days, but she was still stressed about Nemrak's visit. Why would they put Charlie in charge of the passage if he was a screwup. They should be afraid of him letting out the secret, thought Monica.

Monica began to understand why she was there. Charlie was figuring out too much and the flock was frightened that he may begin to talk. They tried the pills to keep him in a trance but he refused them. That pay stub I found may have something to do with the willpower that Charlie carries himself with. I must look into this more, to see if I can find something out that Nemrak doesn't know; that would put me back in good standings with him. Monica began going through Charlie's house again.

Chief Ward, Daphne, Rachael, and Officer Huber went into the cave to investigate. Daphne showed the officers the pile of wood, and then the place where she had smelled the opium. She didn't smell it anymore. "Does anybody smell anything unusual?" she asked. No one did.

The K-9 search went deeper into the caverns, and suddenly the dog began to bark. They all followed the dog.

Rachael spoke up. "Do you smell that?"

Chief Ward stopped and took a deep breath. "I do," he replied.

"Hopefully it's an animal carcass. Otherwise we may find something we really don't want to."

The dog stopped barking, and all they could hear was Officer Huber hacking. Daphne went as fast as she could toward him. "Oh my God," echoed through the cave walls as she came upon the discovery.

Chief Ward and Rachael headed toward them. There was a black sheep's head lying in the middle of a pentagram, with Sister Stephanie's bloodied pajamas wrapped around the sheep's body.

Daphne pointed out an urn with a bloody handprint on the outside. Chief Ward asked her what it all meant.

"It's not good. Marcy was here with the others last night. That's why I smelled the opium then and not today. Amy saw this and freaked out. Fran and Sister Stephanie are in grave danger. Marcy knows we are on her trail. Time is limited until she kills one or both of them. She may have already. This is a sacrificial ceremony setup. We may be too late."

Rachael knelt down and said a prayer by Sister Stephanie's pajamas. She was interrupted by the K-9 dog sniffing them.

"Wait," Officer Huber said. "He has another scent." The dog took off down a corridor with the humans following. By the dim light of their flashlights they saw bloody drag marks. Daphne looked down and shook her head. "We're too late."

Officer Huber began hacking again. When Daphne, Rachael, and Chief Ward caught up, they saw Sister Stephanie lying face down, motionless, with a pentagram carved into her back Daphne went and rolled her over and saw her throat had been slit and there was a pentagram carved into her forehead also.

Rachael screamed. "Look!" She pointed to a makeshift altar containing Sister Stephanie's heart and liver; she had been eviscerated. They all hung their heads and prayed for a moment.

Chief Ward swallowed the lump in his throat and made the dreaded call to Father Pelfrey, who was outside the cave with the volunteers. "We found Sister Stephanie," he said. "She is dead. Call my men off so we can recover the body and look for clues."

After making the call, Chief Ward told Daphne that she and Rachael should go back to the seminary, that he and his men could handle it from here.

"We aren't giving up on Fran," she snapped back. "There was only one body dragged down this corridor. There must be another way out, and we need to find it." Daphne and Rachael headed out to Father Pelfrey.

Father Pelfrey was outside the cave crying when Rachael and Daphne approached him. "We need to search around the cave for another exit," said Daphne. The three of them began to search around the outside of the cave.

Sure enough, on the other side of the cave there was a second entrance. It was small, but big enough to crawl through. They found no drag marks, which confused Daphne. Could Marcy have the power of mind control, or was Fran's body in the cave too?

Father Pelfrey and the women returned to the seminary; Chief Ward and the volunteers stayed and searched the cave. They found neither Fran's body nor any more clues. The officers covered Stephanie's body and removed it out of the cave. Then they too returned to the seminary with heavy hearts.

Chief Ward told Father Pelfrey he was calling off the search. His thoughts of Fran and Marcy working together made his decision, with no clues to prove otherwise. Father

Pelfrey was angry, but he had a funeral to plan.

Rachael went to talk to Marsha about the phone call that morning. After learning what it was about, she headed back to her room, where Daphne was already asleep. Rachael woke Daphne up to pass on what Marsha had told her. "We must go to the hospital and see," Rachael said.

"You go," Daphne said. "I must get some rest."

"Don't you have an herb or a spell or something to give you energy?"

"I'm only human."

"Okay," Rachael said, "but what do you want me to do if it's her?"

"We'll think of that later."

Father Pelfrey was planning the funeral for Sister Stephanie. She was so young, he thought. I have to notify her family and see what they want done with her body, if they want me to handle the funeral, or if I need to ship the body elsewhere. So much to do and we still have missing people and a police chief who just gave up on the case.

Dr. Collins walked into Father Pelfrey's office. "You're looking kind of stressed tonight," he said.

"I've got a lot on my plate," Father Pelfrey replied.

"I know," said Dr. Collins, "but Amy is recovering well, so make a list of things you need to get done, and take two of these." He handed Father Pelfrey some pills. "We all need a good night's rest. I'll split the list with you in the morning."

Rachael went to the hospital's registration desk. "I'd like to see the woman that was brought in earlier by Officer Cortez."

"Let me look that up," the receptionist replied. "I'm sorry, we didn't have anybody brought in today by an officer."

"What? Officer Cortez responded to a call this morning about a woman acting strange on Highway 32."

"Oh, I know who you're talking about. She was transported here by ambulance. I can call for an escort to take you up to see her. There will be someone right with you."

About ten minutes passed before a security guard finally introduced himself to Rachael. "Hi, my name is Mr. Davis."

Rachael introduced herself, and said she thought the Jane Doe might be one of the missing students.

"Officer Cortez didn't think she was," Mr. Davis replied, "but I'll let you take a look just to be safe. I was sorry to hear about Sister Stephanie."

"Thanks," Rachael said.

"Before you see the patient, you should know that she is very beat up and you may not be able to recognize her right away. You may want to wait until tomorrow to see her. I know you want to find the missing students, and sometimes hope brings false conclusions."

They were outside the door. Mr. Davis opened it, and Rachael took a deep breath and followed him inside. She had to do a double take at the person lying in the bed. "It's Marcy," she said, "but there's no way it could be Marcy." She turned and ran crying from the room. She stormed out of the hospital, flagged down a taxi, and headed back to the seminary.

Mr. Davis went to the nurse's desk. "By her reaction, I think we do have one of the missing students from the seminary here. Call Chief Ward so he can inform Father Pelfrey and get him here for positive ID."

Rachael paid the cab driver and let herself into the seminary, where everyone had turned in for the night. She went back to her room to wake Daphne. "Daphne, wake up," she said. "I just got back from the hospital."

"What?" Daphne moaned.

Rachael began to cry. "I just got back from the hospital, and it was Marcy."

Daphne sat up and said, "Marcy. Are you sure?"

"I'm almost positive...no, I'm positive it was her," replied Rachael.

Daphne was confused. "It can't be Marcy. That would mean that Fran's dead too, and her body can't be too far from where we found Sister Stephanie. We must go back tomorrow to know for sure. You've had a long day, and your eyes may be playing tricks on you."

Daphne got out of bed, pulled an incense candle out of her bag, lit it, and began to chant. Rachael was asleep before she knew it.

CHAPTER 15

Daphne awoke eager to get out and look for Fran. "Wake up, Rachael," she said.

Rachael yawned and stretched. "What's up?"

"We need to get an early start on searching for Fran. We need to find her before anybody else does."

Rachael looked puzzled. "Why?"

"She isn't safe as long as Marcy is around."

Father Pelfrey saw the girls leave; he put his hand to his chin and shook his head. Just then, he got a phone call from Chief Ward.

"Marcy is missing from the hospital," Chief Ward said. "No one has seen her since 2:00 a.m. We don't think she left on her own. It looked like a struggle took place in the room. I think Fran was involved in this."

Father Pelfrey thanked him for the information, then headed to Dr. Collins's office to tell him what was going on. "So not only are they looking for the wrong person, now Marcy is back on the loose. We all may be in trouble, and Daphne and Rachael are out now looking for Fran."

Dr. Collins got up out of his chair. "Well, what are we waiting for? After Stephanie's ceremony, let's get those girls in here and let them know what's going on. Our reputation is at stake here. We've already had one murder, maybe two. We don't need any more."

Father Pelfrey and Dr. Collins knelt and said a prayer

for Fran, Rachael, and Daphne, just in case they didn't make it back in time. "Father, please protect your three children as we mourn the loss of another. Let them all return to us safely. Amen."

Daphne and Rachael had returned to the seminary to clean up and were ready to leave for Sister Stephanie's service when they heard something. Rachael turned quickly to the window. "What was that?" she said.

"Shh!" Daphne said. The two of them sat quietly, and soon they heard it again.

"Someone is out there," Rachael whispered.

Daphne got up quietly and went over to the window. "No one is out there," she replied.

The two of them hurried to the ceremony. "Let's sit in the back pew just in case," Daphne told Rachael.

"In case of what?"

"In case we need to split."

Rachael headed into the church but Daphne hesitated. "I'll be right back," she said.

Rachael went in and took her seat. A couple of minutes later she was joined by Daphne. "Where'd you go?"

"You'll find out later," Daphne replied.

Father Pelfrey was in the priest room talking to Dr. Collins. "I hope those two made it back for the ceremony."

"I'm sure they did," replied Dr. Collins. "Rachael was close to Sister Stephanie and I don't think she would miss her chance to say goodbye."

Father Pelfrey headed to the altar and the whole crowd stood. Holding back his tears, Father Pelfrey gave a eulogy for Sister Stephanie. "Where do I begin? In all my years here at the seminary I've never had an assistant such as Sister Stephanie. Her faith was strong, and she passed that on to each and every student that went through her classes. She was always in good spirits, and you could tell she deeply enjoyed what she did. She touched the lives of so many people."

Just then Father Pelfrey broke out in tears. "Excuse me a moment," he said as he stepped back from the altar to come to grips with his emotions. After a few moments he was able to continue.

"As you can tell she meant a lot to me also, and she will be deeply missed." Father Pelfrey led the crowd in prayer, then one by one people came down the aisle to pay their respects.

Daphne nudged Rachael on her shoulder. "Come with me," she said.

Rachael replied that she wanted to pay her last respect to Sister Stephanie. Daphne told Rachael there would be another time for that. The two of them headed back to Rachael's room.

After the ceremony, Father Pelfrey and Dr. Collins returned to the priest room. "I didn't see Rachael or Daphne come through to pay their respects," said Father Pelfrey.

"I didn't see them in the congregation either," Dr. Collins said. "They must still be out searching. I could go out and search since it will be a few hours until everything is wrapped up."

"I don't think it's such a good idea for you to go out on your own."

"They're probably on their way back. I shouldn't have to go very far."

Father Pelfrey reluctantly agreed, but asked Dr. Collins to be back before 5 p.m. "If you haven't found them, we can search together."

Dr. Collins returned at the stroke of 5:00. Father Pelfrey asked if he had any good news.

Dr. Collins told him he had none. "Those two must be really deep in the woods, or I searched in the wrong direction. We only have a few hours of light left."

"We'll stay here and wait," Father Pelfrey replied.

"Let's check Rachael's room. If they don't return by the morning we will call Chief Ward and organize another search."

Monica woke up eager to cast a spell on Charlie to find out what was going on with him. It failed. She was discouraged, but it would be only a few more days until she had help.

After watching Charlie take his medication, she went to rummage through his garage. It's obvious he's hiding something and that would be a perfect spot to hide it, Monica thought.

She searched all around the garage and found nothing. She was almost ready to quit when she looked up and saw two boxes sitting in a makeshift loft. She grabbed a ladder and took down one of the boxes. She took it into the house and began to search through it.

Monica found nothing useful in the first box. She retrieved the second from the garage. She didn't have to dig very far before she found a Bible from St. Mary's Catholic Church. She leafed through the Bible and noticed that several scriptures had been marked. She continued searching through the box and found some books about Satanism, witchcraft, and Satanic cults. In the one about Satanic cults she found a piece of paper with a name and phone number on it. The name on the paper was William Hurst. This name was not familiar to Monica, but maybe Nemrak knew something about him.

Nemrak was sitting at his desk when the phone rang. The person calling was Mr. Vanhooven.

"Yes, Larry," Nemrak said. "What can I do for you?"

"My daughter is in the hospital. They are admitting her to the O.B. floor right now. I thought you might want to know.

Nemrak snarled and slammed the phone down. Five days from All Hallows Eve and now this? He picked up the phone to call James and inform him of the event.

James was irate as well. "We need a replacement, and I don't care how you go about getting one," he told Nemrak.

Nemrak racked his brain for hours. Finally he decided to go for a drive. Nemrak went out to his car and headed into town. If I were pregnant on such a beautiful day, where I would be?

He drove to the park and noticed a lot of people there. Ah, the Harvest festival. My luck is beginning to change.

Nemrak parked his car and went into the festival. He looked at every woman he walked by. Not pregnant. Not pregnant. Not far enough along. Then, finally, he saw what he needed. The woman was sitting on a bench.

"Lovely day," Nemrak said as he approached.

She replied that it would be lovelier if it wasn't so uncomfortable. Nemrak looked at her and said, "Oh, so when are you due?"

"In a week or so, but not soon enough," she replied.

Nemrak's mind went to work. "Do you mind if I sit with you?" he asked.

The woman said she didn't mind, so he sat. He found out she was there with her husband and daughter, but couldn't stand being on her feet anymore, so she decided to rest while they went off to have fun. Nemrak asked if she knew the gender of her baby.

"A boy," she said with a smile.

Nemrak smiled also, but it wasn't for joy for the woman. Yes, his luck had definitely changed. He congratulated the woman and asked her if she would like some water.

"That would be great."

Nemrak went to get some water from a nearby concession stand. On his way back he put a powder into the water. He gave it to the woman and she drank it down; a few seconds later she became lightheaded and dizzy. Nemrak took her hand and told her he would take her to the medical tent. Instead he led her to his car and sped away with her passed out in his backseat.

When he got home, Nemrak called Sam to come over and help him bring the woman into the house.

"You have a way of figuring it out when things get tough," Sam said.

"That's why I'm at the right hand of James," Nemrak replied.

They brought the woman into the house and placed her on the bed in the guest room. Nemrak called James and told him everything was under control.

Nemrak was seeing Sam out when the phone rang; it was Monica. She told him she had found something at Charlie's that may interest him. Nemrak told Monica he would send Sam over.

Sam arrived at Charlie's and was met at the door by Monica. She handed him a box and told him it all was inside. She explained about finding a phone number for St. Mary's Catholic Church, and another phone number for William Hurst. "I figured they may be important to Nemrak," she said.

Sam thanked Monica and went back to his car. Monica headed back into the house with a smile on her face. She gloated the whole time she was tending to Charlie, telling him he was going to be figured out, and would have to pay the consequences.

Nemrak opened the box Sam handed him. "So, William Hurst is involved with Charlie."

Sam looked puzzled. "Who's William Hurst?"

"An old acquaintance from college. James and I both know him. We need to find a way of tricking William into believing we are Charlie, and then maybe we can find out what's going on. But that's for later. We need to concentrate on All Hallows Eve. All our concentration needs to be on the ceremony."

Sam went out to his car. He didn't want to wait until All Hallows Eve to find out what was going on with Charlie. He decided to investigate; his first stop would be St. Mary's Catholic Church.

Sam knocked on the rectory door and was greeted by Father Sandler. Sam introduced himself as a concerned parent. Father Sandler invited Sam in so that the two of them could talk.

Sam said he thought his son was in with a Satanic cult, and that his son was now under some kind of mind control. "He won't come out of his house and he speaks of evil spirits passing though his closet. He had a girlfriend, but she left, and when I was over at his house I found this phone number written in her handwriting."

"What is your son's name?"

"Charlie," Sam replied.

"Oh yes," Father Sandler said. "His girlfriend was in here asking us to do an exorcism. We refused, but we gave her a phone number."

"Could I ask whose phone number?"

"I'm afraid I can't tell you that. Rest assured your son will be fine in a few months."

Sam thanked Father Sandler for his time and headed back to his car. William Hurst must be the one whose phone number they gave. Francisca must be involved in this somehow, but she hasn't been seen around here for months.

Sam lay in bed that night trying to think of a way to get William Hurst's phone number from Nemrak. Maybe he could trick William himself. But how would he get the number back from Nemrak? That would be impossible since Nemrak told him they needed to put this aside until after All Hallows Eve. Sam tossed and turned that night until he finally fell asleep.

"My wife! Has anyone seen my wife?" screamed a panicked man. Two officers came up to him.

"What's going on here?"

"My wife is missing. I left her over there on the bench and now she is gone."

The officers asked him if he had searched anywhere for her. The man said he had already searched the grounds for her, and he didn't see her. The officers called on their radios to the other officers in the area and gave a description of the man's wife. The officers took the man to the temporary headquarters on the festival grounds to fill out a report. "The other officers will be searching for your wife so you don't need to worry. If she is on the grounds they will find her."

The officers returned with no news for Mr. Jenkins. They announced over the PA that they had a missing person. They gave a description. "If anybody has seen this woman please come to the police trailer."

Mr. Jenkins was fit to be tied. He paced back and forth, and his daughter kept asking him where her mommy was. "Don't worry honey, she'll be right back."

The officers asked Mr. Jenkins if there was anybody they could call to come and get his daughter. Mr. Jenkins replied that his family was new in town, and they had no relatives that lived nearby. The officer asked if they could call a social worker to pick up his daughter so she wouldn't have to be there for the investigation.

"Investigation?" Mr. Jenkins asked. "You mean missing persons, don't you?"

The officer looked Mr. Jenkins right in the eye. "No sir, I mean investigation. We have a description of a man that resembles you walking with Mrs. Jenkins back to your car."

Mr. Jenkins stared at him. "I was with my daughter the whole time, and while you guys are investigating me, who knows what will happen to my wife?" He grabbed his daughter and left the police headquarters, ignoring the officers telling him to stop.

It was well into the evening and there was still no sign of Daphne or Rachael. Father Pelfrey knelt on the floor, bowed his head, and prayed. "Heavenly father, please protect those two young women out searching for their friend. Please bring them back to us safely. Thank you, Lord. Amen."

Dr. Collins came into Father Pelfrey's office just as he finished praying. "No sign of them," he said, "and still no response when I knock on Rachael's door."

"We will open the room in the morning if they don't show up for breakfast," Father Pelfrey said.

"Why don't we check the room tonight? I would sleep much better if we did."

Father Pelfrey said he didn't want to infringe upon their privacy by looking in the room at night. "They may be sleeping, and I just wouldn't feel right about it."

Monica was writing an entry in her journal when Charlie began screaming. "No, no, no!"

Monica woke Charlie and gave him a drink of water. She asked what he was dreaming about.

"Nothing," he replied.

Monica went back downstairs and continued her journal. I wish Charlie would open up to me. When the witches get here they will find out what's going on. Hopefully they don't hurt him.

Charlie dreamed that night of a woman screaming and a baby crying. When the woman stopped screaming, the crying of the baby became muffled, fading into gurgles before fading. The dream fed Charlie's anger. It pushed him to the edge, and he liked it. He didn't quite understand the dream or what it meant, but he felt good inside for the first time in a long time.

CHAPTER 16

Monica was awakened by the smell of bacon and eggs. What's going on? She hurried into the kitchen and saw Charlie making breakfast. "Good morning Charlie," she said.

Charlie looked around at Monica. "Don't you mean great morning, or awesome morning? Because that's the way I feel this morning."

Monica was confused, and then she realized she had done it by herself. Her spell had taken effect; Charlie was in their control now, and there was more evil than good in his soul. "Yes, I mean awesome morning, because I feel awesome this morning also."

They sat down and ate breakfast. Charlie thanked Monica for taking care of him while he was sick, then asked what day it was. Monica told him it was October 24th.

Charlie asked Monica how long she had been at his house. Monica told him, then asked why she found the phone number to St. Mary's Catholic Church.

"One of Charlotte's friends came to visit after she died," he said. "I told her that Charlotte had died, but she stayed here a few days. She was freaked out one night when she came upstairs and saw the passage. She must have gone to the church after that."

Monica then asked about William Hurst. "Who is he?"

"He is a man she contacted. He came and picked her up

and I haven't seen her since."

Monica was puzzled. Was Charlie holding something back or did she get excited over nothing?

Charlie and Monica spent the whole day cleaning. Monica told Charlie about how she was still learning her witchcraft, but has doubts about her feelings toward it. "So I'm kind of like you, Charlie. I don't know if I belong in the cult or not."

Charlie's eyes lightened a little as if he wanted to say something, but they darkened just as quickly. "I know my place in the flock. You should know yours. If you fall astray from us, you will become vulnerable, and who knows what will happen? Look at me for example."

Monica looked like she was ready to cry. Charlie then told her that she was young and inexperienced, so he would say nothing about their conversation. Monica got up from the table, ran off to the guest room, and slammed the door. Charlie couldn't believe how good he felt. He grabbed a glass of water and went to watch television in his recliner.

Charlie had fallen asleep in his recliner when he heard a faint but familiar voice. It was Charlotte, but he was unable to answer. Then he heard the sound of a running horse, then he heard the horse neigh, then he felt a vibration.

Charlie awoke in a sweat. He grabbed another glass of water and went to the passage. "Can any of you hear me?"

The familiar spirit appeared. "Yes, father, I can hear you."

"Why do you keep calling me father?"

"In due time, father, you will know. I'm proud of the progress you have made. Tomorrow you will finish your journey, and all your questions will be answered." Then the spirit disappeared.

Charlie felt strong. He wanted to go for a late-night walk, but he couldn't go outside no matter how hard he tried. Damn it Monica, don't you trust me?

Father Pelfrey awoke in the morning and headed to the commons for breakfast. He noticed that Daphne and Rachael weren't present. He was soon joined by Dr. Collins. "Well, no sign of them this morning," he said.

"No," Dr. Collins responded, "but I heard some noise outside last night. I wasn't able to sleep after that so I made a few rounds."

"Maybe you heard them coming back, and now they're asleep in their room. Let's finish breakfast and then we'll go look."

They were just outside of Rachael's door when Father Pelfrey reached into his pocket for the key. Dr. Collins asked if they should knock first. Father Pelfrey replied that his nerves were already shot, that he needed to know if they were back or not. He turned the doorknob and it was locked, so he slid his key into the knob and turned. The door came open.

They called for Rachael and Daphne, but there was no response. They went through the room and found no sign of them. In fact, it looked as if something was missing. Dr. Collins thought for a moment. "Daphne's bag isn't here. I don't recall seeing her with it yesterday."

"They probably took it with them."

They went back to Father Pelfrey's office. Father Pelfrey picked up his phone and called Chief Ward. "I want to report two more missing persons from the seminary," he said.

"I told you that this would happen," Chief Ward said, "and that Francisca is responsible. We will step up our search, but I order you to stay out of our business."

This angered Father Pelfrey. "I will not stop searching for them, and there is nothing you can do to stop me."

Chief Ward snickered. "Really?"

Father Pelfrey slammed the phone down. Dr. Collins's jaw dropped. "What was that for?"

"Chief Ward said he would step up the search. Then he said I'm not supposed to be involved in the search for Daphne and Rachael, and that he would make sure that I'm not."

"If I didn't know better, I would think he is involved in some way," Dr. Collins said.

"Let's not make accusations."

Later, Father Pelfrey was in his office when Dr. Collins told him he was wanted at the front door. Father Pelfrey asked Dr. Collins who it was. Dr. Collins replied that it was a couple of police officers. Father Pelfrey thought maybe they were there to give him some news.

Father Pelfrey arrived at the main entrance and was informed by the officers that he was wanted downtown by Chief Ward for some questioning. "At this hour?" he asked. "What is so important that you need to escort me downtown for questioning? He could have just come here."

One officer spoke. "Sir, are you refusing to come with us?"

"Yes," Father Pelfrey replied. "We are in the middle of crisis here."

The other officer replied. "Well, then you give us no choice." He read Father Pelfrey his Miranda rights. "Place your hands in front of you and join them."

Father Pelfrey did as the officers said as they placed the handcuffs on him. He calmly walked out with the officers. Dr. Collins told him he would contact the archdiocese to arrange for an attorney. The officers placed Father Pelfrey in the backseat of the cruiser and pulled away.

When they arrived, the officers led Father Pelfrey into the station and the booking room. "Wait a minute," Father Pelfrey said. "I thought I was here to answer a few questions."

"That's right," replied one of the officers, "until you refused to come with us. We booked you on obstructing police business."

"What?"

"Your little search is interfering with ours, and you're disturbing possible evidence."

"These are bogus charges," Father Pelfrey said, "but as a man of the lord I'll let him sort things out." He calmly went through booking and the humiliating strip search. In his cell, he prayed until he could no longer stay awake.

Father Pelfrey was awakened by Chief Ward. "It's time to prepare for your plea hearing."

"What hearing?" Father Pelfrey asked. "What is going on here?"

"You need to go before a judge and enter your plea," Chief Ward told him.

"Don't I get a phone call?"

"I guess."

Father Pelfrey went to the phone and called the seminary, but no one answered. That's strange, he thought.

"Dr. Collins AWOL on you?" Chief Ward asked. Just then, he was informed that he had an emergency call from Officer Huber. They had found the body of a woman in the creek that ran through the woods surrounding the seminary. Chief Ward told Officer Huber he would be right there.

Officer Kennedy went up to Father Pelfrey's cell. Hello Father, my name is Officer Kennedy. I'll be escorting you to the hearing." He opened Father Pelfrey's cell. "I need to cuff and shackle you before we go to the courthouse."

Chief Ward arrived at the scene of the emergency and was greeted by Officer Huber. "I think it may be the girl we're looking for."

Chief Ward bent over and rolled the woman onto her back. He pulled the picture of Fran from his pocket. He compared the woman's face to the one in the picture. He looked up at Officer Huber and said, "The case is closed, as far as I'm concerned. I positively identify this woman as Francisca." He told Officer Huber to contact the coroner, that he needed to get back into town for some unfinished business.

Father Pelfrey and Officer Kennedy were just about to enter the courtroom when Chief Ward came busting through the doors. "Wait here," he told Officer Kennedy.

Chief Ward walked into the courtroom and came back a few minutes later. He told Officer Kennedy to uncuff and unshackle Father Pelfrey. "You're a free man. I dropped all the charges. We got her."

"Got who?" Officer Kennedy asked.

"Francisca," Chief Ward replied. "She's been found dead in a creek in the woods surrounding the seminary, so I closed the case. Father Pelfrey is free to go." Without saying a word Father Pelfrey darted outside to get a ride back to the seminary.

Father Pelfrey thanked the driver outside the seminary gates. Something didn't seem right. He was still wondering why no one answered the phone when he called.

He passed through the main entrance and went to see if Marsha was in her office. Indeed, there she sat. She had to do a double take when she saw Father Pelfrey. "I'm surprised to see you," she said. "I figured Chief Ward would have you locked up for a while."

"Chief Ward had a change of heart," he replied. "Have you seen Dr. Collins?"

Marsha replied that she hadn't seen him all day. Father Pelfrey's strange feeling came back. "I'll go to his office," he said. "I'm not feeling right today so I should see him."

It looked as though no one was in Dr. Collins's office, but the door was unlocked. Father Pelfrey opened the door and fell to his knees. Dr. Collins was lying on his back; his throat had been slit. He had been cut from his nipple line down to his naval and was eviscerated, his heart was on his desk with a dagger through it, and there was a pentagram on the wall made with his blood. He had the numbers 666 carved into his forehead. In his right hand Father Pelfrey saw his rosary.

He noticed a note on Dr. Collins's desk. It read, "It's Marc…" The last letter was unreadable. Father Pelfrey had no doubt what said it was, but who was he to say? Chief Ward had closed the case and any more interactions with him would probably land Father Pelfrey in jail again.

Father Pelfrey went back to his own office. He had a very big decision to make and it would take a lot of praying to figure it out.

Charlie woke to the sounds of unfamiliar voices. He got out of bed and went downstairs, where he was greeted by two of witches. Charlie tried to ignore their cackling as he went to the refrigerator for a glass of water.

Charlie had just finished his glass of water when he was approached by the witches. They introduced themselves as Rosemary and Samantha. Rosemary asked Charlie how he was doing. "I heard you were under the weather for a few days."

Charlie replied that he had never felt better. He headed to his recliner.

Monica stretched and yawned as she walked into the kitchen. She noticed Rosemary and Samantha sitting at the table sipping coffee. Monica was like a child meeting a movie star when she saw them. She went right up to them with an awestruck look in her eyes. She said hello, but they just snarled at her. Monica was crushed; she had spent the last several days bringing Charlie to their side. She wanted to tell them off, but thought better of that, and left the kitchen.

Charlie was watching television when there was a knock at the door; it was Sam and another witch. Sam introduced Charlie to Wanda. Sam showed Wanda to the kitchen where see joined Rosemary and Samantha.

"Where's Monica?" Sam asked. Charlie told him she was in the guest room.

Sam went to get Monica. He knocked on the door and told her it was time for her to pack and go home. Monica opened the door with bags in hand and tears in her eyes. As she walked by the other witches, she just stuck her nose in the air and said nothing. She gave Charlie a hug before she left.

Charlie spent the whole day waiting hand and foot on the witches but he didn't mind. When they turned in for the night, Charlie lay on the couch and watched the news while he fought to keep his eyes open. A few hours into his sleep he heard the sound of chanting. It was like nothing he had heard at any of the ceremonies he had ever been to. He again heard the clop-clop-clop and neighing of horses.

CHAPTER 17

Father Pelfrey barely slept at all. As dawn approached, he made up his mind. Dr. Collins had no family except for those at the seminary. I'll have a small service for Dr. Collins, and then I'll bury him on the seminary grounds. That way I don't have to deal with Chief Ward anymore.

Father Pelfrey went into one of the student dorm rooms and took a rolling bed with him to Dr. Collins's office. He put the doctor's pieces back into him the best that he could, lifted the body onto the bed, and rolled it to the ice room. Then he returned to Dr. Collins's office and cleaned it up as much as possible.

When it was time for Marsha to come to work, Father Pelfrey met her at the door. He told her what had happened to Dr. Collins, and after fifteen minutes of comforting her, he told her what his plan was. Marsha offered to help him as much as she could. Father Pelfrey thanked her and told her she needed to go home for the day, and return the next day for the ceremony.

Marsha was still teary-eyed when she left. Father Pelfrey set out to dig a grave for Dr. Collins.

Father Pelfrey dug off and on all day and was very tired. He decided to go into his office and relax for a while. He kept getting a strange feeling like he was being watched.

He went to lie down in his bed, but the feeling of being watched persisted. He tossed and turned for an hour before getting back up. He decided to write a letter to one of his good friends. I may not be around much longer. I need to let someone know what's going on.

Father Pelfrey wrote his letter and walked it to the mailbox. He returned to his room and was finally able to fall asleep.

Charlie woke in the morning to the sounds of Rosemary, Samantha, and Wanda cackling in the kitchen. Charlie got and noticed Wanda stirring something on the stove. Charlie asked her if she was making breakfast.

"You could say that," she replied.

Charlie went back upstairs to change. When he returned there was a bowl of oatmeal on the table for him. Rosemary told Charlie he should eat it before it got cold. Charlie asked if any of them were going to eat with him. They all replied that they already ate.

Charlie grabbed a glass of water and sat down to eat. "It's delicious," he told Wanda.

"Eat up," she replied. "There's plenty."

Charlie ate three bowls of oatmeal. He got up and started to walk to the living room. Suddenly he became light-headed, and the last thing he remembered was falling face first into his couch.

Charlie was in a deep sleep when he heard voices chanting spells. Charlie was familiar with the spells, but he wasn't able to place the meaning of them. The chanting seemed to go on and on. The longer the chanting went on the stronger Charlie felt.

James called Nemrak to ask him how everything was going. Nemrak replied that it was all going fine, and gave him an update on the situation at Charlie's house.

James told Nemrak he knew that things were fine, but something had been troubling him. "I've been having weird visions lately. I've also been having trouble concentrating. I've been waking myself up at night citing from the Bible. I can't be doing that for the ceremony. I want you to take me to a doctor, so you need to call Sam to watch over the woman until we're done."

Sam was in the middle of lunch when the phone rang. Nemrak told him what he needed. Sam asked what was going on with James.

"Nothing unusual for him," Nemrak replied. "You need not worry. He'll be fine for the ceremony. I'll see you when you get here."

Later, Sam was getting up to check on the woman when Nemrak returned. Sam asked if everything was all right.

"James has been admitted to the hospital to correct his medication," Nemrak said. "It looks unlikely that he will be able to do the All Hallows Eve ceremony."

"What do we do now?"

"Not to worry," Nemrak replied. "I'll perform the ceremony in James's absence."

"Is there enough time for you to learn everything?

"I'll be burning the midnight oil but I'm confident I'll be able to handle it. The witches do most of it anyway."

Sam stayed with Nemrak as he prepared for his role in the ceremony, which was only two days away. Sam was exhausted. "As many times as I heard you repeat the ceremonial words I could do what you're doing," he said.

"Don't be smart with me," Nemrak hissed. "You know as well as I do that everything must be perfect." Sam apologized and spent a few more hours at Nemrak's until he left for the night.

At 10 a.m. Father Pelfrey rolled Dr. Collins out to the gravesite. Marsha had brought flowers to place on the grave. Father Pelfrey and Marsha held hands over the body and began to pray. "Father, please welcome our friend into

Heaven with open arms. He was a good friend and a great believer in our faith. Help us cope with his untimely death, and please return those who are still missing to us safely. Father, please protect us from all who try to harm us. Amen."

Father Pelfrey and Marsha loaded Dr. Collins into his grave. Marsha was concerned that the grave wasn't deep enough. Father Pelfrey said he was afraid of that, but he had another idea. He went to the tool shed and brought back a can of gasoline and a book of matches.

Marsha looked at him. "Have you gone mad?" she shouted.

"I can't stand the thought of my friend being chewed on by the animals around here, and I'm too old to dig any deeper."

Marsha threw her arms in the air and headed back to her car as Father Pelfrey doused his comrade in gas. He waited until she left before he threw in the match. He fell to his knees as Dr. Collins's body burned. He prayed for God to forgive him for this act.

Father Pelfrey stayed outside until Dr. Collins's body finished burning. He reminisced about all the times they had together. Darkness was approaching as he went in for the night. It was the loneliest he had ever felt when he entered the halls of the seminary. Father Pelfrey collapsed into his bed and cried himself to sleep.

This time, as Charlie slept, after hearing the familiar chanting he heard the screams of children. The more the children screamed the more excited Charlie became. Soon he was belting out an evil laugh.

He awoke to the faces of Samantha, Rosemary, and Wanda. Samantha asked Charlie how he was feeling.

"Fine, witch," Charlie replied in a very deep voice. "Leave me to my business."

The three witches cackled as they left Charlie in the living room. Charlie felt great but there was something missing. He felt the urge to go upstairs to the passage.

He opened his closet and sat in front of the opening. "Master I'm ready to serve you." Suddenly the spirit of the boy appeared. This time Charlie recognized him. "You're my son."

"Yes," the spirit said. "I need you to do something for me."

"Anything, my son."

The spirit told Charlie that he needed to sleep and a vision would appear to him. "It is up to you to make the vision a reality." Charlie said he would not let him down, and the spirit disappeared.

Charlie lay down in bed and was asleep in no time. Just as the spirit said, he began to dream. In his dream his son was there, but he wasn't a spirit. Charlie could touch him. He saw his son and a bunch of his friends running around causing mayhem. This made Charlie laugh. To have one day with his son Charlie would do anything. Unknowingly, he did give something for that: Charlie lost his soul that night, and from now on he would be responsible for more than he could ever imagine.

Father Pelfrey rose at dawn to cover the remains of Dr. Collins. He went out to the gravesite and was greeted by a mess. He picked up what was left of Dr. Collins's bones, placed them back into the hole, and began to cover them. When the dirt was filled in, he placed Marsha's flowers on the grave. He knelt down and said goodbye to his longtime friend for the last time.

Father Pelfrey decided to leave the seminary and restart his life in a different country or city in a regular church. He went inside and called the archdiocese. The archbishop they would relocate him, but it wouldn't be until November first. Father Pelfrey thanked the archbishop and hung up. What's a few more days, he thought. Maybe his luck would change and Daphne and Rachael would show up with some encouraging news. Still, he needed to get away from the seminary. He arranged for a ride into town to eat at one of his favorite restaurants, and have some time to relax.

Charlie awoke feeling wonderful. He went downstairs, and as he entered the kitchen the witches knelt before him. "We are at your command, master."

Charlie went into the bathroom and looked into the mirror. He had to look twice, because his face was back to normal.

Charlie went back into the kitchen. "Wanda, make my breakfast. Samantha, you make my coffee. Rosemary, come over here and give me a shoulder massage." The witches hurried to do his bidding.

After breakfast, Charlie decided to test his powers. He ordered Samantha upstairs with him. She followed Charlie upstairs and the two of them had sex. Then he ordered her back downstairs.

Charlie let out an evil laugh. Then his fun was interrupted by his son's spirit appearing in the passage. Charlie knelt in front of him.

"Have you figured out your duties yet?" the spirit asked. "Or do you want to return to your old life?"

"Yes, master. I know my responsibilities and accept full responsibility of them."

The spirit told Charlie to rise. "Welcome, soul harvester. Your big day is tomorrow. You need to harvest as many souls as possible."

"Don't worry, son. Daddy will take care of you."

"Sleep, soul harvester." The spirit snapped its fingers, and Charlie was asleep.

Sam was glad the ceremony was tomorrow. He didn't think that he could spend one more day with Nemrak being so particular. At least he finally had it down pat.

Nemrak told Sam he was going to the hospital to check on James. Sam asked if he could go. Nemrak told him he could, but he would have to help him place a stronger spell on the woman to keep her from waking up for a few hours.

"A few hours?" Sam asked. "What hospital are we going to?"

"Not the one in town."

Sam and Nemrak arrived at the hospital, where they still had James in a medically induced coma. Nemrak left Sam in the room and went to talk to the doctor. After fifteen minutes he came back and told Sam it was time for them to go, that the ceremony would definitely be under his control. Sam asked Nemrak why James was in a coma. Nemrak said it was for his own good. The two of them headed home for the night.

Chapter 18

Nemrak was up at dawn the next morning. "Today is All Hallows Eve," he said with a smile. "I must prepare myself for tonight." He started making a list of things he needed to do. He was so focused on what he was doing that he forgot to take care of the woman. He looked at the clock; it was almost 8:30 a.m. He hurried into the room where the woman was and began to put the pre-ceremonial spells on her.

Father Pelfrey was up early. He didn't sleep well the night before, and he felt as if he wasn't alone. As he grew more and more uncomfortable, he decided to go out for a walk.

As he walked he thought he saw someone in the distance. "Hello!" he hollered. "Who are you, and what is your purpose on the seminary grounds?" He received no response, so he headed toward the figure. He kept yelling, but he never received a response.

When he was about a hundred yards away, the figure disappeared. Father Pelfrey figured he was seeing things from all the stress he was under, so he headed back to the seminary.

He made it about thirty feet into the seminary when he was again overwhelmed with the feeling that he wasn't alone. He headed into to his office and locked the door.

He decided to write down everything that had happened, in the hopes that someone would find it and none of their deaths would be in vain.

Charlie spent a lot of time thinking through the night on how he was going to carry out his mission. He awoke with a plan and told Rosemary and Samantha to go to the store to get Halloween decorations and candy. While they were gone, he took Wanda up to his room for sex.

When Samantha and Rosemary returned, Charlie ordered the three of them to decorate the outside of his house so little trick-or-treaters would stop for candy. He laughed an evil laugh, and the witches cackled with him.

Charlie would need the help of someone the kids wouldn't be afraid of. He thought for a moment, and then he made a phone call to Sam.

Sam was sleeping when his phone rang. "I need you to do me a favor," Charlie said. He went on to tell Sam his plan to harvest souls, but he needed someone the kids wouldn't fear to lure them into his house.

Sam asked if Charlie had someone in mind. "Monica," Charlie replied.

"Why Monica?"

Charlie replied, "Even though she is a witch she still has her innocence." Then he laughed his evil laugh. Sam told Charlie he would call him back after he talked to Nemrak.

Sam soon called back to let Charlie know Nemrak approved his plan.

"Good," Charlie hissed. "All phases are go." She will never expect anything, he thought.

Sam was driving to get Monica when a thought dawned upon him. "No, that would never work," he said to himself. "I don't know where James's hospital is located anyway."

Monica was outside on the steps when Sam arrived. She was eager to go back and spend some time with Charlie. Sam was ready to pull over and leave Monica at the side of the road after fifteen minutes.

Charlie went up to the passage and summoned his child's spirit. "Well done, soul harvester," the spirit said. "My friends and I will be ready. Don't let us down. Afterwards you will feel so energized with evil you will feel like you've never felt before. You will yearn to remove the innocence from this world."

Charlie laughed as the spirit left. He then went to the stairs and called for Rosemary to come and take her turn.

Sam pulled up to Charlie's house. He opened Monica's door and escorted her to the front door. Charlie invited them both into the house; Sam declined, saying he had some unfinished business to deal with. Charlie thanked him for getting Monica as he left. The witches made Monica feel at ease as Charlie unveiled his plan to her. She hesitantly agreed to it, and the five of them began to put it into motion.

It was nearing 4:00 p.m. and trick or treat would start in two hours. Charlie went back up to the passage. "I the soul harvester offer you my son the souls that will be harvested tonight, so that you and your friends may walk the Earth among us and put an end to the innocence that keeps us down. Please help us in all ways possible so the great one can walk again on Earth controlling what is rightfully his." Charlie knelt in front of the passage, made a pentagram on the floor from his own blood, and meditated.

As he was meditating, he heard a woman's voice, so faint that he couldn't make out what it was saying. This angered Charlie. "Who dares interrupt me?" Charlie got up and went downstairs. "Who interrupted me?" he yelled.

The witches looked at Charlie and said they had all been downstairs.

"Don't lie to me!" Charlie screamed. "One of you was up there and when I find out who it was they will pay." He went back upstairs to finish his meditation.

An hour later Charlie was pacing around the house, looking at the clock every five minutes. He asked everybody to recheck everything to make sure they hadn't left anything out. When they were done Rosemary, Samantha, and Wanda left for the ceremony.

Charlie and Monica were alone at the kitchen table. Charlie asked Monica if she remembered when they last sat at the kitchen table and she said they were alike because neither of them had a place in the cult. "Tonight you find your place." He got up from the table and left. Monica sat at the table wondering what it was.

James awoke in the hospital. "What I am doing here?" he asked the nurse.

The nurse looked at James and told him he was brought there by a fellow named Nemrak. "He said you weren't acting normal so we tried a few different medications for your bipolar disorder."

"I feel great," James told the nurse. "May I talk to my doctor so I can get out of here? I need to return to the church to help Father Sandler."

The nurse told James she would contact the doctor and update him on his condition.

She returned a few moments later. "Good news, James," she said. "You've been dismissed. Do we need to call someone to pick you up?"

James gave her William's phone number. As he gathered his things, he thought to himself, this isn't my stuff.

The nurse came back and said that William wanted to talk to him. James picked up the phone in his room and waited for the call to be transferred. William asked James how long he had been in the hospital. James turned to the nurse. "Four days," she said.

William asked if James had any clue what day it was.

James looked at the calendar in his room. "Oh my god," he said. "It's October 30th. Where did August and September go?"

"Exactly," William replied. "I'm on my way. Do you need anything?"

James told William he needed some clothes. The hospital must have gotten his mixed up with someone else's.

William stopped by the patient records office when he arrived at the hospital. He asked the secretary if she could tell him who brought James in. The secretary explained that she couldn't. William told her James had been missing for two months.

The secretary looked at William. "Okay, but no one else can know that I told you." William agreed, and the secretary told him, "He was brought to the hospital by a man named Nemrak, on concerns that his medication wasn't right." William thanked the secretary and headed upstairs.

James thanked William for bringing him different clothes. William told him they needed to talk, but this wasn't the time or place. James agreed they could talk on the way home. The nurse had release papers that needed to be filled out before they could leave.

"Do you remember the girl who came to ask about an exorcism?" James said when they were in the car. "What happened to her?"

"Francisca," William replied. "Father Sandler and I sent her to Rome to take classes to become a nun, so she could help her boyfriend Charlie with his problem."

"Is she in the class that is supposed to graduate in a few days?" William said she was. "Good," replied James.

"What is your involvement with Nemrak?" William asked.

"Who?"

"Nemrak," William replied. "He was the one who brought you into the hospital saying that your medication wasn't right."

"I should thank him for taking me to the hospital," James said.

William pulled the car over and got out. He opened the trunk and pulled out James's bag containing the unfamiliar clothing from the hospital. He looked in the pants and found a wallet. He opened it to James's ID. James was stunned. William flipped through the business cards in the wallet and pulled one out: it was for the high priest of the First Church of Satan.

William dug back into the bag and found a necklace with a pentagram on it. William showed the business card and the necklace to James and asked him to explain them. James couldn't. William again asked James what kind of involvement he had with Nemrak. James had no response. William suspected something but didn't want to push the issue due to the stress James was under from being in the hospital. He started the car and drove on.

Father Sandler greeted William and James at the rectory. "James, where have you been?" William and Father Sandler escorted James to his room and made sure he took his medication.

Father Sandler and William went downstairs. William pulled the business card and the necklace out of his pocket and showed them to the priest.

"Where did you get these?"

"They were in James's personal belongings," William told him.

"But why?"

"I don't know," William replied, "but I don't like my gut feeling. Have you ever heard that James has a twin brother?"

"Of course."

"Have you ever met him?"

"No, I haven't."

"I've known James for over twenty years," William said, "and I've never met him, or seen him, even though he lives here in town."

"What you are getting at?"

"I think James and his twin are the same person, but I need more information to prove it."

"What about Francisca?" Father Sandler asked.

"What was taken the night of the break-in?" William asked.

"Nothing," Father Sandler replied. "It looked like somebody just went through the files."

William stood up. "We need to call Father Pelfrey in Rome. I just have a bad feeling."

Father Pelfrey was still in his office when the phone rang. "William," he said. "I'm glad it's you. We have some major problems going on here, and I need to tell you because I don't know how much longer I'll be around."

He told William everything that had happened. "Now, Marcy, the Satanic Princess, is on the loose. Francisca, Rachael, and the Pagan High Priestess Daphne are all missing, and I'm here all alone."

William told Father Pelfrey to hang in there, and that he would pray for him. Father Pelfrey thanked William and hung up.

Father Sandler asked William what he had learned. "We're too late," William said. "My suspicions are becoming clearer, but I need to make one more phone call."

William called the hospital and asked the nurse what medication James was on. The nurse told him the medication was for bipolar disorder. William asked the nurse to explain that further. The nurse said it was a multiple personality disorder, that the person could lose control of their mind like they were somebody else, and not be able to recall anything that took place.

"We have big trouble," William told Father Sandler.

"James is bipolar. He is himself and his twin. That means he is into Satanism. He is the one who broke in and went through the files. He knew we sent Francisca to Rome. He is the one responsible for what happened there."

Father Sandler's mouth was wide open. "What happened in Rome?"

William repeated what Father Pelfrey had told him. Father Sandler lowered his head. "There is nothing we can do."

"We can make sure James takes his medication."

Father Sandler and William continued discussing the events that had taken place. "If Fran is still alive," William said, "maybe she will try contacting one of us. If we hear from her, we should let each other know."

William left for the night. Father Sandler checked on James before he went downstairs to the library. He was deep into his reading when he heard footsteps upstairs. He went to investigate. Father Carey was sound asleep, but James wasn't in his bed. Father Sandler looked all over upstairs but couldn't find him. Not again, he thought as he went downstairs. Then he heard someone in the kitchen.

"Hi, Father Sandler," James said. "I have a lot of explaining to do."

"Yes," Father Sandler replied, "but not tonight. We both need a good night's rest."

They turned in for the night.

Father Pelfrey put away his diary and headed off to his room. When he got there, the feeling of being watched disappeared. Writing in my diary must have worked. I feel as if I could sleep for days.

He put on pajamas and knelt to pray. His prayer was abruptly interrupted when someone grabbed his hair and pulled his head back. Marcy was holding what looked like a femur bone with its end sharpened. "You must die," she said as she raised her hand with the bone in it. There was no pain for Father Pelfrey. All he could hear was screaming and scuffling.

Trick or treat had started and kids by the handful were coming to Charlie's for treats. Monica had strict orders to lure kids without parents or adults into the house for a special treat. Halfway through, they only had two kids in the house. Suddenly a group of four rang the doorbell. Monica answered the door; with a snap of her fingers they were under a spell.

"We still need seven more," Charlie told her. Slowly but surely more and more kids came, and they ended up with thirteen by the time it was over.

Monica asked Charlie what he was going to do with the children. He told her it was none of her business. "Just send them upstairs one by one for their special treat. When one comes back down, send the next one up."

Monica sent the first child upstairs. Charlie handed the child a candy bar and told her it would make her feel like she had never felt before. The girl ate the candy bar and passed out. Charlie summoned a spirit from the passage to take over the body. She went back downstairs and Monica sent the next.

After 45 minutes all the children were back in the living room. Charlie then came downstairs. "Now, my children, go have fun. Cause mayhem. Treat this like it is your last day on Earth until Satan rules again."

Monica looked at Charlie. "What did you do to them?" she asked.

"I gave them what they wanted: one more night on the Earth to roam free and cause mayhem."

"What will happen to them?"

Charlie's look of joy turned to one of anger. "I told you that you would find your place in the cult, and I'm about to show you."

He grabbed Monica's arm, took her upstairs, and tied her up. "Tonight and every All Hallows Eve afterwards you will fulfill your duty to the cult."

"Let me go!" she screamed. Charlie ignored her and prepared for the ceremony.

Charlie's children of the night were running around town causing mayhem. One of them went up to a house and rang the doorbell. "Trick or treat!"

The old lady who answered the door replied, "I'm sorry sonny, trick or treat is over."

"So it must be trick time," the child replied in a very deep voice. His head did a complete 360-degree turn, and the woman fainted. The other children smashed pumpkins or left flaming bags of poop on people's porches. These were minor acts compared to what was to come.

Nemrak was preparing the woman for the ceremony, placing her in a black gown. He called Sam to come and help him load her up. Then he got himself dressed. I wish James were here, he thought. Sweating, his fingers fumbled with his buttons.

Charlie prepared himself for the ceremony. "Tonight at the ceremony you will find your place in the cult," he told Monica, "so you need to clean up." He untied her and handed her an old black dress. Charlie followed her downstairs and waited outside the bathroom door so she wouldn't try anything.

Charlie's children decided to put some real fear into the living. They broke up into two groups of four and one group of five. The first group thought they would terrorize a couple out for an evening walk. One of the female children fell down and acted like she was hurt. As the couple bent over to comfort her, the other three kids attacked them, knocking them unconscious and dragging them into a nearby abandoned building.

The couple woke up in an unfamiliar place. The husband

looked at his wife. "Kim, are you all right?" he asked.

"Yes Jason, I'm fine," Kim replied, "but where are? What happened?"

"I don't know."

Suddenly a voice came to them out of the darkness. "Nothing's happened yet," it said.

"Who are you? What do you want with us?" Jason asked nervously.

"We wanted to show you something." A dim light appeared in the distance and three shadows appeared. One was a girl lying on a bed with her legs open. The second was a boy up by the girl's head. The third was another girl down by the girl's legs. It looked like they were delivering a baby; sure enough, the girl down by the legs pulled out a baby and laid it on the other girl's chest. Then the boy pulled out a knife and stabbed the baby.

Kim screamed. Jason got up. "What is going on here? Who are you people?"

"I'm your son," replied the voice.

"My son isn't born yet."

"Exactly," the voice replied. "Not yet."

"That's enough," Jason replied. "Show yourself."

Suddenly he was surrounded by four kids. He looked at them. "You're just kids. What are you going to do?"

One of the girls grabbed his testicles and twisted. "You will listen to us or you will suffer." Jason grabbed the girl by the hair and began pulling it. The two other children quickly subdued him.

The other boy was very interested in Kim. "What you want with me?" she screamed.

"Oh Mommy, I just want to see you."

Kim began to hyperventilate and passed out.

"It's time for phase two," said the boy to the others. The four of them grabbed Jason and everything went black for him.

Kim awoke to see the children but not Jason. "What did you do to him?" she asked.

"Nothing yet," the children responded.

"What do you mean, yet?"

The boy who called her 'Mommy' came up to her. "We want to make a deal with you."

"A deal?" Kim asked. "What do you want?"

"The soul of your unborn child for the soul of your husband." The other children brought Jason out on a cross made of 2x6s with his hands and feet tied to it.

Kim looked at him. "Honey, are you okay?" she hollered.

"Don't do it!" he yelled. Just as he said that he was cracked with a whip on his bare flesh.

"Don't hurt him!" shrieked Kim.

"The soul of your baby or your husband's life," the boy said more forcefully. Kim hesitated; again Jason was cracked with the whip. He struggled to get loose, to no avail.

Crying, Kim screamed, "No, I won't."

Two of the children came out with hammers and spikes. "Your baby's soul or your husband's life," the child said again.

Kim still couldn't answer the question. The two children drove the spikes through Jason's hands. Jason screamed and then passed out from the pain. Kim finally saw enough. "Take my child's soul and let him go," she said, then passed out. The children took Jason off the cross and called the police for an ambulance.

The second group of children went back to the older lady's house from earlier. "I'm going to give that bitch a heart attack tonight," said one of the boys. The four of them waited patiently until she let her cats out. When she closed the door, they grabbed her cats and went to a dark spot in the neighborhood.

The little old lady was watching TV when she heard a meow outside the door, so she got up to let her cats in. When she opened the door she grabbed her chest and fell to her knees. She finally fell face first on the sidewalk as the blood from her two gutted cats fell upon her back, as they hung from the tree above. The kids placed a knife in the woman's hand to make it look as if she had gone crazy and done it herself. They then headed back to the meeting place.

The last group of kids decided to have their fun at a farm just outside of town. The silence was broken by sounds from the animals. "What's going on out there Maybelle?" asked her husband Zeke. He got up out of bed, grabbed his 12 gauge, and headed out to the barn. "Damn coyotes," he said.

Zeke entered the barn and stared in horror. There were pentagrams painted on the wall with the number 666, and on the barn floor ahead of him was one of his heifers. It had been eviscerated, and had a pentagram and 666 carved into it. He headed out of the barn to go call the police. He just closed the barn door when he looked up to the upstairs window and saw shadows in his bedroom.

He ran into the house and upstairs. As he opened the door to his bedroom he saw Maybelle lying on the bed with her rosary twisted tightly around her neck. Zeke shook her. "Are you okay?" he yelled, but she didn't respond. Zeke called the fire department.

The thirteen children met up at their meeting place. They had stolen a wheelchair to put Kim in. One of the boys spoke up and said they needed to make one more stop. They went by one of the houses and stole a sign saying, "It's a boy!"

When Sam arrived to pick up Charlie and Monica, he noticed something familiar about Monica's dress. He kept it to himself. Charlie already had a lot on his mind. The three of them headed to the ceremonial grounds.

At the grounds, flock member after flock member arrived. Samantha, Wanda, and Rosemary had the altar set up. Charlie, Sam, and Monica arrived shortly after Nemrak. Sam helped Nemrak with the woman as Charlie kept an eye on Monica. The four of them were preparing for the ceremony when Samantha came up to Charlie. "What's the brat here for?" she asked.

"Mind your business," Charlie replied.

They had just finished preparing for the ceremony when Charlie's children showed up. "Children," Charlie said. "How was your time on Earth?"

One boy came up to Charlie. "Father, we have a surprise for you," he said. They wheeled Kim up to him.

"A woman," Charlie said. "What do I want with a woman?"

"Not the woman," the boy said. "The future baby. She gave us the soul of her child in return for her husband's life. Now I can be with you all the time."

"How?"

"Rosemary can tell you. I never was born, like this child who hasn't been born yet. I'm a Satan spawn who needs to be on Earth to gather a following so that my true calling can be achieved, so that our father Satan can once again rule the Earth."

Charlie went over to Rosemary for an explanation. Rosemary told Charlie on the thirteenth hour of Halloween the woman must go through the passage while a witch chants a spell. "Your son will come back out of the passage, but you must be wed so your child has a mother."

"I have that part almost taken care of," Charlie said.

"She must be a member of a Satanic cult and must not be impure. She must be able to lead the child to fit into society. We have fifty minutes before the ceremony begins. Let me know your decision."

Fifteen minutes before the ceremony, Charlie approached Rosemary with Monica on his arm. "This brat?" Rosemary cackled. "She's only fourteen. What kind of mother would she be to your son?"

The look in Charlie's eyes became dark and piercing. "You said the mother must be pure, and she is the purest person I know, besides Charlotte."

"You're making a mistake," Rosemary replied, "but if that's what you want, fine. You'll need her parents' permission first."

"I'm the soul harvester. They will bow before me."

Rosemary just laughed. Charlie and Monica went to her parents to ask permission. They wouldn't grant it until the boy appeared. "I, the spawn of Satan, command you to let my father Charlie marry your daughter to raise me. I will not stop until I'm on Earth to rule those who don't believe."

Monica's parents then agreed. Charlie accepted their permission and went back to Rosemary. "We will perform the ceremony after All Hallows Eve is done."

Nemrak approached the altar. "All rise and bow your heads to our father. Satan we are all gathered here so we can praise you and give you the encouragement that we do want you back on Earth as the rightful ruler. Give us the power to carry out your word."

Everyone took their seats as Nemrak made the announcement of Charlie and Monica's wedding after the All Hallows Eve ceremony. "Bring the virgin forward," he commanded.

Samantha and Wanda wheeled the virgin to the altar on a gurney. Nemrak took the dagger and began chanting. "Satan, take this virgin as an offering. Take her and have your way with her pure soul, as we share her with you." He took the dagger and cut her throat, as Samantha and Wanda caught her blood in urns.

Nemrak took a saw and cut her sternum. He reached in and ripped the heart out of her chest. Nemrak took the heart and held it in the air. "Look! It's still beating the last of her innocence before she becomes a servant of our father."

Before the heart stopped beating, he pierced it with the dagger and sprayed blood on the flock. "Receive your shower my children. Believe the virgin blood and Satan will protect you. He will take care of you as long as you believe and help us bring him back on Earth to rule." He took a bite of the heart. "Now, my children, I want to offer you some of my pleasure. Take a drink of the blood. Cherish it. The virgin keeps me happy, so she should keep you happy too. Drink her blood, my children."

One by one the flock members came forward to drink the blood and eat small pieces of the heart. They all knelt on the ground and with their hands they drew pentagrams on the ground. They all placed their heads in the pentagrams and began to pray.

"Now, my children," Nemrak said when they were finished, "we will head to the creek." All the members got up and followed him. They found the woman was lying on the ground. Nemrak used his dagger to draw a pentagram around the woman; a glow came from the pentagram. The woman then began to give birth to the child.

The crying of the baby woke the child's mother, but she didn't snuggle it. Instead she got up and walked the baby toward the creek. Nemrak began chanting. "Satan, we offer you the ultimate sacrifice: a baby boy. We worship you and give you thanks for all that you do for us. We will always follow you, and you will one day rule again, and we will be your right hand. Please take our sacrifice, father."

The baby was still crying as Nemrak finished his chant. The woman walked into the creek and held it underwater. The muffled crying made Monica tear up. Charlie put his arm around his future bride to comfort her. The crying stopped and the mother let go of the child, letting it float away with the current. Nemrak then handed her the dagger and snapped his fingers. She drove the dagger through her own chest, into her heart, and fell face first into the water.

Monica looked as the water turned red. She took Charlie's hand off her shoulder and ran off. Charlie turned as if to run after her, but he knew that the ceremony was almost over and didn't want to miss the baptism.

One by one the flock members walked into the creek. Nemrak took an urn of bloody water and blessed each one of them. Charlie was baptized and then went after Monica. He looked all around and couldn't find her. It was five minutes from the time they were to be married when he found a note. "Charlie: I found my place in the flock. I didn't belong. If I was to raise a son to continue this, I couldn't live with myself. Monica."

Charlie had just finished reading when he felt something wet fall on his head. He looked up and saw Monica hanging from the tree with a rope around her neck. Charlie fell to his knees. "No!" he screamed.

Sam came running to him and asked what was wrong. Charlie looked at him with tears in his eyes and just pointed. Sam looked and saw Monica hanging there, but there was no comfort from him. "Well," he said, "it looks like Satan got a bonus tonight."

Charlie looked at Sam. "Why can't I love without pain?"

Nemrak approached them. "You can still love her as you do your son," he told Charlie. "You are the soul harvester. Every All Hallows Eve you can spend time with them, as long as you do what's expected of you."

Charlie's son then ran up to him. "Father, I will take care of her as long as you keep your promise," he said. He gave Charlie a hug; Charlie ignored him. He ran off with the rest of the children.

The children headed to a vacant house several blocks away. The children made their way into the house, drew a pentagram on the floor, and began chanting. "Thank you, father, for our last night on Earth. We are ready to join you, and we became stronger tonight to help you with your quest." One by one they fell face down on the floor, never again to see the light of day.

The ceremonial grounds were cleared of all evidence of any activity that had taken place there. Charlie was still under the tree. The longer he knelt the more he began to hate, not the cult for what happened to Monica, but people in general. He fully gave his soul to Satan. He slept under the tree that night, and through the night he heard demonic voices telling him not to trust anyone that wasn't affiliated with the cult. The demonic voices would then taunt him to anger him more. Charlie's mind raced with visions of bloodied skies, people begging for their lives and bowing to him in the name of Satan.

Chapter 19

"Charlie, wake up," broke the morning silence. "Wake up, boy. We need to leave here before the sun rises."

Charlie awoke to Sam and Nemrak standing over him. He got up and stretched, then looked up at Monica's body still hanging there. "She doesn't know what she is missing," he said. "So young and naïve. I can't believe I was stupid enough to think that she could have raised my son."

"Fran…what? Am I dreaming?" said a groggy Father Pelfrey.

"No, Father, you are not dreaming," Fran replied. "It's really me."

Father Pelfrey sat up to see Fran, Rachael, and Daphne in his room waiting for him to wake up. "Marcy," he said. "What happened to her?"

"She is under a very strong spell," Daphne told him. "She will not bother anybody until I want her to."

Father Pelfrey got up out of his bed and gave Fran a big hug. "We thought we had lost you," he said. He looked at the three of them standing in front of him. "With the three of you here, my prayers have been answered."

Daphne told Father Pelfrey there was a lot that they needed to talk about, but she would feel more comfortable if they went into town and talked about it over lunch. Father Pelfrey agreed, but he still couldn't believe his eyes.

Last night he thought his life was over. Now his prayers were answered. Father Pelfrey told the girls that he needed to clean up and pray, that he would meet them in an hour at the main doors.

Fran, Rachael, and Daphne discussed their time with Daphne's family, and how much Fran and Rachael had learned about Wiccan traditions. "I hope we learned enough to go back to the States and release Charlie from the cult," Fran said.

"Maybe we can talk Father Pelfrey into going with us," Daphne said. "Between him and Rachael's brother, there may be a good chance of releasing Charlie as long as they are able to keep Marcy with them and under a spell. She is the biggest piece to our puzzle.

"I don't know how Father Pelfrey will react to bringing Marcy along after what she did," Rachael said.

"I'll handle that," Daphne replied.

Father Pelfrey and the girls got out of the cab and headed into the restaurant. Inside, Father Pelfrey asked, for a very secluded table. The greeter took them to a table in the corner with no one else around it. They took their seats and ordered their drinks. Then Father Pelfrey asked for an explanation.

Fran told of being kidnapped by Marcy, and witnessing Sister Stephanie's murder. Just as she finished, the waitress returned with their drinks. When she left, Fran said she had escaped the cave through a small opening in the back and headed back toward the seminary. "But I didn't let anybody see me, knowing that Marcy would come back to look for me."

"When we went back to the cave," Rachael said, "we found some clues Fran had left, but we kept them quiet because Chief Ward was on a witch hunt for the wrong person."

Then Daphne spoke. "By the time Marcy came back

to the seminary, Rachael and I had taken Fran with us to England to stay with my family. We stayed in England until All Hallows Eve. That's when we figured she would make her move. We waited patiently, watching your every move, until you got into your bedroom. We had a feeling she would attack you there. Rachael was already inside. Fran and I waited outside your door."

Rachael then spoke again. "Marcy came out of your closet when you turned out your light. I was beside your bookshelf. I tapped three times on the wall, and Daphne put a sleeping spell on us. After the spell was out of the air, Fran and Daphne came in and put you to bed. They took Marcy to Dr. Collins's office and put her under a spell. Now she's under the watchful eye of Daphne's Aunt Demy."

Father Pelfrey was silent for a moment. "You knew Fran was alive," he said finally, "but to protect her from Chief Ward you kept it a secret. By not turning Marcy over to the authorities, she was able to kill two of my closest friends and colleagues."

"We need her," Fran said. "And we need you."

"For what?"

"Remember my boyfriend Charlie?"

"I remember," Father Pelfrey replied, "but what do you need me for? And what do you need Marcy for?"

At that moment, the waitress brought their food. "We'll finish our discussion at the seminary," Father Pelfrey said. "It's getting busy in here.

Charlie, Sam, and Nemrak were in the middle of breakfast. Nemrak took a drink of his coffee and then began to talk to Charlie. "Taking the lives of those children so your son could roam the Earth for one night showed us that you would kill for Satan. Then you offered to marry Monica so your son, who you know is not yours, but a spawn of Satan, could live upon Earth to fulfill his destiny. That showed us you were trustworthy. So when Monica killed herself last night you became confused, you began to feel, and we became worried."

Charlie interrupted. "Why are you worried for me to feel?"

"Monica wasn't worthy," Nemrak replied. "She was too innocent, too pure. As you said, she was young and naïve. She wouldn't have made a good mother for your son."

"So what does this have to do with my dreams last night, and the voices I heard?"

"Charlie," Nemrak replied, "you died last night. Those were the voices of the souls in Hell. They were heckling and making fun of the old Charlie. The old Charlie doesn't exist anymore. Now, no more questions." They finished their breakfast in silence.

Sam, Nemrak, and Charlie went to Nemrak's house. Sam took Charlie into Nemrak's office, and the two of them waited for Nemrak to join them. When he did, he was wearing the same ceremonial dress he had worn the night before. Following him were Wanda, Rosemary, and Samantha.

"What are they doing here?" Charlie asked Nemrak.

"They're here to finish the transformation, Charlie," Nemrak replied.

Sam told Charlie to lie on the couch. Samantha came up to Charlie and began chanting. "You're no one. You don't understand our language. You don't want to be innocent. You can hear the voices but you just tune them out. Now go with the enemy, arise with the almighty."

Charlie's eyes rolled to the back of his head, and his whole body began to convulse. Wanda began chanting, "You are our enemy, our hated enemy. Leave us. Take your innocence with you. Your soul is afraid to awake because your purity holds it back. You can hear the voices but don't tune them out. They will fulfill your destiny."

Charlie looked down on the scene as he floated above.

He saw Rosemary begin chanting over his own convulsing body. "I can see inside you. The sickness is rising. Don't try to deny what you feel. Your human side is slowly melting away and decaying. We want you to open up your demon side."

Charlie's body stopped convulsing, and with one final jerk he awoke. He sat up, very groggy. "What happened?" he asked.

"Arise, my son," Nemrak said.

Charlie stood up. Sam, Rosemary, Wanda, and Samantha all knelt before him. "Hail Natas," they said.

Nemrak looked at him. "Yes, my son, demon spawn of Satan, you are here to fulfill your destiny." Charlie was no more; the demon spawn that was to be his child now possessed him. His body was just a puppet so that a destiny could be fulfilled.

Father Sandler, Father Wilson, and Father Carey were watching television when the news came on. The top story was thirteen children found dead in an abandoned house, all around a pentagram: possible cult suicide, and autopsy to come. They followed with news of a teen found hanged in a tree in Cut Deep Park.

James's eyes went blank, and he began to sweat. "No!" he shouted. "No, no he didn't!"

Father Sandler got up and tried to calm James down. "He didn't do what, James?"

James calmed down and told Father Sandler they all needed to talk. Father Sandler called William to tell him James was ready to talk. James told Father Sandler they were up against a huge nemesis, and that he would discuss it further when William arrived.

When they arrived at the seminary, they all went to Father Pelfrey's office. Daphne picked up where the conversation left off. "Rachael's brother used to be a priest. We need you to help him conduct an exorcism at Charlie's house. We need Marcy to help us figure out what exactly is going on there. After we're done, we will turn her over to the authorities."

Father Pelfrey thought it over for a moment. "I can't help you," he said finally. "I've been transferred to a different church and I leave tomorrow. But I know someone who can help you. He is the one that sent you here, Fran."

"William," replied Fran. "How is he going to help? He sent me here because they wouldn't help me before."

"When you get back to the States, you will understand," Father Pelfrey said. Then he called William and explained that Fran was planning on returning and bringing a few friends. "She is determined to set Charlie free. She is bringing a fellow student, a Pagan High Priestess, and a Satanic Princess. They plan to meet with a former priest to perform an exorcism. I believe in the cause, William, or I never would've called you."

"I know," William replied. "I'm headed out right now to talk to a few priests, in fact. Have them let me know when they make their travel plans."

Father Pelfrey hung up the phone and told the girls that William would help. "You girls have to make your travel plans. This seminary is to be closed until further notice and they want nobody here after tomorrow."

Daphne asked to use the phone to make a phone call. "It's all taken care of for Fran and Rachael," she said when she was done. "I'll meet up with you two after I acquire passports for Marcy, Demy, and myself. We will head back to England to get everything together and we will contact you."

Fran then called her aunt to see if she and a friend could stay with her for a while. Her aunt agreed, so Fran gave her the details of their flight back to the States. Fran wrote the phone number down for Daphne. Father Pelfrey wrote down William's phone number down for Fran and Daphne. Fran and Rachael then headed to their rooms to pack.

Fran was excited to be going back to the States with a chance of having her Charlie back and letting him know she was carrying his child. She and Rachael boarded their plane. Just after they sat down, Fran took Rachael's hand. "Thank you," she said.

Rachael smiled. Then she asked Rachael if she would be the godmother of her child. Rachael had tears in her eyes as she said yes. She gave Fran a big hug, but it was cut short by the announcement that it was time to buckle their seatbelts. Before they knew it, they were taking off. They decided they should try to get some sleep because of the time difference; they wanted to be well rested when they arrived so they could start planning right away.

William wasn't aware of the news he was about to receive at the rectory. He went up to the door and was greeted by Father Sandler.

"James has something we all need to talk about," Father Pelfrey said. "It has something to do with what we saw on the news today."

They went into where Father Carey and James were sitting. William sat down across from James

"I can't believe he did it," James said. "Nemrak summoned the spirit of the Satan spawn to take over a person."

"How do you know?" William asked.

"Didn't you see the news this afternoon?" James asked. "Thirteen children were found around a pentagram in an abandoned house. The thirteenth spirit is the son of Satan. Someone is then ridiculed and made to feel inferior so they invite the spirit into themselves."

"What we can do?" asked Father Sandler.

"You can't do anything about this," replied James. "It's all my fault."

"How is it your fault?" Father Sandler asked.

"William, do you remember that card you found in my wallet from the First Church of Satan? As you all know, I suffer from split personalities, and apparently my alter ego is a High Priest of a Satanic cult. I think he was responsible for what happened last night."

"But you were here last night," Father Sandler replied.

James told them about Charlie and Charlotte's wedding, Charlotte's rape, and her subsequent death, as well as her unborn child. "I looked hard and long through all the available writings of Satanism but I couldn't find a spell on how to bring the Satan spawn back. I then contacted the First Church of Satan and was given the information to carry out the ceremony. We knew we had a suitable person to perform it on: Charlie."

William broke in. "Charlie? The same Charlie whose friend Francesca came and asked about an exorcism?"

James looked down. "Unfortunately, it is."

William told them about his phone call from Father Pelfrey. He looked at James. "Are you responsible for the Satanic Princess sent to Rome to keep Fran from finishing classes?"

"No," said James, "but I wouldn't put it past Nemrak."

"Two people died from that stunt," William said.

James lowered his head farther. "That's quite unfortunate," he said. He suddenly got up, went to his room, and came back with a book. He handed it to Father Sandler. "Everything you need to know is in this book. If the ceremony was successful, only one of his own blood may save Charlie."

James then stormed out of the rectory. Father Sandler started to go after him but William stopped him. "Just call the cops," William said. "He is better off being locked up in jail. The cult will just kill him when they find out he told us."

After Father Sandler called the police, William finally asked the question. "Are you two willing to help in the quest to free Charlie?"

"You heard James," Father Carey said. "He can only be saved by someone of his own blood."

"He did say everything we needed to know was in this book," Father Sandler replied. "And that the ceremony had to be performed flawlessly. We will never know unless we try. I'm willing to help, William."

"Thank you, Father Sandler," said William. "How about you, Father Carey?"

"Let me read some of the journal and then I'll make my decision. I don't want to jump into something without knowing what's going on first."

"Fran is supposed to contact me when she gets back into the States so we can get a plan together," William said. "Both of you study that journal and learn all you can. If you hear from James, let me know. We need to find out more about Nemrak."

Sam and Natas left Nemrak's house. "How does it feel to have your father sacrifice himself so you can be on Earth to fulfill your destiny?" Sam asked.

"He wasn't my father," Natas said. "Only a puppet to do my dirty deeds. Each soul he took made me stronger. The runner. The two neighbors. He was too stupid to stop it."

This angered Sam. He knew the flock was stronger with Natas than they ever were with Charlie, but he had raised Charlie himself.

Natas sensed Sam's feelings. "So, you have sympathy for that weakling. You need not say anything; I can read your feelings. I can tell how strong your willpower is. It's pathetic, Sam. You're nothing but a follower."

Sam dropped Natas off at his house and then pulled away as fast as possible. He was on his way home when he passed a familiar face; it was James. Sam slammed on his brakes and backed up. "James, do you need a ride some-where?"

"Yes, I do," James answered before he recognized it was Sam. "Sam! What are you doing?"

"I just took Charl—oh, I mean Natas home," Sam replied.

"Did you say Natas?"

"Yes. Why?"

"Sam, we need to leave town. Nemrak isn't a Satanic High Priest. There is a good chance the ceremony wasn't performed right, and Natas may be more powerful than he is supposed to be. Or he may not be very strong at all. Either way, he is going to begin craving souls."

Sam's jaw dropped. "How can we stop him?"

"If he is stronger then he is supposed to be, he can only be stopped by someone of his own blood. If the ceremony didn't go as planned, a very determined exorcism my take care of it."

"He has no blood relatives that we know of," Sam said. "That's why he was chosen for his duties. Is there anything that we can do?"

"We may be able to slow his hunger for souls," James said, "but I need your full commitment."

"Anything," Sam replied. "I raised Charlie, and I don't like seeing him like this."

"Let's go to a church in Mercer. We'll be safe there, and I'll explain what we need to do."

Father Sandler and Father Carey blessed the room, put the journal on the table, and then sat down to read it. "Today is the day we wed the two teens whose birthday is today, 7/7/36, in hopes that she will conceive a replacement for me in my old age."

They read on, but James had already told them most of the story. Then they came to an entry about the passage. "We hired a stripper to find out what is up with Charlie and his strange behavior. We cannot afford for him to communicate with the spirits; they may let some of our intentions slip."

Father Sandler stopped reading. "This is useless," he said. "We already know what he knows about Fran."

Father Carey took the journal and leafed through the pages until something caught his eye. A page had been ripped out. He read the next page. "I have bad feelings about performing this ceremony, Nemrak has become uncontrollable. I hope I find the courage to stand up to him, but he keeps me on more medication than I need to keep me in this state of mind. If this ceremony is performed, look in the Old Testament. The answer is there."

Father Sandler put his hand on his chin and thought hard for a few minutes. He ran to James's desk, but his copy of the Old Testament was gone. "Nothing here," he told Father Carey.

They headed into the church. After about ten minutes of searching, they realized James hadn't held a mass since before that entry was written. They went back into the rectory, where Father Sandler called William to inform him of what they had found in the journal. William told him he would be back in the morning.

Father Carey had never done an exorcism, so he and Father Sandler went back to their rooms to read up on them. They both eagerly awaited a phone call from the police so they could question James about where his Old Testament was.

When they arrived at the Catholic church in Mercer,

James asked Sam, "Would you be willing to renounce your belief in Satan and be baptized in as Catholic Church if it could help save Charlie?"

Sam agreed, and they went into the church and met with Father Amberge. James told Father Amberge that Sam was here to be baptized and renounce his faith in Satan.

As Sam approached the altar, his skin began to burn a little. Father Amberge began the baptism. "Sam, do you believe in one father, the lord and giver of life?"

"I do," Sam replied.

"Sam, do you believe in Jesus Christ, the only son of the father, who will rise again in fulfillment of the scriptures and will take his place at the right hand of the father?"

"I do."

"Sam, do you believe in the holy spirit, the maker of things that are real and unreal who is seated with the father and son in heaven?"

"I do."

Father Amberge took holy water and dumped it on Sam's head. "In the name of the father, and the son, and the Holy Spirit. Amen." Sam, Father Amberge, and James all did the sign of the cross.

Sam was now officially baptized. The burning was gone and the years of hatred melted from his body. His shoulders felt as if the weight of the world was off them. He looked at James. "I feel like my old self."

James patted Sam on the back and congratulated him. James asked Father Amberge if he and Sam could stay the night at the church, as they had some soul-searching they needed to do. Father Amberge took them over to the rectory to show them their rooms.

Sam sat in James's room so they could talk about what to do next. "I've done some strange things in my lifetime," James said, "but getting mixed up with Nemrak was the worst thing I've ever done. I turned my back on my true friends tonight. I revealed to them the secret life that I have regretted horribly. I was bound to it by Nemrak, who kept me so medicated I didn't know what I was doing."

"I'm sure by now that Father Sandler and Father Carey have discovered what I wanted them to, but I also have a funny feeling that they may not. Sam, I need you to go to Nemrak's and find my Old Testament. It is the only way we will have a remote chance of helping Charlie.

The next full moon is the week of Thanksgiving. That's when Charlie will begin to feed."

Sam looked overwhelmed. "Did we turn Charlie into a werewolf?" he asked.

James didn't like Sam's humor. "Werewolves don't exist," he said. "We both know that."

Sam apologized.

"Charlie will kill his victims ceremoniously," James continued. "He will invite people to his house and lure them up to the passage. Then he will push them through, leaving their bodies to be fed upon by spirits."

"But how does he harvest their souls?" Sam asked.

"I must be very tired," James replied. "I left out the most important part. He will put something into their drinks. When they pass out in front of the passage, with inhuman strength, he will inhale over the heart of the victim and suck the soul from the body."

Sam was in shock. "How many times can he feed in a day?"

"No more than twice."

"What if he feeds more than twice in a day?"

"I don't know," James told him. "If you get me that Bible, we can find out."

CHAPTER 20

Fran and Rachael boarded their second flight. It took off at 2 a.m., and they had about two hours before they arrived in Ohio. Rachael fell asleep, but Fran couldn't. Something was bugging her, but she didn't know what it was. Fran didn't want to wake Rachael, so she closed her eyes and forced herself to fall asleep.

She had been sleeping for almost an hour when a vision came to her. The woman was familiar, but she couldn't put a name to the face. The woman told her to stay away from Charlie, that he had changed.

The vision frightened Fran, and she woke up before the person had told her everything. She dismissed it as nerves and managed to fall back asleep. She had just reached a deep sleep when she heard the announcement that they were approaching Dayton, and that all passengers must buckle their safety belts. Fran woke Rachael to tell her that they were preparing to land, but she didn't mention the vision.

As they gathered their luggage, Fran's Aunt Agnes and Uncle Gerald greeted them. The car ride to Gerald and Agnes's house was silent, because Fran and Rachael crashed in the back seat. Again Fran had a vision of the woman, who again warned her to stay away from Charlie. Then another vision flashed in front of her eyes, one that caused Fran to wake up screaming.

Rachael took Fran's hand. "What's wrong?"

"Just a bad dream," Fran said.

They arrived at Gerald and Agnes's house around 7 a.m. and they went in and fell asleep.

Nemrak was up early. He called Sam's house, but there was no answer. He thought maybe Sam was just sleeping in, but being an impatient person, he tried again and again for an hour. Nemrak then called Natas and asked if Sam was there.

"Why would he be here?" Natas asked, and hung up.

Nemrak went over to Sam's house and let himself in. He looked around and noticed that Sam's stuff had been ransacked. That son of a bitch had second thoughts and ran off, he thought. I will let everyone know that if they see Sam they are to report it to me.

Nemrak went back to his house and into his office, which also had been ransacked. What the hell? Nemrak looked at the books scattered throughout the room. He collected himself and began to inventory the books, and became really irate when he discovered that the Old Testament, which had been stolen from rectory, and the First Church of Satan book were both gone.

"James," Nemrak said to himself. "When I find him I'll kill him. Better yet I'll have Natas find him and suck his soul out as he begs for mercy."

Sam woke James to let him know he had stolen the books from Nemrak. "Thank you," James said. "Now we have some work to do."

James asked Father Amberge to call Father Sandler and have him come to the church. When Father Sandler answered, Father Amberge introduced himself and explained that Father Wilson was staying at his church and wanted to talk to him there. Father Sandler said he would be there in an hour.

Father Amberge, James, and Sam were just sitting down for coffee when there was a knock on the door. It was Father Sandler, Father Carey, and William. Father Amberge led them into the study. When they entered, they noticed James sitting there with someone unfamiliar to all except Father Sandler.

Father Sandler looked at Sam and said, "I know you from somewhere. You came to me as a concerned parent whose son was tied up in a cult. His name was Charlie, correct?"

"That's right," Sam replied.

Everyone sat down. James held up his Old Testament. "I think you guys are looking for this."

"Yes, we were," Father Sandler replied. "We looked all over the church and rectory for it last night. We looked through all the copies at the church and found nothing."

"I know," James said. "What you were looking for isn't in just any Old Testament." He held the book by the cover so the pages faced down, and out dropped a slip of paper folded long and skinny.

"That looks like a bookmark," Father Sandler said.

"Yes, it does," James said. "I purposely did that to confuse anyone who tried to find it." James unraveled the paper, and inside was another, very old piece of paper. "This is what you need." James handed it to Father Sandler. James then put the First Church of Satan book on the table. "This is a bonus. This is the book Nemrak performed the ceremony from. Sam took it from Nemrak's house this morning."

"What are you doing here?" Willam asked Sam. "Aren't you Nemrak's right hand man?"

"I was," Sam replied, "until he took my son away from me."

James told William that Sam had been baptized by

Father Amberge, and that he would make a strong ally.

Father Carey looked at James and Sam. "How can we trust you? You two are pretending to need us to set us up for our demises."

"I'll swear on the Bible that I've changed," James said. "Nemrak isn't around to force medications down my throat to keep control of me."

"We all need to work together," William said. "We have more people coming to be involved with this and we all need to be on the same page when they get here. Sam was at the ceremony,, so he can give us an idea if it was performed correctly, and James wouldn't have called us out here if he didn't want to help. He and Sam really put their heads on the line, so let's put aside our differences and work together."

James asked William who else was coming. "There's Fran," William said, "who is Charlie's girlfriend. Rachael was a student at the seminary with her, and her brother, who was a priest in California. Daphne is a Pagan high priestess." He paused. "There's one more. Marcy is her name and not a lot is known about her."

"We don't need all this help," James replied. "We don't know if the ceremony was performed right, and we don't know any blood relatives of Charlie's. That's the biggest obstacle."

"Hold on," William said. "These kids went through a lot in Rome, and Fran is pregnant with Charlie's kid. We owe them the opportunity to be involved in the exorcism."

"How far along is she?" James asked.

"Only a couple of months," William told him.

Sam stood up. "You're not thinking what I think you are," he shouted at James. "You are not going to sacrifice my only chance to have a grandchild."

"Calm down," James said. "No harm will come to the fetus. It's too young."

Fran awoke eager to call William to let him know they had arrived. She dialed the phone and waited but there was no answer. She tried again and again until her aunt told her to calm down and eat something. Fran sat down and ate, but her mind was wandering a million miles per hour trying to figure out what the woman in her dreams was trying to tell her and who she was.

Fran finished eating and tried again to call William. Still no answer. Fran was disappointed that William wasn't answering his phone but her mood soon lifted when her aunt informed her that Daphne was on the phone for her. Fran took the phone from her aunt.

Daphne informed Fran that she and Marcy would be arriving on Tuesday. She also said Marcy had some information that would be very useful. Fran wanted Daphne to tell her what it was, but Daphne said she had to go.

Fran hung up and told Rachael what Daphne had said. She was interrupted by her aunt saying there was a William on the phone that wanted to talk to her.

"Hello, William," Fran said.

"Fran," William replied. "I need to talk to you and Rachael in private."

"How about at supper tonight?"

"Sounds good. I'll pick you up around six."

Fran told Rachael they had a date that night.

Nemrak wanted to pay a visit to Father Sandler at the church to find out if he had seen James, but finally he decided that wouldn't be a good idea. He decided to have another person in the flock do the dirty work for him. He picked up his phone and called Tom. He told Tom to go to the rectory and ask for Father Wilson, and he wasn't there to ask if they know where he was. Tom said he would call back with any information.

Tom headed to the rectory as soon as he hung up with Nemrak. He was greeted by the receptionist. "May I help you, sir?"

"Is Father Wilson here?"

"Father Wilson has been gone for several months," she replied.

Just then, Father Sandler came into the office. He asked Tom if he could help him. Tom again asked to speak to Father Wilson. Father Sandler didn't recognize Tom as anybody who went to the church. "Father Wilson isn't here. He has gone for several months and no one has seen him."

Tom thanked Father Sandler and left. Father Sandler let out a sigh of relief. The receptionist asked what that was all about. Father Sandler said he didn't know, but he had a feeling it wasn't good. He called James to ask if he thought Nemrak would send people out looking for him.

"Why?" James asked.

Father Sandler told James what had happened. James said that Nemrak would do that kind of thing, and if anything else strange should happen to inform him immediately.

Tom went back and told Nemrak that no one had seen Father Wilson for several months. Nemrak slammed his fist down. Tom started backing away from him. Nemrak held up his hand and .apologized. "I owe you an explanation," he said. He told Tom that James and Father Wilson were the same person. "Since the last high priest was murdered we had no one to take his place. There was no one in training. I went to college with James and we both dabbled in Satanism so I knew he had some knowledge about it. He quit college and went to a seminary and became a priest, but he also had bipolar disease so I knew I had an edge on him. I went to his church one day and asked him to go fishing with me. I changed his medications. I was able to hypnotize him and he was under my control."

Tom was still confused. "How was he able to perform the ceremonies?" he asked.

"He didn't, you fool," Nemrak replied. "He was just my puppet. Didn't you notice me mouthing the words as he said them? I think James is nearby and that traitor Sam is with him. I knew he couldn't be trusted. How was he ever chosen to raise the next high priest?"

"I thought Charlie was the next high priest," Tom said. "Is he?"

Nemrak pointed his finger at Tom. "No more. I've told you too much already."

Nemrak was frustrated as Tom left. He almost let the secret slip. "I've told him too much," he said to himself. Could Tom be trusted? Then he remembered: with Natas around, all his worries could be taken care of.

Agnes greeted William when he arrived, then went to the steps and called for Fran and Rachael. Fran was delighted to see William; she had so many questions to ask him. He escorted the two young ladies to his car.

As they drove to the restaurant, Fran asked William about Charlie. William began to explain to Fran that Charlie had changed; he wasn't the same person anymore. That's what the voice was telling me, she thought. William went on to tell the girls that he had talked to some priests this morning and he wanted the girls to meet them.

Father Carey was still very skittish on committing to the whole idea. Father Sandler sensed Father Carey's hesitation. "If it is out of the boundaries of your beliefs, you don't have to participate," he told him.

"The participation isn't bothering me," Father Carey replied. "I just have trouble trusting James."

"I don't trust him either," said Father Sandler. "We are

doing this to help this woman and her boyfriend. As God's servants we must help his children by any means possible. We must not let our own feelings affect the way we go about our business."

William, Fran, and Rachael had just finished their meal when William spoke. He wanted the girls to go with him to be informed of what was going on by someone who knew more about it than he did. They agreed to go with him.

Fran was very curious about what was going on with Charlie, so she asked William if she could see him. "Charlie as you know him no longer exists," William told her. "He is a spawn of Satan."

Fran began to hyperventilate. Rachael calmed her down by holding her hand and telling her to take slow, deep breaths. Finally, Fran was able to ask William, "Will we be able to save him?"

"That's why you need to go with me."

Sam asked James what he thought the chances of saving Charlie were. "There is strength in numbers," James replied, "but only one holds the key to Charlie's future." Seeing that Sam was confused, he continued. "We can only hope that the keyholder is among the people we have accumulated. If not, our chances are slim."

William and the girls had arrived at William's house. He showed them the guestroom. "It will be a long and mentally draining day tomorrow," he said. "So get plenty of rest." Then he went to call Father Sandler and Father Amberge to make arrangements for the next day.

Fran was already dreaming. She saw Charlie in front of the passage with his back toward her. She grabbed him and he turned around; he looked so evil. She fell to the ground screaming. Charlie picked her up and carried her toward the passage. He almost had her to the passage when she was awoken by Rachael.

"Ouch!" she said. "Fran, are you okay?"

Fran told Rachael about the nightmare. Rachael could see she was very upset.

"Are you sure you want to go through with this?" she asked. "The stress isn't good for the baby. At least when you have the baby you'll always have a part of Charlie with you."

"I need to see for myself," Fran replied. "If I can't handle what I see, I'll make my decision then."

William was making breakfast when the phone rang; it was Fran's Aunt Agnes. She wanted to let Fran know that Daphne had called and planned on being in town on Friday. William told Agnes he would relay the message.

Chapter 21

Father Sandler was finishing the first mass of the morning when something came to him. Back when he was in the seminary he overheard a person talking to a man named Nemrak, but he couldn't put a name to the face.

Father Sandler went into the rectory and looked at his class photo. To his disbelief the face that appeared to him was William's. He then remembered William was the one who sent Fran to Rome. He was the only one who knew how everything happened there. He then remembered his phone call from William the night before, saying he had Fran and Rachael with him.

Father Sandler hurried to get Father Carey so they could leave. "What's the rush?" Father Carey asked.

"At the end of mass this morning I had a vision. I remember a guy in my class talking to a person named Nemrak. When I looked at the class picture the face I saw was William's, but I don't recall him being in my class."

They were greeted by Father Amberge when they arrived in Mercer. They went into the rectory and sat down with James and Sam. James looked at Father Sandler. "You look like something is bothering you."

Father Sandler was about to speak when he was interrupted by the arrival of William, Fran, and Rachael. William received a penetrating stare from Father Sandler. The three of them joined Sam, James, Father Sandler, and

Father Carey at the table. Fran whispered into William's ear that she was uncomfortable with Sam being around. William assured her that Sam was on their side, and he wanted to help Charlie as much as she did.

James stood up and told everyone how he had been involved along with Sam in what had happened to Charlie. He went on to explain that his right-hand man in the cult had taken over and performed the ceremony on All Hallows Eve, and that something had gone terribly wrong according to Sam.

Sam said that thirteen children's souls were to be sacrificed, along with the soul of a newborn baby boy, but a fourteenth child's soul was sacrificed as well.

"What does this have to do with Charlie?" Fran asked.

"Charlie is now being controlled by his son's spirit," James replied, "and on full moon nights he regains strength by sucking the souls out of people."

Fran's face became white. She turned to Rachael. "Remember last night when I had a terrible dream? In my dream Charlie was holding me by the throat and I felt like he was draining my life."

James asked Fran if she had any other strange dreams. Not fully trusting him yet, she told him no.

Sam then told them about Monica's suicide, the fourteenth soul to be sacrificed. "This broke Charlie's heart. He assumed you were dead, and then Monica. He was an easy target for his son to take."

"Poor Charlie," Fran sobbed. "I wish I could've been there for him."

"You would have been killed," Sam said. "You know too much. You aren't safe as Nemrak is around. You are carrying the brother of Natas, the son of Satan, in your womb."

"What does that mean?" Fran asked.

Sam stood. "You're carrying the heir to the throne that

Natas will be ruling."

James told Sam he needed to sit down.

"You two-faced son of a bitch," Sam said to James. "Do you think I would actually change to help Charlie? He got what was coming to him. I took him under my wing because his father was in charge of the cult at the time. His mother took him and his sister away and put them under the protection of the Catholic Church. We got her and her daughter, but Charlie wasn't there. He was put into an orphanage and we eventually got him back."

Father Sandler stood and said, "While we're at it, William, I believe you are in this whole conspiracy on the wrong side."

"I have no idea what you mean," William replied.

"Come on, William, tell them," Sam said.

Father Carey had enough. He took Fran and Rachael and left. This left Father Sandler with James, Sam, and William. William told Father Sandler that he should get the girls and himself out of town. "They are not safe. Someone here can't be trusted."

"You're the only hope for salvation," James told Father Sandler. "Pray hard, and hope that what I wrote in my Old Testament is accurate. This is by the body of Christ."

Father Sandler sprinted out of the church just in time to catch up with Father Carey.

Nemrak arrived at the church about 25 minutes later. "So, William, where is everyone?"

William apologized to Nemrak. "But we still have James," he said. "He and Father Amberge are gagged and bound in the trunk of my car."

"Does James know the plan?"

"Yes, Father. If we can get the other James back, we can ruin their plans."

Nemrak and Sam took Father Amberge and James out of William's trunk and put them into Nemrak's trunk, and the two of them headed to Nemrak's house.

Father Sandler, Father Carey, and the girls arrived at their own church. "We have to leave town," Father Sandler said. "We were set up."

"I told you I didn't trust them," Father Carey replied.

Father Sandler ran into the church and retrieved James's Old Testament. He noticed some papers folded up in it. He went back to the car and they left the church.

Father Carey asked what they were going to do with the girls. "We can't take them back to Fran's aunt and uncle," Father Sandler replied. "William knows where that is."

"No," Fran said. "It would be okay to take us there. They have to get someone from the airport, so we can stay there."

She gave Father Carey directions as Father Sandler began to read the writing from James. Apparently James was fascinated with Satanism long after he became a priest. He wasn't mentally stable, and the diocese covered for him quite a bit. The James at the church in Mercer was more genuine then Father Sandler had ever known him; it was like he was a totally different person. James normally kept to himself but recently had been very open. He said he was bipolar, Father Sandler thought. He said he was in charge, but Sam referred to him as a puppet. Father Sandler shook his head and kept reading. He found stories on Charlie's parents.

"Paul Tansa, age 30, was found dead in the St. Mary's river off Cut Deep Rd. in Hickstown. His body was grossly mutilated."

"The body of Shelley Tansa was found in an alley. She was raped and bludgeoned to death with a tire iron. Witnesses say she was seen with her two children at the five and dime store. Her children were not found."

Father Sandler then opened a newer piece of paper it

read. "I met Charlie Tansa today for the first time. I married him to Charlotte at tonight's ceremony. The boy is nothing like his father. This boy is genuine and innocent. I believe Nemrak is wrong about him."

Father Sandler looked at Fran and told her to read the rest of the paper. She did so, and her jaw dropped as she read. "Marcy!" she exclaimed. "We have a Marcy coming with our friend Daphne." She explained who Marcy was and what had happened in Rome. "William knows when and where they're arriving. They need to change their flight, and we'll set up a new meeting place."

Nemrak and Sam took James and Father Amberge back to Nemrak's house. They threw Father Amberge into the basement and locked the door. They took James into the guest bedroom.

Sam tied James's hands and feet to the bed while Nemrak called his witch Alice, asking her to come and put a spell on James until his medication wore off. Then they headed down to the basement.

Nemrak tied Father Amberge to a chair, then taunted and spat on him as Sam watched. "Satan's time to rule has come," he said. "Anyone who won't bow down to Satan will be destroyed."

The doorbell rang about 45 minutes later. They let Alice in and led her to the bedroom where James was. She pulled some herbs and several candles out of a bag. She placed the herbs in a small dish containing water and placed the dish over the candles. When the water and herbs began to boil, she began to chant. "I confront you with my master Satan. Your mind is weakening. Satan controls you."

Alice led Nemrak and Sam from the room, and told them they needed to stay out for at least five hours. She explained that one of the herbs put him to sleep and the others would clear his mind, and then she would take care of the rest. She went to meditate and prepare, while Sam and Nemrak headed to William's house.

Fran, Rachael, Father Sandler, and Father Carey arrived at Agnes's house. Fran informed her aunt and uncle that maybe they should leave town for a while. Something in Aunt Agnes's eyes told Fran something was wrong. Suddenly, William came out of the kitchen. "Welcome," he said.

"You son of a bitch," Fran said. "You lied to us."

"Did I?"

"You betrayed us back at the church," Father Sandler said.

"No," William replied. "I gave them James because he is more of a liability than an asset. With Sam around I wasn't comfortable. I made other arrangements."

They sat down around the kitchen table.

"You look familiar to me," Father Sandler told William. "It's like I saw you a long time ago, but I don't remember you."

"You know me from the seminary. I was a first-year the year you were finishing."

"Where did I get the name Nemrak?"

William realized it was time to come clean. He took a deep breath and let out a sigh. "Nemrak is my stepfather," he said.

Father Carey stood up. "You want us to trust you and then you tell us this?" he yelled. "This is getting too deep. I don't know if I want to trust you or even help in this whole situation."

William asked Father Carey to sit down. "I said stepfather," he said. "Actually he is my ex-stepfather, and I was very young when he came into my life. I looked up to him and actually went by his name after he and my mother divorced. I was very hurt when the divorce happened. He was a good man until he met James. James drew him into Satanism, and Nemrak became fully consumed with the cult. My mother wouldn't convert so we left in the middle of the night."

"I don't trust you," Father Sandler told William, "but we have no one else to turn to."

William asked Rachael when her brother was supposed to be in from California. "Not for another two weeks," she said. "Closer to the full moon."

William told her to call him and get him to come as soon as possible. Then he asked Fran when Daphne and Marcy were scheduled to arrive. "Friday," she replied.

"Great," he said. "Then I'll have Father Pelfrey show up on Friday also."

"Really?" Fran said. "How did you manage that?"

"When Chief Ward put Father Pelfrey in jail, that kept his transfer from going through. Since the seminary is closed he has nowhere else to go, so he is coming here. We'll pick him up on Friday along with Daphne and Marcy."

Sam and Nemrak pulled up to William's house. Nemrak pounded on the door, shouting William's name. There was no answer; Nemrak insisted that Sam kick in the door. They went into the house, but William wasn't there.

"Traitor!" Nemrak shouted.

They returned to Nemrak's house just as Alice was finishing up. "The rest is up to you," she told Nemrak as she left. Nemrak told Sam to go down in the basement to cut Father Amberge's wrist and catch the blood in a glass.

Sam reluctantly agreed, but when he got downstairs he suddenly changed his mind. Instead, he cut the ropes that were holding the priest to the chair. He told Father Amberge to meet him at his car. Father Amberge asked no questions, just squeezed out through the basement window.

Sam then took the knife and cut himself and let his blood flow into the cup. He put anti-coagulator into the cup of blood and took it to Nemrak. Then he left the house and met Father Amberge at his car.

When they were some distance from Nemrak's house Father Amberge asked Sam why he did what he did.

"I don't know," Sam replied. "I think it has to do with the way you opened your doors to me and made me feel like I belonged. I haven't felt that way in a long time. To Nemrak I'm just a servant, but you made me feel like a person." Sam then told Father Amberge that he had cut himself and given the blood to Nemrak. Then he laughed. "I am no virgin. That blood won't work."

Father Amberge smiled. "I am no virgin either. People tend to think we were priests our whole lives. They forget we were teenagers once."

Sam chuckled a little. "Come on, Father. You're pulling my leg."

Father Amberge shook his head. "I lost my virginity to the neighbor's wife when I was sixteen."

"The neighbor's wife?" Sam said, incredulous.

"I wasn't always a priest," Father Amberge replied, and they both laughed.

Sam dropped Father Amberge off at the church, then tried to think of where he could hide. Finally, he had an idea.

Nemrak commanded James to awake. "Master, take this blood, the blood of an unwilling virgin, and drink. This blood will give you the power to stay yourself."

James took the blood and drank it. He immediately spat it out. "This is not virgin blood." He began to choke.

Nemrak didn't know what to do so he hit James over the head with a chair and fled the house. He waited an hour before going back inside. He first went to the basement and saw that Father Amberge was missing. He grew angry with Sam. Then he went upstairs to check on James. He was dead.

After dark, Nemrak's temper had cooled, so he decided to find a place to dump James's body. "Ah, Tom," he said to himself. "I need to catch up with him anyway, plus he has a key to the meat market. Maybe I'll be able to take care of my dilemmas after all."

When Tom arrived, Nemrak showed him James lying dead on the bed. Tom asked if Nemrak needed him to help set up arrangements, or call people.

"No, we need to get rid of the body!" Nemrak shouted. He told Tom that they would take the body to the meat market and grind it up. Tom reluctantly agreed and the two of them loaded the body into Tom's trunk.

William was thumbing through James's Old Testament when he stumbled upon a stack of papers. He opened the folded papers and realized they were more articles about Charlie's family.

"Body of Female Tansa Child Found in Hickstown," the headline read. The article said the body was found badly decomposed. If this is true, William thought, then the Marcy that is coming isn't Charlie's sister, and we'll be in over our heads. William pondered that for a moment, and decided to go to James's house to see if he had a diary or any other information that may be useful.

William went to James' house and found nothing. Even though he hadn't slept all night he wanted to find the death certificate of this person in the article and then go to the Sheriff's Department and see if he could go over the police report.

CHAPTER 22

Tom unlocked the back door of the meat market, then got a rolling tub to make it easier to move the body. Tom and Nemrak wheeled James body to the shredder. It took all the two of them could muster to get the body close, but they couldn't get it in. Nemrak ordered Tom to get a ladder.

Tom brought the ladder and Nemrak ordered him to climb it. He pushed James's body up until Tom could grab it under the armpits. Tom pulled the body until he was able to rest the shoulders on the intake of the machine. He was then able to grab the midsection as Nemrak lifted the feet. Finally they were able to get the body situated.

Nemrak turned on the machine as Tom, who was still on the ladder, pushed the body into the machine. The bones made Tom have to push harder to get them through the blades of the machine. This gave Nemrak his opportunity. He pulled the ladder out from under Tom's feet. Tom struck his head on the machine as he fell, knocking him unconscious. Nemrak then used the ladder to push Tom's head into the slicer. After Tom's head was gone Nemrak placed the ladder to make it look like an accident.

Brent, the manager of the meat market, went in to open the store. As he entered the building he heard a strange noise. He followed the noise and it led him back to the shredder, which was running. He turned it off and got onto a ladder so he could peer into it. He noticed something funny in the mass of flesh that was stuck in the machine.

He used a broomstick to fish it out. As he removed the flesh from the object he saw it was a shoe, with a foot still in it. Brent dropped the shoe and became very nauseated as he ran to the phone to call the police.

Twenty minutes later Officer Phillips arrived to take a statement. Two more officers arrived and went to the machine. They had the painstaking task of sorting through the flesh for clues. Soon they found a wallet caught up in the blades. Luckily, it hadn't been harmed. Officer Phillips opened the wallet and noticed that the ID was still it in. It belonged to Tom Jansen.

William went into the coroner's office and talked with the receptionist. He was filling out some paperwork when Dr. Jarvis came in and told his receptionist to take messages on all phone calls today, that he had a big case to work on and didn't want to be interrupted.

William had known Dr. Jarvis for a long time. He asked how things were going; Dr. Jarvis told William about what happened at the meat market.

When Dr. Jarvis told him it was Tom Jansen, the name was familiar to William from his childhood. Dr. Jarvis went on to say that Tom must have been a very big man because there was more flesh than would have been expected from a normal man.

William told him that Tom wasn't very big, that he had the same build as the doctor.

"Well, I may have my work cut out for me," the doctor said with a puzzled look.

William motioned Dr. Jarvis closer and whispered in his ear. "Let me know if you discover more than you're anticipating."

Dr. Jarvis told him he would. William got the information he needed and headed to the Sheriff's Department.

William asked a Sheriff's Department secretary for information on the Tansa case. He explained that he had found some old clippings about the case that didn't add up. The secretary went back into the file room and pulled what information she was allowed to. William signed all the paperwork he needed to sign, thanked the secretary, and headed home.

Dr. Jarvis went back to his autopsy room and began by grabbing the teeth out of the mess. One by one he put the teeth into a container. Then he decided to weigh the flesh. It came to 430 pounds.

Dr. Jarvis thought for a moment. William told me Tom was the same size as me. There is over 400 pounds of flesh and bone here. Something is not adding up.

He counted the teeth: 35. There had to be more than one person in the machine. Dr. Jarvis called the police department and told Officer Phillips they were looking at a homicide, not a suicide as earlier thought. Officer Phillips wanted to know what evidence that he had to support his claim. Dr. Jarvis told him about the weight and the teeth.

Officer Phillips returned to the meat market. He went into Brent's office and asked if he noticed anything else fishy. He told Brent about Dr. Jarvis's belief that at least two victims were involved.

Brent was in disbelief, but then he remembered that Tom's car wasn't parked anywhere on the property. This raised the eyebrows of Officer Phillips. He called the station to have another officer begin a search for Tom's car. Then he started looking around the market for more clues.

The only clue he found was a cross necklace. He took it to Brent and asked if it belonged to anyone there. Brent said he didn't know of anyone that had a necklace like that. Officer Phillips told Brent he would stay in touch.

Officer Davis got the task of looking for Tom's car.

He called the Sheriff's Department for help outside of the town's jurisdiction. He talked the Deputy Hangman; the two of them would work together to find the missing vehicle. Both officers headed out. Officer Davis decided to look in the wooded area around the meat market; Deputy Hangman decided to look around the country in river or pond areas to see if there were any fresh tire marks leading into them.

Nemrak awoke in a panic. He needed a way to get rid of Tom's car, but he didn't want to contact anyone else in the cult to help him. He decided he would just have to burn the car, but where would he do that? He would have to do it within walking distance of his house, but that would draw unwanted attention.

The more he thought about burning the car, the more he decided it wouldn't be such a good idea. He got into Tom's car and parked it in the barn. He could hide it there long enough to find Sam.

He hopped into his own car and toward Sam's house. He almost had a stroke when he saw a deputy sheriff's cruiser pass him, heading toward his house, but he drove on.

Nemrak saw that Sam's car wasn't at the house when he arrived. He got out of his car and looked around. There was no sign of Sam being home at all. Nemrak then decided to try Natas's house to see if Sam hiding out there since Natas would be resting. He almost had another stroke when he saw a city police cruiser passing Natas's house.

Nemrak saw no sign of Sam's car, though. He kept looking for several blocks, thinking Sam may have parked away from the house and walked, but he had no luck there either.

He thought for a moment. Where would Sam go if he needed to get away from everything? Finally it dawned on him.

Sam's car was not at his ex-wife's house. Nemrak drove down the road and stopped so he could keep an eye on the place. It wasn't twenty minutes before he saw Sam drive by. Nemrak decided to wait until it was dark before he made his move.

Officer Davis returned to the station without finding the car. Officer Phillips called him into his office and showed him the cross necklace.

"What does that mean?" Officer Davis asked.

Officer Phillips told him that Red's Meat Market used to be run by a cult, and apparently still was.

"What makes you think that?"

"Do you know what kind of jewelry your co-workers wear?"

Officer Davis thought for a moment. "No, I don't," he said.

"Exactly," replied Officer Phillips. "Brent told me right away that this didn't belong to anyone at the market." Just then his phone rang; Dr. Jarvis asked him to come to his office.

When he arrived, Dr. Jarvis took him into his office and showed him a ring he had found in the mess of flesh. "This could belong to anybody," Officer Phillips said.

"Not just anybody," Dr. Jarvis told him. "It can only belong to a priest. This is the ring they get upon completion of classes at the seminary."

Officer Phillips told him about the cross necklace and Brent's reaction. "It makes you wonder if anything ever changed at that market." He took the ring from Dr. Jarvis and headed to the rectory to see if he could find out who owned it.

Father Sandler came down the stairs as Officer Phillips arrived at the rectory. "How may I help you, officer?"

They went into Father Sandler's office and sat at the

desk. Officer Phillips took the ring out and showed it to Father Sandler. "What can you tell me about this ring?"

Father Sandler took the ring. "I have one just like it," he said. "This is the ring we receive after we graduate from the seminary. Where did you get this?"

"Did you hear about what happened at Red's Meat Market this morning?"

"You mean the suicide?"

"Well, that's what we thought, until the autopsy showed that there was more than one victim. This ring was found in the flesh at the market."

Father Sandler felt a crushing pain in his chest as he wiped away the blood on the bottom of the ring and saw the initials JDW. He gave a look like a little boy who just lost his dog. "It belonged to Father James Wilson," he told Officer Phillips. "He was a priest here but has been gone for a while. He had some kind of involvement in a cult around here. I can give you a person to contact that may be able to give you more information. His name is William Hurst."

William was at home going over the information he had received from the Sheriff's Department when the doorbell rang. He invited Officer Phillips in and they sat down at the kitchen table. Officer Phillips pulled out the ring. "This belonged to Father James Wilson."

"Belonged?"

"Yes," Officer Phillips replied. "It was found at Red's Meat Market this morning in a machine with almost 400 pounds of human flesh. Father Sandler said you might be able to tell me what happened to him."

"I hope you have a lot of paper," William replied. He explained how Nemrak had used James as a puppet to run the cult. He went on to say that the last people he had seen with James were Nemrak and Sam Decker.

After Officer Phillips left, William headed to the rectory. He got there just as Father Sandler finished telling Father Carey what happened to James. The three of them sat down to decide how they could all keep safe until it was time for their plan. They decided to stay together at the rectory; they all felt safer in numbers.

William then told them what he had found about the Tansa case. The body they had found wasn't the Tansa girl at all; it was a cover-up by the old corrupt sheriff. "I feel very confident that the Marcy the girls found is actually Marcy Tansa, Charlie's sister."

"That's the only good news I've received today," Father Sandler said.

Sam knocked on his ex-wife's door. It opened. "What the hell do you want?"

"Julia, I'm in trouble. I need a place to hide out for a while. Also, I haven't seen the kids in years. I know it's my own fault, but I fear for my life and would like to see them if I could. Please."

The woman told him he could stay the weekend but that was it. Sam entered the house.

In the living room he saw his daughter Samantha and his son Jacob. It had been at least four years since he last saw them. Sam asked Jacob if he knew who he was. "I'm your daddy."

"No you're not," Jacob replied.

This hurt Sam, but he knew he deserved it. He went over to Samantha and asked her if she knew who he was. Being older, she did. She asked Sam where he had been.

"Sweetie, daddy has been very busy."

Samantha gave her dad a hug said she missed him. After Julia explained to Jacob who Sam was, he warmed up a little. Sam sat down and played marbles and jacks with his kids. He loved it.

Soon, Julia asked Sam if she could talk to him in the

kitchen. "So what's with the change in you?" she asked. "Why all of a sudden do you want to spend time with the kids?"

"I had a life-changing experience," Sam replied, "and I wanted to fulfill what I've been missing for all these years. There has been a big void in my heart ever since you and I split. I've missed the kids dearly but I fully understood why you didn't want me around."

"I hope you are sincere, because they'll need their dad in their lives." Julia began crying.

"What do you mean?"

Julia looked at Sam. "I have cancer. They're only giving me a month to live. I've tried to contact you but I've had no luck." Sam began to cry also.

Suddenly there was a knock at the door. "Who could that be?" Julia said. She went and opened it. "Sam!" she yelled. "There is a man at the door for you."

Sam's face turned as white as a ghost when he saw it was Nemrak. He stepped outside with him. "What are you doing here?"

"You know why I'm here, Sam," Nemrak replied. "You screwed with the wrong person, and now James is dead."

"I'm trying to turn my life to the better," Sam said. "Just leave me alone and I will keep my mouth shut."

"You know I can't do that."

"Nemrak, I just found out that Julia has cancer and they only gave her a month to live. My kids need me. Have a heart, man."

"She has more time with the kids than you do," Nemrak snarled.

Sam attacked Nemrak. The two of them fell off the porch fighting and rolling around. Sam saw the kids and Julia watching through the window. This was his last chance to prove that he had changed, and now he knew Julia wouldn't trust him. He felt a sharp pain in his chest.

Nemrak stood; Sam just lay there like a beaten mule. The last thing Sam saw was Julia leading the kids away from the window. Nemrak loaded his dying body into the trunk of his car and headed home.

Chapter 23

Officer Phillips was on his way to Nemrak's house when he noticed smoke coming from about three roads over. When he got there, he saw a vehicle matching Tom's engulfed in flames. He called it in so he could get backup and the fire department. He noticed a person at the steering wheel, but the flames were too hot for him to do anything but wait for the fire department.

By the time the fire department arrived and extinguished the fire, the body was destroyed beyond recognition. There was no way any ID would have survived. They would have to wait and see if Dr. Jarvis could perform another miracle.

Officer Phillips left the scene and went to Nemrak's house. "How may I help you tonight, officer?" Nemrak asked when he opened the door.

"Sir, I would like to talk to you down at the station in regards to the murders that took place this morning at Red's Meat Market."

"I don't know anything about any murders," Nemrak said.

"Sir, either cooperate and come downtown or I will place you under arrest and take you there myself."

Nemrak replied that he would meet the officer downtown but would have to stop by his son's house first to take care of his dog, because his son was out of town. Officer Phillips told Nemrak to be at the station in 25 minutes. Nemrak said he would be there.

An hour passed and still no Nemrak. Officer Phillips slammed the door of the police station on his way out to his cruiser. He searched for nearly two hours before calling it a night.

At the police impound yard they inspected the burned vehicle, trying to see if the serial number survived the fire. They brushed debris away from the site where the serial number would be. Digit by digit the serial number appeared. They double counted the numbers and letters to make sure they had them all.

As they inspected the rest of the vehicle they noticed some fibers that in the trunk and saved them as evidence. They learned the back seat area burned hotter then the rest of the car, which told them the fire was set purposely, likely to cover something up. They called the police station and left a message for Officer Phillips to call them first thing in the morning.

Dr. Jarvis inspected the body taken from the burning car. He decided from the bone structure that it was a male's body, but it was burnt so badly that there was no way of identifying the victim without dental records. Dr. Jarvis made molds and drawings of the teeth with each filling or crown noted. He then called Dr. Mackey, a local dentist.

When Dr. Mackey arrived, Dr. Jarvis brought him back to the autopsy room to show him what he was dealing with. Dr. Mackey noticed something on the left shoulder of the body. It was faint from the burns, but he recognized it. "Look here," he said to Dr. Jarvis.

"It's a tattoo," Dr. Jarvis said. "A lot of people have them."

"Not this kind. I think I've seen this one before. I just wish it wasn't so damaged so I could be positive."

Officer Phillips got his message and called the impound

yard first thing in the morning. Officer Frank answered the phone told Officer Phillips what their investigation had turned up. Officer Phillips hung up and headed to the coroner's office to see what he had found.

Dr. Jarvis entered his office to find Dr. Mackey waiting for him. The dentist said he had figured out where he had seen the tattoo before: on a patient named Sam Decker. "Here are the X-rays to prove it." He handed Dr. Jarvis a set of teeth X-rays that matched the molds and drawings. The name on them was Sam Decker.

Just as Dr. Mackey was preparing to leave, Officer Phillips walked through the door. Dr. Jarvis told him they had identified the body.

"Sam Decker?" Officer Phillips. "I've heard that name recently, but I can't place it right now." He scratched his head. "Have you discovered the cause of death?"

"It's pretty obvious the guy burnt up in a fire," Dr. Jarvis said.

"Don't be too sure," Officer Phillips said. "We have evidence to suggest otherwise. We believe the fire was a cover for a murder." He told Dr. Jarvis what the impound yard had said.

Dr. Jarvis told Officer Phillips he would look into the situation more and keep him updated. Officer Phillips told Dr. Jarvis he'd try to remember why the name Sam Decker was familiar.

Back at the station, Officer Phillips went through his recent reports, trying to find the name Sam Decker. Finally he stumbled across William's explanation that Father Wilson was last seen with Nemrak and Sam. "Bingo!" he shouted. He grabbed his phone and left a message for Dr. Jarvis.

Dr. Jarvis began the autopsy by sawing through the chest cavity and making an incision all the way down the abdomen. He cut through the fat and muscle layers until he reached the internal organs. He took each one out, looking for any cause of trauma, but there weren't any obvious signs until he reached the heart. There he found a puncture wound, which resembled one from a small pick.

He pursued the autopsy up the neck. As he pulled layers of burnt skin, he noticed bruising in the soft tissue, consistent with being choked. This evidence backed up the theory that the fire was a cover-up for something more sinister.

Dr. Jarvis cleaned up and went to his office. His secretary told him Officer Philips had called about two hours ago. He must have found what he was looking for, Dr. Jarvis thought.

Officer Phillips answered the phone when Dr. Jarvis called. He told Dr. Jarvis that Father Wilson was last seen with Nemrak Sigmund and Sam Decker.

"That's interesting," Dr. Jarvis said, "because your theory has proved to be true. I found a hole in Mr. Decker's heart that's consistent with a small pick of some kind. Then in the neck area I found bruising that suggests strangulation."

Officer Phillips thanked Dr. Jarvis for the information and hung up. He put out an all points bulletin to find Nemrak for questioning. Now all the local departments would be on the lookout for him.

That done, Officer Phillips decided to go to Nemrak's house for a little investigation. Upon arrival, he noticed that Nemrak's car wasn't there, so he tried to gain entry to his outbuildings to see if it was hidden. He didn't find the car, but he did notice some tire tracks in the barn. Officer Phillips took pictures of the tracks and called into the office to let them know he needed an evidence team out there immediately.

He didn't want to disturb the tracks in the barn so he continued his investigation elsewhere. He found nothing in the shed, so he continued to the house. He checked the door and noticed that it was unlocked.

As he was about to enter, the evidence team arrived. Officer Phillips took Sgt. Fox and his team to the barn and showed them the tracks. Then he headed into the house.

In one of the bedrooms he noticed the flat sheet was missing from the top of the bed, and there was a stain on the fitted sheet. He determined it had the consistency of a bloodstain. He also noticed all the candles in the room, and the strange odor. He then went down to the basement, where he saw a chair with tied and untied rope lying around it. He took photographs of that, as well as the bedroom upstairs, before calling the evidence team inside.

Officer Phillips continued his search, but found nothing more of interest. As he was driving home that evening, he realized that William might know more places he should look for Nemrak. He drove by William's house, but all the lights were off and there was no car in the driveway. Officer Philips drove home.

William could sense Fran's excitement when he arrived to pick her and Rachael up in the morning. "You better calm down," he told her. "That baby is going to come early."

"I know," she said. "I just can't wait to see Daphne and Father Pelfrey."

William told them that James was dead, likely by Nemrak's hand. This dampened Fran's mood a little. She asked if it had any effect on their plans. William said no. "James was too much of a liability to do any good," he said. "Besides, he already gave us all the information we need."

William and the girls arrived to learn that Rachael's brother's flight delayed an hour, but the other flights would be on time. They headed to the terminal to meet Daphne and Marcy, who would arrive first. Fifteen minutes later

Daphne and Marcy appeared. Fran gave Daphne a huge hug. The five of them sat down to catch up while they waited on Father Pelfrey's plane.

Daphne told them how well Marcy was adapting to the pagan life. Marcy apologized to Fran for everything she put her through; she also let Fran know she would do anything to help.

Fran accepted Marcy's apology from Marcy. "Just promise me you will do everything in your power to help save Charlie."

Daphne had talked to many elders in her village for ideas on how to take care of the situation. Before she could outline all of them, Father Pelfrey's plane arrived.

Father Pelfrey was amazed at the change in Marcy. She apologized to him, saying she knew she could never bring his friends back but was willing to do whatever it took to make it up to him.

An announcement over the P.A. alerted them that Rachael's brother was about to land. Rachael was the first to greet him and then she introduced him to everyone else. "This is my brother Darren."

They all crowded into William's car for the ride back to Agnes's house. Seven people made for a tight fit. "It's a good thing you all packed light," William joked.

They were almost there when a bulletin came over the radio. "We have a statewide search going on for a white male, age 65, about 6 foot 1 and about 200 pounds. His name is Nemrak Sigmund and he is wanted for questioning about his involvement in three murders in Mercer County."

"It's about time," William said.

"What's that all about?" Daphne asked.

William explained Nemrak's role in the cult. "Now he will be on the run, so we can move much faster and easier with our plan."

He dropped everyone off at Agnes's house. They invited him in, but he declined. "You're probably all tired from your travels. Get some rest. I'll see you tomorrow."

The next morning Officer Phillips was planning to drive by William's house again when he saw William enter the station. "William!" he called.

William looked and saw it was Officer Phillips. "Hi Greg," he said. "I wanted to ask you some questions about Nemrak."

"That's funny," Officer Phillips said. "I need to ask you about Nemrak too."

They went back to Officer Phillips's office. William asked about the bulletin they had heard on the radio the night before. Officer Phillips explained what he and Dr. Jarvis had found to make Nemrak the prime suspect. "I've looked all over town for him. That's what I wanted to talk to you about. Do you know anywhere we should look for him?"

William thought for a moment. "Did you try the old cemetery on Cut Deep Road? Or the one on Carson Road? Maybe one of the cult members is hiding him. It's hard to say. That's all I can think of off the top of my head."

From there William went to the rectory. Father Carey asked William what was he doing there so early and where everyone else was. William said they were all still at the safe house and that he wanted to talk to them by himself first to discuss the recent happenings.

The three of them sat down at the table. "Now is our time. We need to strike while Nemrak is on the run."

"Will we be able to do it with so little preparation?" Father Carey asked.

"Yes," William replied. "We'll have something on our side that we weren't counting on: time."

Father Sandler got it right away. "With Nemrak on the run, there will be no way for him to find out our plan or interfere. So tomorrow it's a go."

"I'll get everybody here tonight. They will all stay at the rectory, and tomorrow afternoon it's a go."

When William arrived at Agnes's house, he got everyone together. "We need to move tomorrow," he told them all. "Can you be ready?"

Daphne said that would be pushing it, but she could do it.

"Great," William replied. "Let's get to it."

Fran and Rachael had to deal with Marcy. Fran remembered the torture Marcy put her through in Rome. She asked Marcy why she did it.

"I wasn't well," Marcy explained. "With everything Daphne was trying to do, I lost control of my emotions. I had no remorse about what I did to you, Sister Stephanie, or Dr. Collins. That has all changed. Since I was with Daphne's tribe I found the real me, the me I remember as a child, before all the ugliness. I haven't felt this good in a long time."

Fran didn't know how to feel about trusting Marcy. "Well, I hope you do the right thing tomorrow," was all she said.

Finally everyone was ready. They piled their stuff into William's car. Fran hugged her aunt and uncle and thanked them for their hospitality, and then they headed to the rectory.

Father Carey was skeptical about going ahead the next day, but he went along. Father Sandler told him they needed to fast for the exorcism. The two priests went to cleanse their souls. They read passage after passage from the Bible, said prayer after prayer, confessed their sins, and prepared all the holy sacraments they would need the next day.

The phone rang. Father Sandler picked up; it was Father Amberge from the church in Mercer. He wanted to know if they had heard from Sam. "He spared my life," he said. "I just want to know he made it safely to his destination.

"Spared your life?" Father Sandler repeated. "When did this happen?"

Father Amberge explained the situation.

"I'm sorry, Father," Father Sandler said. "Sam is dead." He told the other priest what had happened.

Father Amberge was silent for a moment. "I know how I can repay him," he said finally.

Father Amberge took a moment and then called Dr. Jarvis to ask if arrangements for Sam Decker had been made yet.

"No," Dr. Jarvis replied. "As a matter of fact, no one has claimed the body. I've been trying to figure out what to do with it."

Father Amberge said he would take care of the arrangements. "I'll have the funeral director pick up the body in the morning."

Officer Phillips checked the places William had mentioned and came up empty. He was running out of places to look. He was walking back to his cruiser when he ran into Joe, the strip bar owner.

"You're looking mighty stressed," Joe said. "What's going on?"

"This damned murder I'm investigating. I know who did it, I just can't seem to find him. It's like he vanished."

"Who are you looking for?"

"Nemrak Sigmund," Officer Phillips replied.

"I know that guy," Joe told him. "He rented a woman from me a few months ago. I can go back to the bar and get the information if that will help you out."

Officer Phillips followed Joe back to the bar. He waited out front while Joe went back to the office. Soon he came back out and handed Officer Phillips some papers. "Here is the contract for the girl," he said.

Officer Phillips looked at the papers. Sure enough, the names Nemrak Sigmund and Sam Decker appeared on them. This proved Nemrak knew Sam. There was also an address which wasn't Nemrak's. Officer Phillips thanked Joe and headed to the address listed.

Officer Phillips located the house, which looked dark. He got out of his car and knocked on the door. No one answered, but he could see movement. He knocked again. "This is the police!" he said. "Open your door now!"

Still there was no response. Officer Phillips went to a neighbor's house and asked to use the phone. He called the station for backup. The dispatcher told him she would send two more officers to the scene. Officer Phillips thanked the neighbor and headed back to his cruiser to wait.

From his car, Officer Phillips continued watching the house. He could see movement the whole time; he wondered what was going on in there and why they were not answering the door.

Soon Officers Davis and Daniels arrived. They all went to the front door and knocked again. No response. By now the commotion had drawn a crowd. One of the neighbors approached the porch asked to speak to one of them. Officer Phillips stepped into the yard.

"My name is Max Otis," the man said. "I just wanted to let you know that there have been many strange happenings at this house since this person moved in. Some of the neighbors believe the house and the person living here are cursed."

Officer Phillips asked Max for more detail. Max told him about Charlie, about Charlotte's death, about the incident with the neighbors' suicide. "Now he just stands upstairs in front of the closet door like he is waiting on something. He never comes out, but sometimes a strange man comes over."

Officer Phillips asked him to describe the man.

"I haven't seen him in a while," Max said. "He's an older guy, fairly tall, probably in his sixties."

That got Officer Phillips's attention. "When was the last time you saw him?"

"Maybe three or four days ago."

Officer Phillips thanked Mr. Otis for the information and went back to the porch. "I think we may have one of our guys," he told the other officers. "Let's check the garage."

They went back to the garage and kicked in the door but there was no car. This puzzled Officer Phillips. He told Officer Davis they needed to go in the house.

They returned to the front door and forced their way into the house. A man confronted them with an evil look on his face. Officer Phillips asked his name.

"Natas," he hissed.

"Is Nemrak Sigmund here?"

"No, he isn't."

"Do you know Sam Decker?"

"Yes."

"Nemrak killed Sam Decker and we are trying to find him. Can you help?"

"Follow me."

Officer Phillips ordered Officers Davis and Daniels to stand by. Natas led him upstairs and showed him the closet. "Nemrak is in here."

Officer Phillips opened the door and saw several spirits. His face turned white as he ran down the steps ordering Officers Davis and Daniels out of the house.

After Officer Phillips regrouped he huddled with the other officers and told them what happened. They both laughed at him.

"Listen, damn it," Officer Phillips said. "That fellow over there told me some freaky things happen at this house, and I just witnessed it. All I know is Nemrak isn't in there."

William and the crew arrived at the rectory. While everyone else retired, William and the priests went to the rectory office and took out all of James's writings, as well as the articles he had cut out, and tried to piece together what he knew.

Father Pelfrey asked about blood relatives.

"Charlie has a sister," William said. "Her name is Marcy, but we don't know if the Marcy we have is Charlie's sister."

Father Pelfrey wanted certainty. He went and woke Marcy and brought her into the office. He asked what she remembered of her childhood. She said her childhood was so tragic that she didn't remember any of it. Then he asked her about the ceremony to bring a spawn of Satan into the world via an unwilling willing host. She told them what they already knew: it required the sacrifice of thirteen children.

"What if there a fourteenth child was sacrificed the same night?" William asked.

"The spirit wouldn't be able to fully take over the body," Marcy replied. The host would retain some of their own personality. The right person could exorcise the demon or spirit."

Marcy started to leave the room, then turned around. "Did you ask me about my childhood?" she asked.

"I did," Father Pelfrey said.

"All I remember is that I missed my brother dearly," she said. "There wasn't a night that went by that I didn't cry myself to sleep because I didn't know what happened to him."

"Do you remember your brother's name?" William asked.

"How could I forget? His name was Jeremy."

CHAPTER 24

Dr. Jarvis had just arrived at his office and taken off his jacket when Frank the funeral director showed up to pick up Sam's body. "Poor guy," said Frank. "Father Amberge spoke highly of him, and said that this guy saved his life."

"Really?" said Dr. Jarvis.

"Yes," said Frank. "He kept going on and on about how this guy saved his life, and since he couldn't repay him while he was alive that he would repay him in his death."

Frank signed the paperwork and headed back to the funeral home with Sam's body. Dr. Jarvis called the police station and asked for Officer Phillips.

Officer Phillips went into the locker room when he arrived in the morning. Hanging from the ceiling were several handmade ghosts. As he looked at them, Officer Davis and Daniels burst out. "Boo! The ghosts are going to get you!"

Officer Phillips slammed his bag into his locker. "You guys are juvenile," he said. "I saw what I saw. I don't care if you believe me or not." He put on his uniform and slammed the door on his way out. As he did, the dispatcher told him he had a call.

He went into his office and picked up the phone to find Dr. Jarvis on the other end. "I think you should talk to Father Amberge from Mercer," the doctor said. He told

Officer Phillips what the funeral director had said about Father Amberge and Sam.

"Mercer isn't in my jurisdiction," Officer Phillips replied. "I'll ask Deputy Hangman to talk to him."

Officer Phillips called Deputy Hangman to ask him to speak to Father Amberge. Then he decided to take William's suggestion to call local churches for a list of their registered parishioners. It was a long shot, but it might help him figure out who was in the cult.

Father Amberge invited Deputy Hangman into the priest house. "What brings you out this way, Walt?"

Deputy Hangman said it was in relation to Sam Decker and Father James Wilson's murder. Father Amberge told him about James and Sam coming to hide from Nemrak, Nemrak showing up, his abduction and eventual release by Sam, and how he learned of Sam's death. "I went ahead and made all the arrangements for him since he saved my life." Deputy Hangman thanked Father Amberge for his statement and headed back to the station.

William was helping everyone get prepared for their attempt to help Charlie when it hit him: he knew where Nemrak was. He called the police department, but Officer Phillips was out. William left a message with the dispatcher to have Officer Phillips call him later that afternoon. Officer Phillips was at Red's Meat Market, speaking with Brent to see if he knew where Nemrak was. Brent was uncooperative and told Officer Phillips that Nemrak could be anywhere. "The cult sticks together," he said. "He could be hiding in another state."

Officer Phillips left the market furious. He decided to take the rest of the day off. He went back to the station and told his boss he needed some time to think. His boss told him to go relax. Officer Phillips changed out of his uniform and left. He didn't hear the dispatcher calling his name on his way out.

William and the crew arrived at Charlie's house.

Daphne had mixed up some herbs to make Charlie sleepy, to make it easier to perform the ceremony. She went up to the door and knocked. Even though she could see someone moving inside, no one answered the door. She tried again, then noticed that the door was broken. She cracked it open far enough to put the now-burning herbs inside, then went back to the car. She said they should wait about fifteen minutes and then it should be fine for them to go in.

When they went inside, they found Charlie asleep in the couch. Daphne began a cleansing ritual for Charlie's soul; Marcy was speaking some language no one understood. Suddenly they heard several noises upstairs. Fran took Father Pelfrey and Father Sandler upstairs and showed them the passage. "We're in for a fight," Father Pelfrey said.

Father Sandler couldn't believe what he was seeing. Several spirits crossed through the passage, like they were ready to attack. Father Sandler and Father Pelfrey grabbed their Bibles and started to recite the exorcism passage from the Bible.

"Hail Mary, full of grace, the lord is with thee, our father, who art in heaven, hallowed be thy name, thy kingdom come, thy will be done, on Earth as it is in Heaven. Evil spirits heal to the power of God, leave this home, and leave this person." They held their crucifixes in the air and repeated the reading again and again.

Downstairs, Father Carey and Rachael's brother Darren took over, performing their own exorcism on Charlie. Daphne and Marcy went upstairs. Marcy saw the passage and she pushed Father Pelfrey and Father Sandler out of the way. She began to speak in old German. The more aggressive she became, the less aggressive the spirits became.

Things weren't going as well downstairs. Natas came out of his herb-induced sleep and threw William up against the wall. He then took Darren by the throat and began trying to harvest his soul. Daphne began to chant, and the chanting seemed to calm Natas. She was then able to put him back into his sleep.

Marcy told Father Pelfrey there was one way to close the passage, but they needed Charlie upstairs. The guys dragged Charlie up the stairs and laid him in front of the passage. Marcy began to speak German again, and the spirits in the passage grew calm. Daphne began to chant. Marcy helped the groggy Charlie to his feet and the two of them kissed.

Fran was upset. She ran through the crowd and pushed Marcy and Charlie. The two of them stumbled into the closet, close enough to the passage for the spirits to grab them. Marcy and Charlie were now adrift in the passage with the spirits.

"If something isn't done soon they will both die," said Father Pelfrey.

Fran ran downstairs crying. Rachael followed her.

"What do we do now?" Father Sandler shouted.

"Let them both die," said Father Carey. "This is way out of our league." He went down the stairs and outside.

Daphne thought for a moment and remembered that she had witnessed a passage like this when she was younger, but she couldn't remember how they had closed it. She told William she needed time to meditate.

"Do we have time?" William asked.

"We have a few hours," Father Pelfrey said. "As of right now our job is done."

As Daphne meditated, she had a vision. She was talking to a woman she had never seen before. The woman told Daphne the only way Marcy and Charlie could be pulled out of the passage was if a pure soul sacrificed itself for them.

Daphne came out of her meditation and ran to the kitchen to let them know what she had seen. The woman she described was the same woman Fran had seen in her dreams: it must have been Charlotte.

They had a decision to make. They needed a pure soul; that left out Fran. Father Sandler said that left him out. Rachael and Darren said they were out, and Father Pelfrey said he couldn't help either. This only left William and Daphne.

Daphne said she would do it.

They went up to the passage. Daphne began to chant as she chanted she walked closer and closer. Father Pelfrey told the spirits to accept her sacrifice for the safe return of their friends. The spirits gathered by the opening to the passage, all salivating to receive Daphne and have their way with her. Suddenly Daphne was knocked down. Lying on top of her was Charlie.

Charlie stood and ran straight to Fran. "I love you," he said as she hugged him.

Everyone cheered, but where was Marcy? "She is at home where she belongs," Charlie said. "She asked me to let you guys know that she is very sorry for everything she did, and she hopes this makes up for it. She couldn't stand to see her brother hurt anymore."

Everyone cheered again as they left the house. Charlie had too many bad memories and didn't want to be there anymore. They headed back to the rectory.

Officer Phillips was out by the river hunting deer when he stumbled upon an old man sitting in the woods. He asked the old man if he was all right; the old man replied that he was lost and hungry. Officer Phillips gave the man some of his beef jerky and some water out of his canteen.

The old man said his name was Sig Karmen. Officer Phillips helped him to his feet and they walked to his car. "Is there anyplace I can take you?" asked Officer Phillips. Before Sig could reply, he grabbed his chest. Officer Phillips loaded him into his car and headed to the hospital.

They rushed Sig into the emergency room and left Officer Phillips in the waiting room. About twenty minutes later the nurse came out said they didn't expect him to make it through the night. Officer Phillips asked if there was anything he could do. The nurse told him he could try to find some relatives. Officer Phillips said he would go back to the station and see what he could do.

Fran had missed Charlie so much that all she wanted to do was hug and kiss him, but he wasn't as affectionate in return. After twenty minutes she gave up and asked Charlie if there was something wrong. Charlie said there was too much going on in his head and he needed some time to figure it all out.

Fran went out to talk to Daphne and Rachael. She told them what Charlie had said. Daphne told Fran that he might not be the same person again. "Just give him his space and see what happens."

William sat down beside Charlie and asked him what went on in the passage. Charlie said he didn't recall. "Everything was blurry, but bits and pieces of stuff come back. Stuff I don't ever want to see again."

William told Charlie that he and Father Pelfrey wanted him to stay at William's house so they could keep an eye on his progress. Charlie said that would be fine, since he had no other place to go.

William then went out told Fran that she was welcome to stay at his house with Charlie. "Okay," she replied, "but if things don't go well I'm going to stay with Rachael."

William said he wouldn't stop her. He told Fran they

would have to go back to the house and get some of Charlie's things, because Charlie flat-out refused to go.

Officer Phillips went back to the station and asked the dispatcher for information on a Sig Karmen. Then he went back into his office sat down. He put his arms on his desk and laid his head down; before he knew it he was asleep.

He was awakened by Officer Davis. "Greg, why don't you go home and get some rest?"

Officer Phillips told him about the old man he found by the river.

"There were some Karmens that lived on an old farm out by the river," Officer Davis replied. "I think they're both dead, but I could be mistaken. Come on, I'll take care of this. You go home and rest."

Officer Davis went to check with Valerie the dispatcher on what she had found out. Valerie told him that Sig Karmen had been reported missing to the Sheriff's Department three days before. She said deputies were on their way out to the house to inform the family. Officer Davis thanked her and headed up to the hospital.

Fran and William getting Charlie's things when William heard a ruckus up the stairs. He started to go investigate but thought better of it after what he had witnessed earlier in the day.

"Look at this picture of Sam and Charlie before all this happened," Fran said. "They look happy. Should I bring this for him?"

William thought it might be a good idea for Charlie to have it since Sam was dead. He heard another big ruckus from upstairs. He hurried Fran out the door and they headed back to the rectory.

They were greeted by Daphne. "Charlie left and we don't know where he is."

Fran was upset. "Maybe he just went for a walk. If he isn't back soon, we'll go look for him." This settled Fran a little. William left her with the girls went back in the rectory.

"Something was wrong at the house when Fran and I went back to get Charlie's things," he said. Father Sandler and Father Pelfrey agreed to go back with him to investigate. Father Carey had been absent since the exorcism, so they told Darren to stay with the girls and see if Charlie returned.

William, Father Sandler, and Father Pelfrey went into Charlie's house. They waited downstairs to see if they would hear the noise. Twenty minutes went by without a peep. They all decided to go take a look.

The whole upstairs had been ransacked. William insisted that neither he nor Fran had done it. Father Sandler said it looked like some looters had come and helped themselves. Then William opened up the passage door and saw a book lying in front of the passage. He picked it up and saw it was a Satanic ritual book.

"This wasn't done by looters," he said. "There is only one person responsible for this, and that is Nemrak."

Darren and the girls were sitting in the den when they heard the door open. Darren went out to investigate, then came back and told the girls it was only Father Carey.

Five minutes later they heard the door open again. This time it was Father Sandler, Father Pelfrey, and William. Darren told Father Sandler that Father Carey was back.

Father Sandler went up and knocked on Father Carey's door. Father Carey said he wanted everybody out of the rectory tonight or he was going to call the archdiocese and let them know that Father Sandler had people staying over. Father Sandler said they needed to wait on Charlie to come back and then they would leave.

Father Sandler went downstairs told William about his

conversation with Father Carey. "I'll wait for Charlie," he said. "Will you take everyone to your house?" William said he would.

Father Amberge sat down to write his eulogy for Sam. He also needed to get the obituary published so people would know the time and place of the viewing and funeral. He was working on those things when his phone rang. It was someone named Julia claiming to be Sam's ex-wife. Father Amberge told her he had made the arrangements, and of course he had to tell her the story of how Sam had saved his life.

Julia was in tears. Sam had honestly changed and now it was too late. She told Father Amberge about her cancer. "It was such a blessing when Sam arrived that day. I was hoping the kids would get to know him and have him in their lives, but then the last image they saw of him was him fighting."

Father Amberge was touched by the story. He offered to let Julia and the kids come stay with him for the viewing and funeral. Julia accepted and thanked him for taking care of everything. After Father Amberge hung up, he wished he could think of a way to help her and the kids.

Father Sandler called to let them know Charlie was back. William went to pick him up.

Father Pelfrey told Fran she needed to be strong during the next few weeks or maybe months. "You are a strong woman," he said. "I have no doubt of your ability to raise that child on your own if needed."

Fran frowned, but she knew it was a possibility.

Soon, William arrived with Charlie. Fran asked where he had been.

"I just need my space," Charlie replied. "I went for a walk to help me figure things out."

Fran noticed that Charlie's hand was swollen and bloody, and he had it wrapped in a piece of his shirt. When she asked about it, he replied that he was so frustrated that he hit a dumpster a few times to let out some anger. Fran took him into the kitchen and cleaned it up, and then she took some ice from the freezer and wrapped it around Charlie's hand. "Maybe we should take you to the hospital," she said.

"No! Just leave me alone." He stormed off into another room.

About fifteen minutes later, an announcement came on the radio saying that the police were looking for a person responsible for assaulting a victim in the alley behind the local tire store. Fran stopped breathing for a moment until William shouted her name.

"Do you think Charlie did that?" she asked.

William said he didn't know, but if they pursued it with Charlie he might go deeper into his hole. Fran was growing more and more worried and scared.

Father Amberge called to let William and the rest of them know Sam's viewing would be the next morning, with the funeral the following day. Fran went to tell Charlie, who shrugged it off like he didn't care.

CHAPTER 25

Charlie was actually snuggling with Fran when she awoke in the morning. She lay as still as possible so she wouldn't disturb him, and so she could soak up the attention. Soon, though, her bladder was calling; when she got back into the bedroom Charlie was up and out.

She went into the kitchen to find Charlie making breakfast. This brought a smile to her face. This was how things used to be. Fran and Charlie sat down, and soon William and Father Pelfrey joined them. Charlie wanted to know what had happened to Sam.

William explained it. Charlie asked if anyone had told Sam's ex-wife Julia. William said Julia had been notified and that she would be staying with Father Amberge.

After breakfast Charlie left for a walk. This time William followed, staying far enough back that Charlie wouldn't see him.

After an hour, William was finding it hard to keep Charlie in his sights. He decided to rest on a bench in the park. He could still see Charlie as he went around the block. He cut through the park to follow Charlie as he walked into the neighborhood where his house was. William held his breath as Charlie walked by it, only stopping to tie his shoe. William hustled by the house; it creeped him out.

After a while it was clear that Charlie was heading back to William's house. William took a shortcut to beat him there. Charlie entered William's house and went back into the bedroom without saying anything to anyone. Fran wanted to go see what was wrong, but she respected his request for space.

Daphne and Rachael were both getting ready to go to Sam's viewing with Fran when Darren popped his head in to say he was leaving. He told Daphne to take care of his little sister. "She can take care of herself," Daphne told him.

Charlie came out of the bedroom and was ready to go. He held Fran's hand as they walked to William's car. She was happy even though they were going to a viewing; she had Charlie and her two best friends at her side; what else could she ask for?

When they got into the car Daphne noticed a strange smell. She asked Charlie if he had some new cologne on. He said he didn't. She spent the whole ride trying to place the smell.

On the way to the funeral home Father Amberge suggested to Julia that she might not want the kids to see the body. Julia said she had already decided to let them see it so they have closure.

They arrived at the funeral home well before anyone else. Father Amberge and Julia went in to see Sam themselves first. As they entered, Julia began to cry. Father Amberge held her beside him as they approached the casket.

Julia was quiet for a moment, looking at the body, and then she began shouting. "Damn it, Sam! Why did you have to go and get yourself killed after I told you I was dying and someone needed to be there for the kids?" She hit the casket, then dropped to her knees. "Why, Sam? Why?" she kept saying.

Father Amberge finally helped Julia to her feet and asked her if she needed to step outside. Julia said she would be fine if he could get her something to drink.

William, Charlie, and the girls arrived at the funeral home. William said a prayer for Sam. Daphne, Rachael, and Fran all did the same, but Charlie did something very strange. He placed his hand over Sam's mouth and stood there motionlessly. His eyes rolled back, then suddenly he took his hand off and everything seemed normal.

Father Amberge and Julia came out of the kitchen. Julia went up to Charlie and gave him a hug. "Boy, you've grown since the last time I saw you," she said. Charlie made introductions, and Julia asked Fran if she would like to meet her children. Fran said of course. She and Rachael followed Julia to meet the kids.

As they stood talking, Fran told Julia she was pregnant with Charlie's child. "You need to stay away from that boy and the cult if you want your child to have a good life," Julia said.

Fran looked at her. "You had children with Sam and they seem to be fine."

"Sam wasn't in the cult when we got married and had children. He joined shortly after our divorce, after Charlie arrived."

Fran was shocked; that wasn't what Charlie had told her.

Father Sandler ran into Charlie as he walked into the funeral home. Charlie showed him where to go. Father Sandler turned around to thank him, but Charlie was gone.

More people started to arrive and Fran was in the greeting line with Julia and the kids, but Charlie was nowhere to be found. About 45 minutes into the viewing Charlie finally showed up. He smelled bad, making Fran nauseous. Her complexion grew pale. Rachael and Daphne came to take her to the ladies room. When Daphne got close to Charlie, she smelled the same odor she had noticed earlier, now even stronger.

The viewing was almost over when Charlie again went up to Sam's body and placed his hand over the mouth. This time Charlie began to shake as his eyes rolled back into his head. He stood there for several minutes with a sinister smile on his face. Then suddenly he was done.

Julia brought the kids up to see the body. She told them to stay away from strangers and to stay within the church, and said their father would still be alive if he had done those things. They began to cry. Fran went to comfort them, but Julia told her to leave them alone.

On the drive back to Mercer, Father Amberge asked Julia why she had been so short with Fran. She said she was tired and didn't feel like talking about it. Father Amberge said he would respect her wishes, but he was there if she needed to talk.

That evening, as Father Amberge tried to concentrate on the readings for the funeral the next day, Julia's actions toward Fran kept bugging him.

When they got back to William's house, Charlie again insisted going on a walk. He left without saying goodbye.

Fran was growing more and more distant from Charlie. It seemed he wanted her only at his convenience. He hadn't mentioned the baby or any plans like he did when they first met. She was losing her patience with him. She sat listening to the radio, waiting for him to come home so she could sit him down and have a nice talk with him.

As she waited, she began to have very sharp back pains. She walked down the hallway holding her lower back.

William met her in the hallway. "What's wrong, Fran?"

Fran said she was having some bad lower back pain and spasms. "I'm just stressed out. I want to try soaking in a hot bath to see if that will help."

"Okay," William said, "but if you don't feel any better afterwards, I'm taking you to the hospital."

William walked into the living room just as Charlie walked in the door. William asked where he had been. Charlie replied that it was none of William's business.

"Do you know Fran is so stressed out that she may go into labor early?" William asked.

Charlie just looked at him.

"Do you even care?" William yelled. "What the hell is wrong with you?"

Charlie turned around and stormed back out the door. Fran heard all the commotion and came out of the bathroom with only a towel wrapped around her. She ran to the door and yelled Charlie's name. He came back and walked right by William as if nothing had happened. He and Fran went back to their room and Charlie rubbed her back for her until she fell asleep. Then he went back out for a walk.

Daphne was racking her brain trying to figure out what the smell surrounding Charlie was. Finally, Rachael said that Charlie smelled like Marcy. That jogged Daphne's memory: it was opium mixed with dragon blood and myrrh, plus something she wasn't familiar with.

Daphne wanted to go back to Charlie's house and perform a ritual to see what was going on. Rachael called a taxi.

They let themselves into Charlie's house. They went right upstairs, where Daphne drew a star on the floor of the closet with each tip representing part of Mother Earth. She lit many candles and incense, raised her spell book into the air, and began chanting. "Almighty protectors from the north, south, east, and west, guide me on my journey to find the demon spirit that stays at this passage. Lead me to why it stays, and to who keeps it here. Guardians of Mother Earth, lead me to the maker of this evil, who it is guided by, and for what reason."

Daphne began to shake, and a voice came out of her mouth that wasn't hers. "Get out, get out!"

Rachael looked at Daphne and knew something wasn't

right. Daphne's mouth again opened and said that Natas would be here soon and all would suffer. The spirit of a small child appeared and tried to pull Daphne into the passage, but he was unable to break her protection star.

Rachael ran downstairs and called William. She asked for his and Father Pelfrey's help. William said they would be there as soon as they could.

Rachael ran back upstairs and saw Daphne in the battle of her life. The demon spirit possessing her was drawing her closer and closer to the passage, but could get her out of her circle. Rachael yelled to Daphne that help was on its way.

William and Father Pelfrey rounded up Fran and Charlie and headed to the house. They ran up the steps to see Daphne lying on the floor of the closet, convulsing and growling. Rachael was behind the bed crying.

Father Pelfrey tried to get the attention of the demon so he could perform an exorcism, but the demon was hellbent on getting Daphne to the passage. He started praying, "Hail Mary, full of grace, the lord is with thee." He kept repeating the verse and telling the demon the lord commanded him to leave Daphne's body.

"You are old and weak," the demon hissed. "You are no match for me."

"I may be old," Father Pelfrey said, "but I am not weak. The lord will prevail."

The demon continued to try to pull Daphne through the passage. Fran yelled at Charlie to do something. He ran by Father Pelfrey and pushed Daphne into the passage.

Everyone's jaws dropped. Fran ran up to Charlie and began hitting him. He pushed her to the floor. "My son with Charlotte was supposed to change my life, and he did. Now I must forever be his servant. That pagan bitch will give him some fun."

William pulled Fran away from the closet. They left Charlie there, going out to William's car and back to his house. William decided they all must leave that night. Fran and arranged for her and Rachael to stay at her Aunt Agnes's house. Father Pelfrey would stay at the rectory with Father Sandler and Father Carey.

William dropped everyone off and went back home. He didn't sleep very well that night.

William called Agnes's house in the morning to learn that Fran and Rachael had left for California. William hung up with Agnes and left for Sam's funeral. He saw Father Amberge and told him what happened the previous night.

"Sometimes you have to concede your losses for some sort of a gain," the priest said.

This confused William. He was about to ask Father Amberge to explain when there was a tap on his back. It was Father Sandler, who asked William to join him. William excused himself from Father Amberge and followed Father Sandler into the kitchen.

Father Carey and Father Pelfrey were already in there. Father Carey said Father Pelfrey had filled them in on the previous night's events. "It isn't too late for Daphne," he said, "but we need to get Charlie out of the picture."

"I'll take care of that after the funeral," William said.

"No need," Father Carey said. "I've been following Charlie, and I've been to the house a few times, and I think I have enough evidence to lock him away in the nuthouse for a while. I'll call the police after the funeral."

William asked Father Carey what was up with the attitude back at the rectory. Father Carey said he was only against the way things were approached with the whole situation. "We knew not what we were going against until it was too late. I've done some studying and some praying, and I came up with this plan."

Father Amberge took his place behind the altar and began

the funeral with a prayer. He then began his eulogy about Sam. "Even though I barely knew him, this man made me realize that no matter where your life takes you or what you have done, someday you may make the biggest contribution to another. Not only did I learn this from Sam, he also saved my life. He had no reason to, nor did he owe me in any way, and all he could say is that he did it because I actually was the only person who cared for him in a long time.

"Through my experience with Sam I met his ex-wife Julia and their two kids. She has cancer and is not expected to make it much longer. She has showed me that no matter what may come to you in life, you must grab it by the horns and live life to the fullest. Don't just roll over and take it. Julia, would you please stand? I want to let you know that I have arranged for you to meet a couple who wants to help take care of your kids, and adopt them when you pass away.

"The only way I could thank Sam for what he did for me, under the circumstances, was to do what I'm doing. Now, that's enough about that. Let us pray."

After the funeral, Father Carey called the police department and said he saw Charlie Tansa beating up the kid up in the alleyway. The he outlined the rest of his plan.

"Daphne is just on the other side of that wall," he said. "She cannot enter the passage as a human mass; only spirits can pass through. It's dark in there, so she is likely confused about where she is."

"So the whole thing with Charlie and Marcy was a trick?" Father Sandler asked.

"Yes," Father Carey replied. "Marcy has been keeping Charlie under a spell to keep him normal. She stayed hidden. That's why he walked so much. He had to see Marcy periodically."

Father Pelfrey, since he was the oldest, volunteered to go and get Daphne out of the passage. "It's dark in there,"

Father Carey told him. "Just look for the light. The light will lead you out."

They parked close enough to Charlie's house to see what was going on. After Officer Phillips led Charlie away in handcuffs, they all went in the house and upstairs.

Father Pelfrey walked into the passage. Like Father Carey said, he found himself in darkness. He was on his hands and knees when he found what felt like an arm. He tugged on it and heard a moan. He ran his hand up the arm and found the shoulder. He shook it.

"What? Who's there?"

"It's Father Pelfrey," the priest said. "I'll get you out of here. Just follow the light."

Father Pelfrey helped the person up and the two of them headed toward the light. Father Pelfrey reached for it and felt a hand. The hand pulled him and the person with him through the passage. When they landed on the other side Daphne was lying on top of him. She was very weak and severely beaten.

William and Father Carey helped her off Father Pelfrey. "Can you stand up?" Father Sandler asked.

She shook her head no. Father Sandler and Father Carey carried her down the steps and laid her on the couch. William asked her what happened.

"There were others behind the passage," Daphne said. "A man and a woman hit me with wood and kicked me. It was so dark that I couldn't see them."

"Are they still up there?" William asked.

"No," Daphne replied. "They left." Then she passed out.

William went and got a cool, damp towel from the kitchen and placed it on her head. "We need to get her to a hospital," he said.

"No," Father Carey replied. "In her religion they heal themselves with herbs from the Earth. If we take her to the hospital she would be banned from her religion."

"So what should we do?" asked William.

"I'll take care of her," said Father Carey. "I have relatives from England that study this religion. I've studied it here and there. The first thing we need to do is to get her out of here before anyone returns."

They carried her to the car. At the rectory, they took her inside and laid her on one of the beds. Father Carey got out a book and blew dust off of it. He asked William to open Daphne's bag and hand him things as he called for them. He asked first for two sticks of dragon blood incense and some oil.

"What kind of oil?" William asked.

"I can't remember what kind it is."

William rummaged through the bag. "Do you mean this tea tree oil?"

"Yes, that oil, plus some cat claw, some eucalyptus, some cinnamon, and some garlic. Father Sandler, can you get me some non-holy water?"

When Father Sandler returned Father Carey set up some candles and poured the water into a bowl, then mixed the ingredients. He told Father Sandler and William they should join Father Pelfrey in the den and he would be right down.

"Why?" William asked. Just then Father Sandler began to yawn.

"That's why," said Father Carey.

Father Carey joined them soon after. "She should feel better by morning," he told them. "She will be sore and hungry, but she should feel better."

William said he would make arrangements to fly Daphne to California so she could finish healing with Fran and Rachael.

Officer Phillips had gotten Charlie to admit to the beating of the teenager in the alley. He already knew what was going upstairs in Charlie's house, so with this new information he could lock him up. He asked Charlie if he wanted to go to the hospital for psychiatric evaluation but Charlie declined saying. "As long as I'm not locked up it is not safe," Charlie said. Then he attacked Officer Phillips.

Officer Phillips yelled for backup. Officers Davis and Daniels came running in, and the three of them wrestled Charlie into a cell. He hissed and spat at the officers long enough that he earned himself a spot in solitary confinement.

As the officers worked on their reports, a woman came in to ask for Charlie. The officers told her she would have to come back in the morning to see him. She told them Charlie needed was overdue for his medication, so if he was acting strange or saying strange things, that was why.

Officer Phillips took the medicine and promised he would make sure Charlie got it. When she left, he went downstairs. He opened the door to find Charlie drawing pictures on the walls with his own blood. The pictures were of flames, a child, and thirteen other children dancing around. Written above it was "Monica, why did you have to ruin it?"

Officer Phillips immediately called the psych ward and had Charlie admitted.

Daphne awoke in a strange but familiar setting. Soon she realized she was back at the rectory. Had she dreamed the whole thing?

When she got up, she realized it wasn't a dream. Every step hurt.

"How are you feeling?" Father Carey asked

"I'm a little sore."

"That's to be expected," he replied.

"What happened?"

Father Carey told her. As he did so, William came into

the room. He told Daphne he would take her to the airport so she could go rest with Fran and Rachael.

A few months later Fran found William's number and called him to let him know she had her baby boy. She told him Daphne was back in England, and that Rachael was going to school to be a teacher. William was happy for them and said he would pass the word to Father Sandler and Father Carey. He also let Fran know that Charlie was in the Psychiatric Correctional Ward, but it probably wouldn't be a good idea for her to contact him.

"He's no longer a part of my life," Fran said. "I look at my son and see all of Charlie I want to see. I'll send you some pictures." She hung up. William never heard from her again.

OTHER BOOKS BY AUTHOR:

MOONLIGHT CURSE

ABOUT THE AUTHOR

J.L. Wenning is a Graduate of Celina High School, Celina OH. He resides in Coldwater, OH with his wife Vickie, two daughters, Brianna & Lauren. He is an entrepreneur and works for Mercer Health transport squad. In Jeremy's spare time, he enjoys writing & hunting, volunteers for the local emergency squad and coaches softball.

www.ingramcontent.com/pod-product-compliance
Lightning Source LLC
Chambersburg PA
CBHW031426200626
46814CB00016B/2336